CW00500515

Richard Pierce is a writer, poet and painter. He lives in Suffolk with his wife and four children, a collection of epées and cricket bats, and a cat.

www.tettig.com

Also by Richard Pierce

Dead Men

The Immortality Clock

Tettig's Jewels

The Failed Assassin

BEE BONES

Richard Pierce

NoPapyrus Press

First published in 2014 by
NoPapyrus Press
Spring Cottage, Church Street, Stradbroke, IP21 5HT

For Marianne

ACKNOWLEDGEMENTS

I owe a deep debt of gratitude to many people for this book.

Thank you, Ren Powell, poet, friend and mentor, for pushing me to enter NaNoWriMo in 2005. Without you, this book would never have been written in a mad 23 days in the November of that year.

Thank you, Marianne, wife, friend, everything, for supporting me on this writer's journey.

Thank you to all who supported me on the authonomy web site in 2008, where I first learned the courage to put my writing to a public test, and to develop a thick skin. You all taught me very many useful things about writing, and about myself.

Thank you to Oscar, Charlotte, Kara, and Alex(andra), for letting me be the dreadful father I am, and for illuminating my middle age.

Chapter 1

Memories are open wounds. They don't heal, even when I'm asleep. And then he wakes me.

Tillmann. His mother had been obsessed by that name. I don't know why. Anyway, it doesn't matter. She's dead now. So there's just me and him. Tillmann. My son. I don't think he's ever forgiven us for that name. The kids at his school call him Attila. He's almost as tall as me now. Although he's only twelve, almost thirteen. So he can stand up to the name calling. I reckon he probably likes it deep down. Him and his messed-up black hair and his messed-up friends. I'm not important. I'm just his servant and his driver, however much I rebel. Oh - and his banker.

'Dad,' he whispers, shaking me. 'Dad.'

Strange how they never lose that whining tone they acquired when they were infants, before they could even spit out half-formed words, just those imploring complaining sounds that drive fathers mad and mothers to lactation.

'Dad!'

I'm awake now. Grudgingly awake in the bed that I should have thrown out after she died, but never got round to.

'Do you know what time it is?' I groan.

He's been doing this since he was an infant, too, waking me at inconvenient times, or at least appearing in my bedroom at inconvenient times. 'It's still dark, for Heaven's sake.'

'So?' he says. 'Doesn't stop you waking me when you want me to go to school.'

'It's Saturday, Till. And I was asleep. For a change. Go away.' I try to pull the duvet back over my head. And my head's hurting, too. Not as much as on some Saturday mornings, but enough.

'This is important, Dad.'

This time I manage a glance at my clock. Six o'clock. 'Tillmann. It's even earlier than I thought it was. What the hell are you on? You need to sleep, too.'

He shrugs and grunts. 'I dreamt about her again,' he simply says.

'Oh, Jesus, mate.' I sigh and sit up. He's been dreaming about her ever since she went, ever since we'd been left, heartbroken and alone, we two men – almost men, anyway, - in this sad little flat overlooking this sad little road. Eight years of dreams. Never nightmares. Never bad dreams. Despite the way she died. Although he saw her die. Here, in fact. Here, in this bed, in this room, in this dark room, morning still waiting under the horizon, behind the houses, out past the railway line from London to Bristol. I miss her, too, his mother, his wonderful gentle beautiful mother.

Some things I remember, some I don't. The pub down the road is one of the things I do remember. Her face I remember from the photographs we still have hanging around desolately; dusty trophies from a better time. But I've forgotten her caresses, the pitch of her voice; they're things I can only imagine, living touches from a dead woman's hand.

He's started sobbing by now, unusually, deep, racking sobs that shake me down into the part of me that I try to hide from everyone including him, because it hurts too much to let it out. His crying crashes into my eight years of pain, of trying to forget, of grief. My arms around him, he just lets himself go, like I've tried to teach him, hypocrite that I am, because I've never learned to let go, never accepted that she's dead and gone and buried, and that we'll never ever ever see her again. Because I'm beginning to think grief is pointless. Because the one person you want to share your grief with is the one you're grieving for. Because it hurts to be alone.

'What can I do ?' I say, still cradling him in my arms. 'Is there anything I can do to make it better?'

'This is one pain you can't kiss better, Dad,' he smiles through his tears.

At least I can still comfort him.

Kate's death has made him grow up too quickly, where it made me age too soon. He speaks with the voice of an older boy, with the thoughts of a young man already making sense of a world that's trying to confuse him. 'We've got to go and look for Mum.'

I don't quite get what he's saying. 'What do you mean, look for Mum?' I say. 'She's dead, mate, you know she's dead. What're you talking about?'

I can't think of anything else to say. Because he's totally taken me by surprise. I've often hoped that some day she'd just come knocking on the door again, although I know that's impossible. That I might just get a postcard from her asking me to go and pick her up from somewhere at a certain time. Or a phone call. I've never told Tillmann about those thoughts, because they're stupid. And they make me cry.

'She can't be dead, Dad. Not with all these dreams I'm having. They mean she's alive somewhere, waiting for us. She needs us.' He tries to look me in the eye, but I'm hiding my face until my tears dry. He shoves me, half playfully, half young pretender challenging. 'Come on,' he says.

'What do you mean, come on?' He's never been like this before. 'This is stupid.'

'Ever realised I'm getting older?' he says. 'I'm maybe not quite as stupid as I was when I was five. I'm maybe a bit more together than you think.'

I didn't talk like that when I was twelve, I'm sure I didn't. In fact, I probably didn't talk at all because my parents were tyrants. 'And what does that mean?' I say.

'You got a plan?' How much more hurt does he want to inflict on himself? On me?

'Not really,' he says. 'I just thought we'd get in the car and drive, and somehow we'd end up where we needed to be.'

'That simple,' I say. 'Now that's cool. I wonder why I haven't tried that before. But then I've never had the urge to go out and find her.' Because I know she's dead, because I'd rather not be here without her. Because the pain's too much. Because I'm dead inside.

'You know, Dad,' he smirks, 'you're crap at pretending things don't get to you. You're crap at hiding that you miss her more each day. Time the great healer, my arse.'

'Tillmann, stop swearing.' Inside I'm sort of laughing with him, though, because my language is a lot worse than his, and he knows it. But he's so young. He's probably not even kissed anyone yet. But I won't ask him. I'm sure he'll tell me when he's ready. Just like I'll tell him about his mother when he's ready. I stop smiling and shake my head. 'We can't do this.' We've got to stay in this ivory tower of memories.

*

Now that's one of the things I do remember. The first time I kissed his mother, the first time we met. Fifteen years ago, fifteen long years ago. Children we were, really; naïve children in a heartless and devious world. On Newbury railway station, ten minutes walk from here. Catching the slow train into London because we were both equally impatient with standing on the draughty platform waiting for the next fast train to come. They still had carriages you could have a smoke in, then. Not any more, though, not in this sterile, emotionless world. God, she was beautiful.

We'd both rushed onto the platform just as the fast

train was pulling out. Cursed aloud. She was tall and thin, an undone black coat billowing out behind her, a shroud of black hair whirling around her white face, big blue eyes staring angrily down the track. She'd stamped her foot and cursed a second time before she noticed me.

'What're you staring at?' she hissed. 'I hate missing trains. I hate it! I hate it!' She didn't give me time to answer. 'Don't you hate missing trains?'

'Well, yes, I do,' I said, hands in pocket. ''Specially as I always do. Without fail. In fact it's probably my fault that you missed yours. What with me staring and all that. And being jinxed.'

It was her turn to stare. 'What *are* you going on about?' she huffed. 'What are you babbling about? Do you smoke? Have you got a spare cigarette?'

I pulled the crumpled packet out of my pocket and offered her a smoke. 'Here you go.'

'Got a light as well, by any chance?' she said. 'I'm desperate. Tried giving up half a dozen times, but failed miserably.'

I lit her cigarette, sheltering the flame from the wind with my empty hand. Accidentally – honestly accidentally – brushed against her naked hand in the process. Started. Apologised. Almost ran. I'm afraid of women, you see. Of women and love. Always have been. Always will be.

She smiled. Her anger seemed to have disappeared as quickly as it had surfaced. 'Thanks,' she said, breathing out her first lungful of smoke. 'I needed that.'

'No worries.'

I wondered what to do next. Turned to face the track, holding my cigarette tightly against the wind. I'd always laughed at people who claimed that touching someone you were attracted to was like getting an electric shock. But I was still tingling, and I didn't want it to stop. And I didn't want her to see the surprise and fear in my eyes.

I'd never believed in love at first sight. Just imagining things, I said to myself, just being a stupid lonely old man.

'D'you always do that?' She'd followed me to the edge of the platform.

'Do what?'

'Turn away from people you've just given a cigarette and a light to. It seems kind of weird to me.' She was hugging her unbuttoned coat closed, breathing smoke across to me, but the wind stopped it from reaching.

'Sorry,' I mumbled. 'I'm not really very good at small talk, so I think it's less embarrassing for me and other people if I just keep my mouth shut. Much less stress.'

'You didn't do so badly just then. Must've been quite an effort, that. Talking of being jinxed and stuff. Quite a monologue.' She wasn't smiling.

I shrugged. 'I get carried away with myself sometimes.' I said. Nearly tried to flirt. Managed to stop myself.

She threw her half-finished cigarette end onto the track. Her coat blew open. She was dressed entirely in black. Black coat, black boots, black trousers, black top.

'You shouldn't be so hard on yourself,' she said. 'Meeting strangers is never easy. 'Specially not when you're jinxed.'

I thought I heard a suppressed chuckle.

'How is it you're jinxed, anyway?' she said. 'You look quite normal to me. Like someone who's just missed a train should look, anyway.'

I stared at her in that way that Tillmann says can be frightening and endearing at once. Shrugged again. 'Not much luck with women and things.' The words just sort of came out of my mouth before I realised what I was saying, before I could stop myself. Should've been strangled at birth, I thought, blushing. Should've stayed in bed this morning. Should've been anywhere but here. 'Keep myself to myself,' I added, sort of in self-defence.

'Like it best that way.' Shut the hell up, I was saying to myself. She doesn't want to listen to you banging on about all sorts of rubbish.

'Been there,' she said. 'Don't worry about it. There'll be someone somewhere; bound to be.'

But already it was only her I wanted. But I was afraid, so afraid. And now she's dead.

*

Tillmann drags me from my daydreams.

'Come on, Dad,' he shouts. 'We've got to do this. We've got to go.'

He's already dressed. I'm naked and unshaven, still clinging to the duvet, as always. 'No. It's early, too early. I'm tired.'

'Come on,' he shouts again, pulls the duvet off me – what do they feed these kids at school? 'Get dressed. Then we'll go shopping, get some nosh for the journey, and off we go.'

His madness is enthusiastic and worrying. I can't let him do this.

'And how long would this sudden magical mystery tour last?' I say despite myself, as I drag on yesterday's clothes, lifted from the floor.

'Who cares?' he says. 'Who cares? Let's live a little. Let's do something we've not done since before Mum died. Let's have an adventure even if it leads nowhere.'

'No.'

'Then I'll go on my own.'

'What?'

'I'll go on my own. Simple.'

We're face to face now. I can't give in. He stares at me. I stare back. Don't even have to look down at him.

'No.'

'I will. Nothing wakes you. I can just leave.'

'And then?'
'Hitch.'
'At your age.'
'Been done before.'
'Don't you care about how I feel?'
'Don't *you* care about how *I* feel? What have we done since Mum died? Nothing. Vegetate.' He takes a step back. 'Laugh? Never.'
I shrug. I can't say anything. He's right. All I've done is work, from out of this house. All I've done is send him to school. In the holidays all we've done is watch the telly or read, or go for short walks round the town. But never away, never away from here. Because, even though I hate it, she's still here, and I don't want to leave her.
'So?' he says. 'Still no?'
'I don't know.'
'Why?'
'I don't want you to hurt yourself.'
'I've been hurt already. You don't know what I know. You think I've forgotten her, but I haven't. She's in my head. All those dreams, and you think I've forgotten. And now I need to do this.'
Maybe he does need this. But it's all wrong. What if I lose him as well? What then?
'D'you promise that you'll knock it on the head if it gets too much, if I say enough's enough?'
'I promise.' He smiles at me.
'I mean it.'
'So do I.'
'On your head be it. Just the weekend. That's all.'
'Ok.'
I put enough dried food and water down for the cat to live on for a couple of days, grab my mobile phone, my coat, my wallet, keys for house and car. Tillmann turns off the lights. We're on our way, and I don't even understand why I've given in to him – again. That's all

we parents do – give in, give, give, give. And that's all children do – take, take, take. It makes me more tired than I should be. And there are so many things he doesn't know that he'll need to find out sometime. Maybe this will be as good a time as any.

The 24-hour supermarket is deserted when we get there. Just a few sullen shelf-stackers and check-out girls listening to the piped music, watching the checkout queue television screens, waiting to get out of their boredom, off their shift, and into their beds again. Tillmann chooses what we're taking with us; I'm useless at that sort of stuff. Used not to be. Used to love shopping. Used to cook all the time. She used to call it foreplay, my cooking. Not been much call for it since she died. Nothing of the sort. Because when she died, so did I. It's Tillmann who's kept us going. Because he's like his mother – determined, unbeatable, loyal.

We head back to the car with our bags of shopping. It's only a small two-door hatchback; modern, boring, and there's plenty of room for what we've got. It's still dark when we nose out of the car park and head towards the motorway.

Tillmann's already stuck a CD in the drive. We hate listening to the radio now, now that John Peel's dead, now that all the good people have gone, now that there's just manufactured pap on, repeat, repeat, repeat. Maybe the times will change and there'll be a new New Wave.

We burned some of Peelie's shows onto CD, but we don't listen to them in the car, because there's too much background noise. Because we don't just like the music; we like to hear him talking between tracks. I used to carry tapes of Peel round with me on my travels, to keep me sane, the same 10 shows over and over, but always something new. But that was even before I met Till's mother, before my real life started.

So we're moving along listening to something

Tillmann's put together, robbed mp3s from the internet, legal tracks from the CDs he buys with his pocket money, stuff from here there and everywhere. He calls them things like 'rocktravel' and 'softtravel' because he needs music when he's moving. And he likes to know what mood the CD is. Doesn't bother with track listings. Problem is that he likes the same music as me. I've been told off for taking away a boy's most potent form of rebellion – music his father hates. And, just on cue, here's The Killers and *Somebody Told Me*. I love loud music.

As we're coming up to the roundabout by the motorway, I ask Tillmann which way to go.

'Head for London,' he shouts over the music, his mouth already full of ripped French bread and ham. 'As good a place to start as any.' He laughs.

And it is as good a place as any. Because that's where everything started, really, after the coincidental meeting at the railway station. It's easy to dream when you're steering a car on a long empty motorway. Easy to lose track.

*

So there we were, on the platform, the black-haired woman and the bleached blond, skirting round each other like nervous animals do. God made this coincidence, I'm sure. Problem is, I've never been able to tell what people are thinking or feeling. My favourite question's always been 'What're you thinking?' but I didn't ask it then.

We had another couple of cigarettes. I was feeling less embarrassed now, more in control of myself, and I knew the slow train was going to arrive soon. Then we'd go our separate ways and that would be that. Another dream, another moment lost.

'So what are you planning up in London?' she said.

'Just looking round record shops, wandering round,' I answered. 'You know the usual sort of thing sad bachelors do on Saturdays to keep themselves occupied.'

'How very sad. I'd have thought you'd at least be going to a football match or something macho like that.'

'Not today. Been there; done that. My heart's not in it anymore.'

I didn't admit to her that I did actually miss doing what I'd used to do when I lived in London; just take a tube to King's Cross and decide on the platform which match in London to go to. But, as I said, my heart wasn't in it anymore.

'And you?' I said.

'No, I don't like football,' she said, deliberately ignoring the real question.

'I meant what are you…'

'I know what you meant. I'm being silly. I live in London. I was just down here last night for a party.'

'And you were in a hurry to leave? Can't have been much of a party if you're not hung over and don't want to stay.'

She shrugged – she had this tendency to shrug. 'These things happen,' she said. 'Can't have great parties all the time.'

Just then the tracks began to rattle, the station announcer muttered some muffled comments through the tannoy and the train pulled in. Before I could stop her, she'd slipped her arm through mine.

'You might as well accompany me to London,' she chuckled (another one of her habits).

In those days the slow trains up to London had separate compartments, all linked on one side of the carriage by a long corridor, but with sliding doors shutting off the compartments. She chose one about halfway down the carriage and sat down opposite me.

While we were waiting for the train to leave, she just stared out of the window onto the platform. Never said a word. Never looked at me. Only when the train started moving again did she turn to me again.

'You've not told me your name,' she said.

'You've not asked me. I'm not sure what you're doing talking to a total stranger, anyway. I could be dangerous.'

She laughed. 'I think I'd know if you were dangerous. London's taught me a bit.' She took off her coat, leaned back again. 'So, what *is* your name?' she persevered.

'You first,' I said, folding my arms over my chest. 'For all I know, *you* might be dangerous, so I need your name and address. Sorry.' I still don't understand, to this day, what had got into me.

'And you say you're crap at small talk! Maybe you're dangerous, after all. A liar.'

'A jinxed liar, if I am a liar. Don't forget that.' I wagged my finger at her playfully. 'Don't ever forget that.'

'I won't.' She giggled and grabbed hold of my finger, stared right at me, face close enough to scent. 'You *are* dangerous, my friend, very dangerous indeed.' She let go of the blushing me, pursed her lips. 'I'm Kate,' she said, 'short for Katherine with a K. And I live…'

'I was joking.' I stopped her. 'And I'm Nairne. God knows what my parents were thinking.'

This time she extended her hand gracefully and waited for me to shake it. The tingling got worse each time she touched me. That's what I remember most.

By the time we reached London we'd persuaded ourselves to have lunch with each other. By the time we decided we'd have dinner with each other as well, we were holding hands. By the time I'd missed the last train home I knew where she lived. And by the time the next morning came, we'd kissed and I'd slept on her sofa.

I believe in gentle beginnings.

*

We're getting close to London. It's only just getting light, and there's still hardly any traffic. The Sex Pistols are telling us now that God should save the Queen, although we'd rather He didn't.

'What now?' I call across to my ever-hungry son who never seems to put on any weight.

'Why don't we drive up to where Mum used to live?' he shouts back.

By now I've given up even trying to argue with him. I don't understand what he's trying to achieve, if him claiming that he thinks Kate is still alive is just a ruse to try to get me to finally confront her absence and start again, or if he genuinely believes that she's alive somewhere and living in London.

'Dad?' he says. 'Did you ever notice anything weird about Mum? Like before she died?'

'What d'you mean – weird? She was dying, Till. She was really ill. There wasn't anything to notice other than that.'

The traffic's worse now. Bloody London. I have to slow down and look at my son when it's the last thing I want to do.

'But did things change between you after she'd got ill, or even before ?' He carries on pushing.

I suppose now's the time to tell him those things that he should know. 'I think we really stopped getting on with each other the minute she got ill, to be honest,' I say quietly, after I've turned down the music. 'It was like she became someone else, just like that. One day she was Kate. The next day she wasn't. I can't explain it.'

'And before that?'

'Well, before that,' I scratch my chin. 'Well, things had sort of been a bit ropey, but I didn't really think much of it.'

'Why's that, Dad?'

'What, why didn't I think much of it, or why were things a bit ropey?'

'Both,' he answers.

'The ropey thing was because Kate wanted more kids, and I didn't. As for the not thinking much about it; well, I guess I reckoned she'd just change her mind after a while, and be happy with just you.'

'Didn't you talk about this stuff before you got married?' He's sounding incredulous now, like he expects everyone to be sensible and rational and organised, when getting married's nothing like that. Just the opposite, in fact. Although it shouldn't be.

'We should've, I guess,' I admit. 'Y'see it's difficult when you're in love and sort of just want to go for it. You don't sit down and discuss things point by point like you should, really.'

'So you didn't,' he states.

'No.' I try to concentrate on driving again. We're heading up to north London. I wonder if I should persuade him that we should just go sight-seeing. It wouldn't work. I'll just drive.

'So how did she react when she noticed that you basically weren't gonna do anything about having any more kids?'

He doesn't give up, does he?

'She stopped sleeping with me,' I say bluntly.

He must be old enough to understand about that stuff by now, mustn't he? Anyway, I've talked to him about it a bit, now and again. Love and respect. Safe sex and all that responsible stuff. It's just difficult to know if they're taking it in. Or even listening. 'I started sleeping on the sofa in the living room.' Back to Square One, I think, but without the anticipation.

'But that's where I always remember you sleeping, anyway,' he says. 'I thought it was because she was ill.'

'Till, mate, can you imagine what I'd have given to be

still in that room with her, even when she was ill?' I say, and all the guilt comes out. 'I should've been there for her, should've been able to care for her more than at arm's length, shouldn't have used her insurance money to pay for a nurse to come in and deal with the worst of it.' I'm almost crying now, idiot that I am. 'And, at the end, all I could do was hold her hand, nothing more. I should've felt close to her but I didn't. It'd all gone, somehow, changed, all changed the minute she got back from the doctor's. Changed even from the friendship we'd still had kipping in separate rooms and having you to look after.'

'D'you love me, Dad?' he says. He's not shaking as much as I am. In fact, he's not shaking at all. He seems quite untouched by all these revelations.

''Course I do! Why d'you ask?'

''Cos it all seems a bit weird to me, that's why,' he says. 'Had the two of you planned to talk about it at any point, and move back into one bed, or were you just two stubborn idiots?' He talks more grown-up than me sometimes, does Tillmann.

'I don't honestly know.' I don't. 'Kate got ill quite soon after we agreed to disagree, so we never really got round to talking about it again.'

'Mmm.'

He turns the music up again. We're just on the road again. A twelve-year-old dude and his inadequate father. It'll probably take another hour to get where he wants to go. And then? All I can do is follow.

Chapter 2

It lasted for several months, the sofa stage after Kate and I first met. It was the right thing to do. If this was the real thing, it'd wait. If it wasn't, there'd be no harm done. I spent a small fortune tripping up to London and back most weekends. Weekends full of kisses and holding hands. During the week we'd call each other and talk and talk and talk. The cats sort of knew that they'd get short shrift once I picked up the phone, and disappeared out into the garden, hunting in the railway embankments for rats and whatever else they could find.

Then, one cold winter evening the following February, Kate cooked us dinner, sat me down at the table and told me she was moving out west. Oh God, I thought, here we go. Another one down. What did I do wrong this time?

I'd had girlfriends before, but they'd all been exercises in brief serial monogamy, or the odd one-night stand, nothing anywhere in the same league as what I felt for Kate – and we hadn't even slept together. Maybe I should've gone for it in a bigger way. Maybe I should've tried to seduce her that first Saturday. All this was going through my head as she was talking at me about moving away from London. Hell, west could even mean the States.

'Are you listening to me?' she said, grabbing hold of my hand.

The tingling was still there. And the kissing over the past few months had been really good. Was this really the end?

''Course I'm listening,' I said. 'I'm just wondering what I've done wrong.'

'What d'you mean, done wrong?' she said, shaking her head. 'I've just said I want to move in with you, you big fool!'

'What?' No, I was imagining things. 'Can you say that all again, please?'

'Dear Lord, what am I letting myself in for?' she said instead. 'What is it that you've got that I just don't want to be without?'

'Stupidity?' I said, smiling, disbelieving. 'A jinx? I'm a good listener?'

She laughed out loud, a shimmering belly laugh straight from the centre of her. A laugh that shook the table. A laugh that made me feel at home. And now she was coming home to me. The logistics of it didn't matter.

That night we drank two bottles of Spanish Cava without getting drunk. And she asked me into her bed. I can still feel her hair stroking my face as she looked down at me. Or I imagine I can feel it, because there's so much I've forgotten. So much I've had to forget to protect myself.

A few weeks later I was pottering about in the flat one weekday evening, trying to get things in shape for when she was due to move in. I'd already tidied up most of the place. Was just passing time until she called me, really. She wouldn't be bringing much with her anyway, because she'd rented her place furnished – cheaper that way. Just a car (which she hardly ever drove), a heap of books, and the usual things that women decide to strangle bathrooms with. I'd already given her a key – she used to come to me sometimes, and I'd sleep on my sofa instead of on hers.

As usual, I had my music on loud. The girl in the flat upstairs – the detached house had been split into flats years ago – spent most of her time with her boyfriend, and wasn't around to complain about the noise. I was listening to some punk compilation – feeling old already. The Only Ones were banging out *Another Girl, Another Planet* when someone grabbed me from behind as I was dancing round the room with one of my old cricket bats.

'Bloody hell!' I shouted.

'Surprise!' she shouted back, chuckling, shrugging, crying, laughing all at once. 'I'm heeeeeere!'

I turned down the music. I always need a soundtrack for my life; I just don't have a track listing for every memory. I grabbed her, grabbed her into my arms, against me, smelt the rain on her hair, kissed her.

'So I see,' I finally said. 'So I see. I wasn't expecting you before the weekend.'

'You won't be seeing me in London this weekend,' she said, 'because, as from now, we're living together.'

I remember bringing in her stuff, scattering her pillows round my spartan living room, piling her books high next to mine. I remember all that, and The Only Ones on repeat because I needed wild music to go with this wild woman who'd found me and saved me. Because I needed something to make a memory.

That's all I remember, for now. It's her funeral I can't remember, refuse to remember. And now she's gone.

*

Tillmann changes CDs as we start driving into Harringay, the Saturday morning traffic slowing us to an almost weekday crawl. The Only Ones, of course. How does he know these things, this kid who spends most of his time playing PlayStation, or out with his mates when he should be at home? I've given up trying to tell him what to do. I'm just thankful that he doesn't get bad marks at school and that he's not on drugs – as far as I know.

'So why d'you want to come up here, then?' I say, although I'd already decided it would be futile to ask.

'Just wanted to see the place again,' he says. 'Pick up some vibes or whatever it is you hippies…' I start growling. '…hippies call it.'

He smiles his cherub smile. Yeah, it was a futile question to a precious twelve-year-old. Stupid, really. I shake my head.

'Don't shake your head, Dad,' he criticises. 'I'm sort of serious. Maybe there's something here.'

I pull the car over. The driver behind me hoots his horn.

'Listen Tillmann,' I say, maybe too harshly. 'I really don't think this is gonna achieve anything other than make us even sadder and more depressed than we are. She's gone, mate, and nothing we do can ever change that.'

'Whatever,' he sighs. 'You're wrong. And, Dad, I'm not talking about ghosts and shit like that. I'm talking about the real world, about then and now. And the real world's telling me she's alive, whatever we might've seen then, whatever that thing was that died in your bed.'

I breathe deeply. I'm getting a bit annoyed now. Mustn't get cross because then I'll lose my temper, and I'm not nice when I lose my temper. No-one is.

'Don't talk like that about her!' I hiss, hitting the button on the CD player to turn it off. 'I don't care what you think about that thing, as you call it, but she was your mother, she loved you right to the end, through all her pain, through all the shit that I put her through, everything. Don't ever ever call her a thing again. You weren't even five, for Christ's sake. You can't even remember her properly.'

He's unmoved by this. Although it's actually bordering on the threatening. He touches my hand – he's electric like his mother, just not in that way. But he has something; power, presence. Maybe I don't think highly enough of myself.

'Sorry it upsets you,' he says, cool, calm, collected. 'But I do remember her. I know you think I'm mad. I know I'm only a kid. I know nothing might come of it. I know it's a crazy idea to have. But what can we lose? Nothing. We'll just be back where we were before I woke you up this morning. And even if we only find out something about her that we never knew, it'll make us wiser, richer, won't it? And maybe you'll be able to start again, meet someone new, stop your pointless grieving.' He doesn't take his hand away when he's finished.

I shake my head. It's impossible to say anything, because I know he's right. With most of it, anyway. I turn the music back on, start the car again. The Smiths hopefully singing *There's A Light That Never Goes Out.* They have that in common with my son. And, deep down, with me, too.

We're in that maze of streets near White Hart Lane now. Kate had lived round here without ever going to see a game. How strange. I thought it then, and I still think it now. But she was never interested in sport. Hated it with a vengeance, for some odd reason. Had a one-track mind for books and a little music, although her tastes had stopped with The Jam.

Here we are now. A street like hundreds of other streets in hundreds of other cities. Shop fronts strung along a straight mile, some of them boarded up, some of them with tables out front laden with fresh fruit and vegetables contaminated by the passing traffic. And above the shop fronts row upon row of windows looking in on student flats, bedsits, empty rooms, full rooms, shabby and elegant at once. The doors, and the staircases behind them, hidden in the blackened facades.

'It's round here somewhere, isn't it, Dad?' Tillmann says, doubting his own memory.

'Yes, it's round here somewhere,' I say, staring at the doorway she used to walk in and out of. 'But she isn't.'

*

We'd met by chance. And now we were living together. I couldn't believe how lucky I was. I'd never thought of myself as handsome or particularly bright. And yet, here I was, sharing a bed, a kitchen, a house, with one of the most beautiful women I'd ever seen, never mind known.

Is there such a thing as coincidence? Is there such a thing as chance, or are all our fates and actions governed by an external force? They say the universe has a finite edge, beyond which there is nothing, and that one day it will all collapse in on us again, after having expanded for billions of years. How can we know? Do we need proof for such things, or is it a question of science ruled by faith, or faith explained by science? I still watch the dark nights for a sign, look for the star that might be the soul of my beautiful wife, ripped away from me by a dreadful illness before we'd had enough time with each other. Wish that that external force which might determine our lives had taken me instead of her, because without her nothing makes sense, and nothing is real.

Is there such a thing as redemption? I don't think so, because I carry the guilt over her death around with me every single day.

Living with Kate was wondrous. She was like a child much of the time, despite the sophisticated veneer she covered herself with. Underneath that outside, she was a playful girl and a grown woman at once. She was my cornerstone, my confessor, my plaything, my lover, my healer. That's why I had to marry her, because I wanted us to be together forever. But there is no forever.

Two months after she moved in with me, I borrowed her passport under false pretences. I'm sure – actually I know now, because she told me later – that she thought I was going to book a holiday for us. What I actually did was to go the local registry office and buy a marriage licence. And set a time for the wedding. A Friday afternoon in May.

We were lucky, really. We had no baggage. She didn't get on with her parents, so I never met them. My parents were old and lived in the North. We were both hermits and loners, deep down. Lucky we found each other.

I surprised her with my proposal. She'd not been expecting it, even after the extended months of sofa sleeping, even after the moving in together. Had she been hoping for it? I don't know. I never asked her. But she said yes, and we dragged two total strangers in from outside the registry office, just like they do in the best sentimental films, to be our witnesses. And that was that.

One thing I remember about that day more than anything else. I managed to find Kate a single black rose which she held throughout the ceremony. And afterwards I took a picture of her in her straight tight dress holding the rose out in front of her. It's that picture that still hangs by the bed – a pale girl all in cream, proffering a black rose out of the photo, and atop it all a mass of black curls, waves in the sand of time.

Our honeymoon was a brief week of paradise in Venice, a city we both loved. We never went back. We talked about it, but did nothing about it.

Life was fairly kind to us after that, for a while. We had decided, at the first, not to have children straightaway because we wanted some time to ourselves. What we didn't realise was how little time we would have, all told.

We can't see into each other's bodies, just as little as we can see out to the edges of the universe. Maybe the disease was already alive in her when I met her, maybe it started the day we got married. Who knows? Despite all the advances of science, despite mankind's intelligence and progress, we really know nothing of the heart of life. No matter how many books we read, no matter what we try to teach ourselves, we achieve nothing.

What is left to me of her? A barren grave in some barren deserted graveyard. A shallow hole with an urn full of ashes in it. I didn't have the heart to follow her wishes and scatter her ashes over some forlorn rocks in Scotland. I wanted Tillmann to have a place he could go when he wanted someone to talk to other than me. All I really have are the bitter memories of her last few months when we had become strangers again. Restless bitter strangers with only one thing in common. A child we thought was too young to understand.

I'm not sure she has forgiven me. I'm not sure she ever will.

*

Tillmann jumps out of the car before I can stop him. I haven't even told him which door it is, of all those front doors. He's obviously been watching my eyes while I've been thinking about the day I married Kate. I can't move. I must be a damn fool to let him go careering off like that in the middle of London, but I'm paralysed. Too many memories. I've not been here since she moved out.

He's banging on the door like a madman. The people in the shop are looking at him like he's a madman. The traffic just keeps pushing its way past me, in my little car, up on the kerb, window closed, head in hands. I can only watch him.

The door opens and he goes in. I can't see who's let him in, but now I panic. I'm halfway out of the car when the door opens again and he comes out.

'She's not been here since she moved out,' he shouts at me across the pavement which has suddenly become an abyss. 'Let's go.'

He jumps into the car before I've recovered from my panic and my inaction.

'Come on, Dad,' he shouts again. 'Let's go somewhere else.'

'Who'd you speak to in there?' I say when I've managed

to wrap myself back into the driver's seat.

'Some old geezer. Says he's been living there for ages. Says he remembers Mum, but he's not seen her for ages.'

'You told him she was dead, then. You did tell him, didn't you?'

'No I didn't.' He looks at me. 'Because she isn't.'

I sigh. I'm exasperated. What was the point of that? I could've told him this would happen, that there'd be no trace of a dead woman in a street she hadn't lived in for almost fifteen years.

'But that's good, Dad,' he says. 'Don't you see? It means she can't have gone back to at least one part of her past, so maybe she's moved forwards…'

'Moved on, more like.'

'Not funny,' he says. 'Not funny at all, Dad.'

'Sorry. And now? What now?'

'You know you said things got all weird between you two before she got ill?'

'Yes?' I don't know where this is leading.

'Well, had things ever been weird between you before, after you'd got it together? Or was everything hunky-dory all the time? Not that I'd believe you if you said it was, 'cos people do have fights.'

He sticks in another CD and grabs some more bread. We're still parked on the kerb.

''Course we argued,' I say, trying to think back. 'Big rows as well, sometimes, but usually over stupid things like being jealous or money or whose bread was better…'

'Now that's what I call stupid. Bloody effin' stupid.'

'Well, you'll find out all about that when you're older, I guess,' I warn him. 'Big things hardly ever cause rows, you know. Big things just cause resentment, something neither of you'll end up talking about. Things that break relationships.'

'Like having more kids,' he simply says.

'Like having more kids.' I start the car. 'And now?'

'Did you ever argue about me?' he says.

'All the time,' I say. 'Like who should be getting up in the night, because I was crap at waking. Like there being too much noise when I was trying to work. All that sort of stuff.'

'Did you like having a baby? I mean, really?' He looks at me again.

'Not really, to be honest. Not really. It scared me; it still does, this responsibility. It's not like you have any job experience when you become a parent. You make lots of mistakes because you don't know any better. You can only do your best. … Look, I don't want to sit here all day. This was your idea – you decide where we're going.'

'Did you ever find out anything about Mum's past before she met you?' he says.

I feel like he's ignoring me.

'Does it matter?'

'It might help me decide where to go next.'

'You're a funny lad. I don't see where any of this is getting us.'

Oh God, her past; if he asks me more about that I don't know what I'll say. Because I hate her past, and she wished she'd never told me about it.

'Tell me some of it, then,' he insists. 'And let's head north. We could always go see Grandma if we don't find anything.'

How the hell will we find anything? There's nothing to find. Eight years of dreaming about a dead woman, and he suddenly decides she's not dead. I can't get over this. How stupid have I been to give in to this child's whim? Still, can't stop now.

We head off again, follow the signs to the North. How far north is north? Where does the world start and end? Tillmann asked me that kind of question when he was small. I didn't have an answer then, either. I guess he's just carrying on from there. I smile to myself. Maybe this'll be a good trip, after all. He turns the music up – *Losing My Religion*, REM tell us. That was one of her songs, too. I remember now that we heard it booming out of some bar in Venice. We'd known it from before, but, from then on, it was the soundtrack of our honeymoon. Long long ago. Before we, too, started losing our faith.

*

Kate and I drove up to Scotland in the January of the second year of our marriage. Eighteen months into it, to be precise. It was almost a celebration of two years of living together. We wanted to be where the cold was crisp, not damp. We wanted to be where the only light you could see would be that of the stars. We hired a cottage for a week, out in the middle of nowhere, in a tiny hamlet called Nethy Bridge. It would take us almost ten hours to drive up there, but we decided to take a break in Yorkshire for one night and sleep at my parents' house.

We finally arrived at our cottage at about three in the afternoon. Dusk was readying itself to settle on the trees and in the bushes. We'd bought supplies on the way. We went for a walk until it grew dark, then opened our first bottle of red wine as we watched the fire in the grate.

'Are you happy?' she said as she leant against me on the sofa.

'Yeah, why shouldn't I be?'

She shrugged, as she always did. 'Dunno,' she said. 'I just wanted to ask you. We need to be happy to have a child.'

We'd decided the previous autumn that we'd try to have a baby. I wasn't entirely sure about it, because I wasn't convinced that she'd be able to give up smoking for nine months. But *she* was sure, even though she'd never managed it before. She'd have a good reason to give up, she said. Better than any other reason, she said. So I'd agreed and she'd stopped taking the tablets.

Of course it wasn't just the smoking that made me a bit dubious about having a child. I was desperate not to lose her. I didn't want to share her with anybody else, anything else. I couldn't bear the thought of not having her near me, of her not being close to me. But back then I didn't know what extremes I would go to to keep her.

Women have this way of making you love them even more. They tell you they want to have your children, and you believe they're showing how much they really really love you; that they're not following a biological instinct. And we men love them more for that, because we're all selfish, all driven by this need for self-confirmation, this macho desire to prove that we *are* men and that our women couldn't exist without us. How wrong we are. And how heavily we pay the price.

Anyway, when she hadn't conceived by Christmas, Kate was getting desperate, so desperate that she was crying herself to sleep nearly every night. She'd convinced herself that there was something wrong with her, that it was her fault. But I knew, and I told her, that it could just as easily be me who had the problem. And that it took ages for the effects of the pill to wear off, and that first babies always take ages. Not that anything I said made her feel better, though. So, at the beginning of January we decided to go up to Scotland, to get away from everything and everybody we knew.

And here we were. I think she asked me if I was happy because she wanted to give me a final chance to retreat from our decision, to give me one last chance to say no to a child. But I didn't, because, above all, I wanted her to be happy. I would cope, I said to myself, I would.

I kissed the back of her head, smelt our walk in that mass of black curls, tasted that unadulterated scent that our lovers have, which is just them, no perfume, no cosmetics, just them. They carry it with them always.

'I love you, Kate,' I said. 'I loved you from the first minute I met you. I always will love you.' It was easy in those days to say what I felt and mean it.

'I know you do,' she said. 'I know you do, and I love you, too.'

She turned round and kissed me on the mouth. The next morning we woke up to snow, and to cells dividing and multiplying in Kate's belly. Although we didn't know about that until 3 weeks later. Maybe that's when the bad cells started multiplying, too.

We walked more than we'd ever walked before, that week. Rambling through the snowy paths in the forest was brilliant, the snow silencing even the little sound of the world that had been around us when we'd arrived. After dark we'd watch the children's videos that were piled up next to the telly, obviously for the families who hired the cottage in the summer. Bambi made us cry. We probably knew even then that Kate'd got pregnant on our first night there. I don't think we'd ever been so happy, so carefree, so joyously without worry.

So, when she'd taken the pregnancy test three weeks later, she stopped smoking. Made me stop smoking in the house. You see, one of my great weaknesses has always been a lack of willpower. That's why I couldn't give up. That's why I blame myself for her death, because she might not've started smoking again if it hadn't been for me.

I started reading books for prospective fathers. We bought name books to choose names. We'd burst out laughing for no reason when hanging out in bookshops (she had once worked in one) and leafing through all the baby and parent books they had. Tillmann's name wasn't in any of those books.

When we went to the local hospital for Kate's first scan, I cried when I saw that tiny black and white scratchy picture moving around on the screen somehow attached to her womb. Although the woman dealing with us explained everything in great detail, it was still a miracle to me, a total wonder that the communion of some of my bodily fluid with Kate's could create something that was alive and moving. That would grow. That would become another human.

But at that moment, too, I realised that I wouldn't, couldn't, ever be as connected to that child as Kate would be. Couldn't ever be as close to any child as its mother. Because it wasn't me who was giving it life, it was Kate. Children are never a part of their fathers. They become one of their mother's vital organs. Men can never understand what it means to carry another creature around inside you for nine heavy months. Can never instinctively understand their children like mothers do. And that's why it's so easy for us to be selfish.

The more pregnant Kate got, the more beautiful she became to me. She hated getting fat as she called it, but to me it was just a blossoming of thinness. I loved to put my hand on her swelling belly, stroke its circumference, feel its primeval heat. And later feel the child inside kicking, moving, turning, hiccoughing. It was then that I started talking to Tillmann, before he was even born, before we even knew what he was. Talking to him so he'd get to know me, and maybe even love me when he was born.

In the end Kate gained nearly thirty kilos in weight. Her stomach was so huge, and the rest of her body so thin, that we took pictures of her from the side just so that we'd remember. It looked weird and wonderful all at once. But it was taking its toll, too, and two weeks before her due date we started working out ways in which we might speed up the arrival of our child.

All the books and magazines recommended sex and curry and champagne. That didn't work, not done separately, not done at the same time. The next suggestion came from a friend who'd driven his pregnant wife down a very long set of stone steps on the back of his motorbike. We didn't have a motorbike. Long walks someone else suggested. After one walk Kate was so tired she reckoned she couldn't have pushed even if she'd had to.

What we did in the end was drive up to Coombe Gibbet in my old car. The car park for this macabre attraction up there on the Downs was a hillside of mud, extremely bumpy when frozen. And it was cold that October. The first frost of the autumn. So I drove my poor old car round that car park as fast as I could for half an hour or more. It was the closest we got to the motorbike. It worked, and an hour later we were in Reading Hospital.

Chapter 3

We decide to find the back way out of London. Tillmann knows I hate motorways. I only drove into London on one because I thought it wouldn't be too busy. For a while we're quiet, just watching those inner city suburbs coming to life. I guess London's always alive, but sometimes more than others. We've still not decided where we're going, exactly, but we're heading north, out of the city, away from its seven million pairs of eyes.

The road signs haven't changed in my memory. On the minor roads, there's the sign that says 'Hatfield and the North'. How north is the North? The North Pole? And round again?

Hatfield is about twenty miles north of London. I'd spent some time there when I was younger. The flat I'd been looking after for some friends overlooked a graveyard. They'd gone to India for a year and had asked me to flat-sit. Me and my mad Welsh flatmate often wandered around in that graveyard after the pubs had shut and we were too drunk and too bored to think of anything else to do. He'd had bright red hair, was into rockets, and worked for an aviation engineering company nearby. He liked blowing things up. The funny thing was that, no matter how out of his head he was, or how disconnected with reality, he always cut his bread into slices half an inch thick. With the help of a ruler he kept in the kitchen. Honest.

Eminem's just getting to the bit in *Stan* where his crazed fan decides to drive off a bridge. Tillmann thinks the song's cool, and I'm not arguing. It's just weird that at his age I'd not developed my own taste in music (some might say he's developed my taste, but that's not true). Maybe it's because kids now get their music players sooner than we got our record players (he hates handling vinyl; I don't). And with us frightened parents trying to keep our kids off the streets, they get more electronic toys to keep them indoors and, so we think, safe. I do try to make sure he plays outdoor team games like I did. He hates it. He's not a team man. But it's something I won't give in on. The only thing, I guess.

'Are you gonna tell me more about Mum, then?' he asks.

I don't know where all these questions have been hiding for the past few years, because he's never asked them before. All the questions used to be about where the heaven was that Mum had gone to. Had Mummy really looked like that – pointing at the wedding picture by my bed – before she'd got ill? Had Mummy loved him? What did Mummy used to eat? All that sort of banal but real questioning that children use to construct their worlds. Where they learn from things that have gone before, and maybe learn to do those things better. Mechanical, real-life things. And trying to build a physical picture of a dead woman not disfigured by illness and pain.

Parenting, of course, isn't one of those real-life things, not to me, because there's no single right way to parent. I know, because I've found all the wrong ways. What will Tillmann think of me when he's older? What will his memory of me be? You see, there it is again, this male selfishness. Who actually cares what children think of their parents? It's unimportant, because what matters is that children feel safe and loved. That they feel they have somewhere they can always come back to and be protected, if that's what they think they need and want. I'm not sure Tillmann's felt that since his mother died, but I could be wrong. I hope I am.

'Mate, you need to ask me more specific questions than that,' I say, knowing even before the words are out of my mouth, that this really does open a can of worms. A huge one. Full of huge worms. 'What I mean… what I mean is that I can't sit here driving, holding a monologue about a woman who was at least as complicated as you and me put together, without knowing exactly what it is you want to hear.'

'If I knew what I wanted to hear, Dad,' he says, and I can feel myself being patronised already, 'I wouldn't need to ask, would I? I'm trying to be like a detective, so I need to know about things that went on when I wasn't around, don't I? You're always saying to me – can't have a future without a past – aren't you?'

I shake my head and try not to smile. 'But that's something different. You're trying to make up a story that'll finish with the happy ending of us finding a woman who we think is dead, but she's actually alive, and us all falling into this huge family embrace at the end. Roll tears. Roll credits.'

'Not true.' He sulks.

'Yes, it *is*. And I wouldn't call that building a future on the past. I'd say it was building a fantasy on the past, and a disastrous and dangerous fantasy at that.'

He doesn't say anything for a while. I'm deliberately driving quite slowly so that time goes more quickly (sounds stupid, but it works), so that I can look at him – sort of – when we're talking. And so he's got more time to change his mind about this crazy adventure before we get too far.

'I won't change my mind, Dad,' he says at last. 'I know that's what you're hoping for, but it's not gonna happen.' He takes a sip of apple juice through a straw. God, I hate that noise. 'D'you remember what she did in Cambridge when she lived up there?' he says.

'She worked in a book shop. I thought you knew that.'

'I did, sort of, but I wasn't sure I was right. Why don't we go there, then?'

'Ok. Not a problem.' And I don't mind, actually. Cambridge is a wonderful place at any time of year (except when it's raining, maybe). And this morning it'll be even more so, because it's one of those wished-for cold autumn mornings now. The edges to all things have sharpened in the sun, and the whole world is more three-dimensional because of it.

It's almost noon by the time we roll into Cambridge. I find a parking space after a while. We get out, huddled up in the coats I'm glad Tillmann decided to chuck into the car.

'Let's just wander round and find some lunch,' he suggests.

'But you've been stuffing your face since we left the house this morning.'

'*You* haven't,' he says. 'And you need some warm food inside you.'

Where does he get it from, I ask myself, this being organised stuff? He's not even a teenager yet. He shouldn't be organising me, should he? He's the one who should be forgetting about eating, and I should be the one reminding him to eat properly and regularly and healthily. And dressing warmly. Oh well. I shrug.

Kate's time here and mine didn't overlap. By the time she wound up here, I'd long gone. Well, I'd been gone a year or so, I suppose, but then I'm not very good at keeping track of time or numbers. She's five years younger than me. Sorry, she *was* five years younger than me. She was only thirty-two when she died. How unfair is that? And I'm still smoking. Tillmann hates it.

It doesn't take us long to find a cafe. We order an all-day breakfast for me and some croissants for Tillmann. I hadn't realised how hungry I am. I wolf down bacon, eggs, baked beans, tomatoes and the extra mushrooms. Just like I did the morning after Tillmann was born.

*

The speed with which the bumpy ride had its desired effect misled Kate and me. When they examined her at the hospital, they told us that we could be in for a long night. It was only six in the afternoon. But Kate was already in a lot of pain, and nothing we'd read had prepared us for how bad the pain would get. Not that I felt the pain. I just felt the helplessness that must grip all men when their wives give birth. There's not actually much we can do. Our presence doesn't make the pain more bearable for them. In fact, they probably hate us for it. Blame us for it. Curse us for it. And then they forget it.

Thirty-six hours later, just as the midwives were preparing to get a doctor in there to get the baby out with forceps, and after I'd been asked to leave because Kate and I were shouting at each other, and after I'd calmed down and come back; after all that, Kate managed one last huge exhausted push and Tillmann was born. Not that he had a name when he was born.

I'd always imagined that it must be revolting to watch the most intimate part of your wife's body open to let go of the child she's been carrying. That the blood and the slime and the distortion would be an end to any attraction. I was wrong. To see our child's head pushing its way out into the world was one of the most wonderful things I've ever seen. I couldn't face cutting the cord, though, so the midwife did it. And then put the new bundle of life on Kate's belly. We both cried. I can't remember it in pictures because the emotion is what I recall, because the joy was one huge red sun rising into my life.

Tillmann was tiny. I'd never seen such a tiny human before. Already he had a shock of curly black hair, already he was making those small snuffly sounds that I would become familiar with. We have no time when children are born, when they are conceived, even, of understanding how much they will change our lives forever. And how badly sometimes we'll wish that they'd never arrived at all to change the way in which we'd decided to confront the world. But all the nightmares come later, all the desperate badness that we spew at those we love. All that comes later and destroys everything we ever manage to build.

But we didn't know that then, didn't realise in our golden hour that life was already demanding its price for the new life we'd created, for the new life that would suck all our will and love out of us, or would at least make us feel that way.

I wasn't allowed to go up to the maternity ward with Kate, so, an hour after our then still nameless boy was born, I tiredly got into the car and drove home. I slept for four hours, was woken by a neighbour asking how Kate'd got on, tried to sleep again but couldn't. So I drove over to the nearest road café and ordered their biggest big breakfast. And gorged myself.

The next few days were a blur. I drove over to Reading for whenever I was allowed to visit. Visiting hours are stupid. Why can't we visit our wives and children when we want?

Kate and I puzzled and puzzled over names. The baby was without a name for three days. Kate was tearful almost all the time. Her breasts were hurting and breastfeeding was an immense effort. On the fourth day she told me she'd decided to call the boy Tillmann. I didn't know why, but, with my name, who was I to argue? And it does sound good when you say it out loud.

On the fifth day, Kate and Tillmann came home. Breastfeeding was becoming harder, not easier. I made a 100-mile roundtrip on that Sunday trying to find something that would ease Kate's pain, something that would make the process of feeding this child more simple. But she wouldn't let me buy formula milk. The next day the midwife told us we could've phoned the hospital to get help. But no-one had told us that before. From there on Kate's pain became less, and we began to settle into life as a family.

Two weeks later my father died. Kate had loved the gruff old man. She'd said, the first time she'd come up there with me, that my parents' house was like the home she'd never had. Not that I knew anything of her as a girl. Not that I ever got to find out anything about her family. About that she was always steadfastly silent. To this day I have no knowledge of that part of her. And never will.

When Kate and I got married, Mum and Dad had only been a little sad that they'd not been there to see it. They understood who I was. They were at ease with me being my own person. I didn't share much with them. Kate was the first and only of my lovers they'd ever met.

Mum was bereft when Dad died. They'd been married for over forty years. They'd met just after the Second World War, and they'd been inseparable from then on. I did the decent thing and donned a shirt and tie and posh trousers to arrange the funeral. I did everything. The only thing I didn't do was cry. I still haven't cried for my father, and I don't think I ever will. Just like I've never really cried for Kate. Sobbed, maybe, but never cried my heart out. Maybe that's because I feel betrayed by both of them.

And so life carried on. I phoned Mum two or three times a week, but that was it. We were too busy with our own lives to understand that maybe we were needed more than we assumed. Too lazy, maybe, to put ourselves out and travel all the way up to Yorkshire from the south to console an old woman robbed of the only person she'd ever really loved. At least she got forty years with him. I only got eight years with Kate, and that was from the first day I met her. What's eight years? Nothing, that's what.

On Tillmann's first birthday we took him to the roadside café where I'd celebrated his birth a year earlier. Even then he'd already developed his insatiable appetite. But he never got fat. Even now he's skinny, just like his mother. We had fun that day, the three of us. Him in his high chair, and we young parents, all of life before us. Would I have done anything differently had I realised there were only four years left of this family life, four years of a love I'd believed would last forever? To be honest, I don't know. We can't ever know how a different past would have changed our now or our future.

But my then was changed that night. After Tillmann had gone to sleep, Kate and I got very drunk. For the first time since she'd got pregnant. We made love on the living room floor, all tears and sweat, and a longing that seemed to stretch so far into the future we couldn't even see the end of the beginning. In the immediate aftermath we felt invincible, I suppose. So invincible that we started talking about things we should maybe never have talked about. The past. I remember exactly how it started.

'Are you glad you married me?' I said to Kate, warming myself against her glow. Looking for self-confirmation again. That self-destructive force we men are born with.

'Of course I am,' she'd smiled back at me. 'I couldn't be happier.' She took another sip of wine. 'But, y'know, you can only be happy if you've been sad. And you can only be very happy if you've been very sad.'

'How sad've you been, then?' I said.

'Ooo, as sad as sad can be,' she said. 'Sadder than all the dead stars in the universe.'

Looking back, it seems obvious now that we'd never really talked with each other about things that mattered. But maybe that's my fault, because I think the past does matter. She never thought it did. She was carefree. I was laden with my mother's madness.

'When was that, then?' I said.

'Do you really want to know, Nairne?' she said gently. 'Do you really want to know? I'm not sure you do.'

'How could I not want to know?' I nuzzled her sweaty neck, her Kate-scented hair, ran my hands up and down her wet, thin-again body.

'Because it may change what you think of me, although it shouldn't.' She leaned back against me harder. 'Because it's before I met you, before you made me happy. And I don't want your love for me to change.'

'Go on,' I said, goading her. 'I can take it. Nothing can make me love you any less.'

'Can I have that in writing?' she said. 'It's your decision. It's not something I need to talk about.'

I thought she'd be telling me something about her family, but that wasn't it. It was something else, something unexpected, something that hurt me, but not as much as it had hurt her. And I had no right to let it hurt me, because it had nothing to do with me. Why does the world make us grow up believing we have the right to have a hold over someone or something? There is our tragedy.

And because she was drunk, because she was in love with me, because we'd come so far in so short a time, she let me goad her into talking about that past of hers that I never should have asked about, that I wish I'd never found out about. That ultimately tore us away from each other.

She wrapped my arms round her, snuggled herself even more deeply into my embrace, took a deep breath, and changed our life. 'That day we met,' she said, 'I'd not exactly been to a party, more like to a wake.'

I didn't interrupt her; I couldn't.

'I went there with my boyfriend. I'd met him in

Cambridge, and we went to this friend's party here. I told him I was pregnant. He told me he didn't want to have kids, that I should get rid of it. That he'd never wanted that kind of relationship; that he wanted to stay young, not become an old man before his time. I'd held off telling him for weeks. I reckoned I was about ten weeks gone. I was in love with him until the moment I told him. We'd been together for ages. He just told me to get lost, that he never wanted to see me again, why hadn't I been more careful, walked out and drove away. I just drank until I fell over. Surprised that I managed to get up in time to miss that train. If I'd got any drunker I might not've met you.' She took another sip of her drink.

'Then I met you at the station and it was like the darkness disappeared. Like everything was light again. You were my light. That weekend with you was a happiness I'd never expected. On the Tuesday after, I had the abortion. An in and out job. Quick scrape, and gone. And then I started taking the pill. After a few weeks I was all fixed again, inside my head. Felt like I was ready for you. And you so gentle and respectful. I never thought I'd get so much time to fall in love with someone before sleeping with them. It felt great. No pressure, no snide comments, no possessiveness. Just me being able to be me.'

Another sip.

'And that's why I got so worried when we didn't manage to conceive straightaway. I thought I'd messed my body up because I'd had an abortion. I thought I was being punished for killing another life, for not being strong enough to have the baby on my own. I thought about telling you about it then, but I didn't dare. However much I love you, I was still scared. But then Tillmann came along and took away all that guilt. And now I'm not scared anymore.'

I should've rejoiced at what I was hearing, should've

felt flattered that she'd felt so safe with me after what she'd obviously been through, but I didn't. All I could think about was that she'd not told me the truth. That she'd really, for everything she said, still been in love with someone else when we'd met. That I'd kissed her while she was still carrying someone else's child. That I'd fallen in love with her the day after she'd probably still wanted to be with that someone else.

*

I've finished my late breakfast now. I put down my knife and fork and drink some orange juice. Tillmann's watching me, leaning back on his chair, arms crossed, half-smiling. He can't see what I'm thinking. Thank God.

'Better?' he says.

I nod. I know he envies me the orange juice, sometimes, but that he understands that he can't have any because it makes him hyperactive. I think he's past caring about it most of the time, though. It used to make him sad when he was little.

'D'you remember which bookshop it was Mum worked at?'

I nod again.

'Should we go, then?' He gets up.

'And what d'you hope to find there?' I say.

'I don't know. I just wanna see it. Be somewhere else she's been. Is that so unnatural?'

'I guess not, if it weren't for the fact that this whole quest seems a bit unnatural. Doesn't it make you hurt more? Like when you got up this morning and cried because you'd been dreaming about her?'

'Dad, I'm used to dreaming about her. I was crying because I realised she's still alive, and because we'd done nothing about it for eight years. That *I'd* done nothing for eight years.'

'But you can't blame yourself for that. Can't blame yourself for not doing anything about something that's not true anyway.'

'It *is* true, and we're gonna find her. You don't have to agree with me, just bear with me.'

I walk him back along the road to the big Heffer's bookshop opposite the two biggest colleges in Cambridge. I hold the door open for him. We walk in.

'If I promise not to leave the shop, will you let me just have a wander round?' he says. How considerate of him.

'Yeah, ok,' I say. 'I'll just have a browse, and I promise I'll not follow you.'

I go one way, he goes another. I love books; old books, new books, any books. There was a second-hand bookshop about ten minutes away from the house in Newbury. Kate and I used to spend our Saturday mornings in there before and after Tillmann was born. It was cold and damp, but it was crammed full of all types of books, and none of them used to cost more than a pound. Most of the books we bought were from that shop. I still have some of them. Others I burned after she died. They couldn't stay in our house without her.

Just as I'm leafing through one of the hardback books on the New Fiction shelf, trying on the words, I feel movement behind me. I check my watch before I start to turn round. An hour's passed already.

'Hullo, Nairne.'

I hear a deep male voice and come face to face with a man in his late sixties. It's Kate's old boss.

'Hello, Bill,' I say and try to smile. Fancy bumping into him. 'Are you still working here? After all these years?'

'Well, I tried and I tried to get away, but they just won't let me retire,' he says, with a nod of his grey-haired head. 'It's sad you never found the time to come and see us after Kate's funeral. We'd have liked to see you.' He stops and starts again. 'We tried to call you, too.'

Tillmann's next to him, smiling.

'You know how it is, Bill.' I shrug. 'Life just passes you by; things get busy – complicated.'

He nods at me. He understands. I always liked him.

'Your young man tells me you're on a search for her, though,' he says, with a twinkle in his old eyes that's questioning and gentle at once.

'He's on a search for her, he should've said, not me,' I explain. 'But I've decided to go along with him.'

'He showed me a picture of her,' Bill says (I raise an eyebrow at Tillmann), 'but I didn't need reminding of her, of course. Such a beautiful woman, such a wonderful mind, such a loss. I did explain to him it's quite common to catch a glimpse of someone in the street and to think you've seen someone close to you who's died. And that this illusion goes on for quite some time, possibly for the rest of your life.'

At this point Tillmann opens his mouth as if to say something, but clamps it shut again.

'I had to tell him, though, that I thought I'd seen Kate a couple of times just a few weeks after she'd died. I was sitting over at my desk up there.' He looks up to the first mezzanine. 'And there was this woman standing down here, looking through the fiction books, who really did look like her. I got up to try to get down here, but when I looked across again, she'd gone.' He looks at me apologetically. 'But like, I said to young sir here,' he quickly adds, 'it was probably just a trick of the light. Sadly. And it was eight years ago.' He shrugs.

Kate'd been very fond of him. He'd looked after her in the early days, when she'd ended up here for one reason or another. I never did find out how, but I gave up asking her about her past after Tillmann's first birthday. She'd always said to me that he'd been like a father to her, only nicer.

'Thanks for that,' I say. 'I'm sure it means a lot to

Tillmann to hear you say that.' I look at my son whose grin is even broader than before. Odd boy.

'You should come up here more often,' Bill says. 'Give me a call next time, and we can have lunch and reminisce a bit. And look forward a bit, too, maybe.' He nods at Tillmann. 'I'm sure he'll be wanting to follow in his father's footsteps.'

'I'm not so sure about that,' Tillmann and I say at the same moment.

Now that's funny. I've not laughed that spontaneously in years. Bill's wrinkled face joins in.

'I guess we'd better be getting on,' I say.

I don't want to get involved in any last-minute invitations to tea or anything like that. I can see Tillmann wants to get going now as well. 'I promise I'll call next time. Honestly. Shouldn't have left it so long, really.' I shake Bill's hand.

He claps Tillmann on the shoulder. 'Look after each other,' he calls as we walk off.

'That was interesting, Dad, wasn't it?' Tillmann says as we're outside in the crisp air again. 'I told you we'd find something, didn't I?'

'What the old boy said doesn't prove anything. He said himself it's just one of those things that happen when someone dies. How often d'you think I've seen Kate and my dad walking down the road at home? It's a figment of our imagination, seeing dead people as if they were alive.'

'I still think you're wrong. I'm gonna write down the approximate dates of when he saw Mum. And I'm sure there'll be more to add.' He gets a little notebook out of his pocket, scribbles in it.

We wander down towards my old college by accident. I'm following him. He's just jay-walking. I don't want to go this way. I find a bench and sit down.

He turns round, looks at me, and sits down, too. 'Did

you and Mum ever bring me up here when I was a baby?' he says.

'A couple of times. Not to see Bill, or anything like that. Just to wander.' He doesn't know we're sitting opposite my old college.

'So why didn't you come up here more often? It's a lovely place.'

'Oh, you know, time, me not really liking it that much, things.'

'And you've not been up here since she went? Why?'

Maybe he is starting to accept that she's dead. I guess it's time to tell, so I tell him the story of his first birthday. He needs to know at some point why things started going wrong.

'Was that why you decided not to have any more kids, then?' he says. 'Because of the way you felt?'

'That was part of it. But I had no right to feel that way, you know.'

'How did you feel, exactly?'

'I was angry at something I'd no control over. Angry that she'd been with someone before I came along. Felt like she'd had no right to be in love with anyone before me. Like she'd been possessed by someone and never got rid of the traces. Especially about getting rid of the baby after she'd met me. But you mustn't ever feel like that. Jealousy is such a wasted, destructive emotion. It's just difficult to shut it out.'

'I wouldn't know. I'm not old enough yet to understand love or jealousy.' He takes a deep breath. After a while, he speaks again. 'But you've always told me to show how I feel. So why's it wrong to show how you feel when you feel jealous?'

'Because jealousy's a sign of low self-esteem. It's a delusion. But, on the other hand, I've never been able to cope with anything but black and white. I've always thought that if you really love someone you want them all to yourself, and that if you don't really worry about someone leaving you it means that you don't care. If you don't care what people do, you can't love them. That's how I felt, anyway.'

'And now?' he says.

'No idea. Everything sort of stopped when Kate died. Before that. I made myself stop caring because it was hurting me so much. Self-pity, I suppose. I'm certain of it. Sometimes. Sometimes not.'

He says nothing, just looks at me with those blue eyes. What's he thinking now? I'll not ask him.

'I don't think that we'll ever get to understand life,' I say when it's obvious he's not going to say anything. 'That's probably the whole point. But some of us think too much about everything. And that's dangerous.'

He still says nothing. We sit in silence for a few minutes, watching the crowds go by. And then I can't stop myself.

'What're you thinking?' I say.

Tillmann just smiles.

'That it's about time I kissed a girl.'

Chapter 4

Of course I never told Kate how I felt about her revelation. I tried to carry on leading life the way we had. Some days I recognised how stupid I was being, how hypocritical it was of me to feel hurt about something that had happened before she had known me, something that really did have nothing to do with me. Other days I'd be raging inside, about the lies, about the betrayal, about love dying, about love never having existed. But I managed to control myself, to never show her what I was feeling, what I was thinking about that one dark mark on our lives. I still loved her, I still wanted her as my wife, as my lover.

But then things gradually began to change. Tillmann, who'd been such a good baby, suddenly began not to sleep through the night. When he'd first been born, the adrenaline had kept me going when he woke, and, after around seven weeks, he'd started sleeping from about seven till seven. Kate had started feeding him bottled milk soon after that because her milk had run out. That's when she started smoking again, too.

Now, over a year on, she, probably reasonably, expected me to share the night duties with her. The only problem was that she didn't actually let me do it without her supervision. Which meant that she was just as tired as before, and that I had to deal with being watched over when I dealt with our son who, by now, had moved into his own room. And I hate being watched over. Hate being told what to do.

One night we had a blazing row about me not being able to hold the bottle properly, that he was waking up at night because I wasn't holding the bottle properly, how useless men were at looking after their children. I was so angry I just gave her the boy and the bottle and walked out. Stood in the cold in my training pants and jumper holding a bottle of red wine and a packet of cigarettes. I wouldn't go back in for an hour. When I did get back in, they were both asleep. In our bed.

I picked Tillmann up as gently as I could and took him back to his cot. There was no way I was going to have him sleeping in my bed. It'd been bad enough having him in our room for almost a year. I felt like I was a bad second to him in a contest for Kate's affections. Maybe I hadn't read enough books about how new fathers are supposed to deal with the imagined rejection that a wife's love for a new baby brings with it.

A few weeks later Kate was really ill, headaches so bad that she was throwing up. I think that's when I started to understand about babies, that's when I started to love Tillmann despite myself, and despite him. I was the only one capable of looking after him for nearly a week. I woke up in the night without feeling dreadful, fed him day and night without being told off for the way I was doing it, held him, talked to him, read to him, played with him. Kate refused to go to the doctor, passed her illness off as a really bad migraine. Not that she'd had any before – ever.

This episode seemed to redress the balance a little, and we developed into a happy enough threesome after this. For a little while. Living in the middle of a town, no matter how small or large, is not ideal with a child or children, whether or not you've got a garden. We used to drive out into the countryside at weekends so that we could go for long walks. I'd carry Tillmann round in a backpack, and he'd hold tight onto my hair and laugh into the wind. Those were great days, those fast few days that I manage to recall.

As time goes on I remember less and less of this, because I try to enjoy my time with the growing Tillmann, not with the baby memories I have of him. Am I trying to forget Kate? I have no idea. I don't think so.

I never could, I don't think, even if I tried.

Tillmann started walking relatively late. He was eighteen months old, and had never even crawled. He'd just bumped himself around the floor on his backside. Then, one day, he pulled himself up on the armrest of the chair Kate was sitting in, and I called across the room to him. We had quite a game for almost an hour, calling him back and forth, before he actually managed to cross that great carpeted abyss without falling. All three metres of it.

And all the time the golden glow of joy had this dark lining, in my head at least, where I would be sitting on my own in the brightness of the desk light, and would suddenly get visions of Kate enjoying herself with another man, calling words to him that she'd never called to me, doing all the things with him that she refused to do with me because she was too tired. I can't go into the details of those dreadful, self-inflicted dreams, because, even now, they hurt me, even now I hurt myself with them, asking myself if what we had ever had a meaning, was ever true.

What is the truth, after all, if not what we tell ourselves it is? Does reality even exist or count? Or is all the reality in the world just what we play to ourselves on the organic screens inside our heads, the pictures we paint for ourselves when we are awake and asleep? We'll never understand, at least not until we die. Kate would know now, I suppose, but there's no way of finding out.

So, amongst the bread-baking competitions we'd started again, much to Tillmann's messy glee, amongst the walks and the new music and the new books, time passed and disappeared without a trace. We have boxes of photos, but most of them are of the growing boy, not of the ageing parents. Not of the dying mother. Although, then, on those Sunday mornings, in those quiet evenings, we couldn't realise she was dying.

Because she was still the beautiful, skinny, gothic Kate I'd met at the railway station a long time ago.

In those early days of Tillmann's life she had asked me once if I wanted more children. I'd said that I thought it was much too soon to be thinking about that. That we should really give all our time to Tillmann and to each other. That to have another child would stop us growing up together. She seemed to accept that, seemed to see the sense in that. What she really thought about it, I don't know.

What do we really know about each other, we who love and live together? In the end, nothing, because we're not each other; we're ourselves, and alone. And, in the end, we die alone, whether or not there's someone there to hold our trembling hands, to listen to our faltering breath, to try to soothe the final fever. I don't think Kate and I really understood each other as well as we thought we did. No-one ever does, regardless of where they meet, regardless of what they do together, regardless of how long they are together.

Tillmann's second birthday came and went, more rows came and went, and we seemed to have settled into that blissful little pattern of self-sufficient and happy families. I never believe anyone who says that they've never argued, because life is incomplete without rows, and totally and utterly unbelievable. This was where we were and who we were, and we were as happy as I think any family can be. Good and bad always co-exist, because none can be apparent without the other. Happy and sad. Black and white. Life and death. There can be no grey.

These are my memories. You always think you'll be able to remember everything when you're living it. Never bother writing it down because you believe it will always stay with you. But it doesn't. Just like love never does, because love can't, just can't, last forever.

*

I laugh when Tillmann says he thinks it's about time he kissed a girl. That's the second time today I've laughed out loud without thinking about it.

'I thought you already had.'

'You encouraging me?'

'Not really, mate. But you've just gotta do what you think you've gotta do. As long as you're sensible and kind, and respectful. Because that's what matters, as far as I'm concerned.'

'I did nearly kiss one of the girls at school.'

'And why didn't you?'

'She looked too much like Mum.'

'They do say that people fall in love with folks who look like their parents, or remind them of their parents at least.'

'Yeah, well, it was just too weird. She is gorgeous, though, this girl, if you can be gorgeous at our age.'

'I never saw any pictures of your mum at when she was that young, but I reckon people are as gorgeous as you think they are, no matter what age they or you are.'

'Haven't you ever thought about getting a girlfriend?'

'That's a strange question from someone who's convinced his mother's still alive. Wouldn't you feel awful if I'd ever thought of it? Or done something about it?'

'I dunno. Not now, anyway. Know, that is. Yesterday, I might not've thought about it so much, but today it'd make me cross.'

'Anyway, it's beside the point. Because I've never thought about it. I still love Kate too much.'

'I won't ask how you've survived for eight years without sex,' he smirks.

'Is there anything you kids don't think about?'

'We grow up much faster now. That's what you're

always telling me, anyway.'

'Well, it's true. I never spoke to my dad about the things you and me talk about.' I shrug and lean back into the bench.

'Why d'you keep staring across the road?' he says.

'It's my old college.'

'You were at college here?' he says incredulously.

'Yes.'

'So why haven't you ever told me?'

'I don't like to talk about it.'

'Why?'

'Because I just don't. I didn't really have a good time there.'

'You know; that makes you just as bad as you say you felt Mum was. Don't I have a right to know about your past?'

'I guess you're right. Though I suppose you have more right to know about me being here than I had to know about your mother's life before me.'

'That's not entirely true. I still don't understand why she never told you about her family. Even if she'd never got on with her mum and dad, she could still've told you about her childhood.'

'Maybe that was something she couldn't bring herself to talk about, not ever.'

'But maybe you could've helped her deal with whatever it was that'd made her so bitter about it.'

'I'm not sure she was bitter about it. More like it was a chapter of her life that was closed, and that she thought should stay closed.'

'Didn't you ever try to get her to tell you more?'

'After finding out about her life just before she met me, and after the way I'd reacted, I wasn't really ever inclined to. Maybe we'd have got there if she'd lived longer, but she didn't.'

'Weren't you tempted to try to discover stuff after she'd

gone? Like I am now?'

'Not really. I think I've always wanted to preserve an image of her in my head of the way she was when we got married. That's probably why I've got that old wedding photo by the bed.'

'That *is* why you've got that photo there. About time you did something about it.'

'But that's why I've got you.' I smile at him. 'To do something about it.'

'Despite not agreeing with me about what we're doing?' He smiles back at me.

'I don't necessarily disagree with what you're doing. It's your motive for doing it that I don't agree with. And talking of what you're doing, what's your plan now, Mastermind?'

'Don't really know. We've got to move on from here, though, that's for sure. Fancy a walk through your old college?'

'No, certainly not. I've not been in there since I left, and I have no plans to.'

'Didn't Mum ever try to persuade you to go back in there?'

'No, she didn't. It wasn't actually something we ever talked about.'

'Why?'

'I didn't really want to. And she never pushed me to talk about it.'

'So what exactly was so bad about the place?'

'To be honest, it wasn't so much the place as the situation I was in.'

'Tell me about it, then.'

'Well, I had a girlfriend back home. I'd started going out with her when I was still at school. Because of her I didn't really want to come down here. And I'd never really been away from home before.' I'm thinking about stuff I haven't thought about in years. Stuff that has nothing to do with Kate.

'And?'

'And she came down here once with her parents. And then nothing. She called me to say she'd started going out with someone her own age, someone I knew, someone who was quite a good friend to me.'

'Did it last?' he says. 'Her and this bloke?'

'She ended up marrying him. They had a two or three kids, the last I heard.'

'Who told you?'

'My mum, but that was some years back, before she went into the old people's home.'

'But if all that happened when you first got up here, why d'you hate it so much? Didn't you enjoy it the rest of the time?'

'Some of the time, I suppose. But not most of the time. Being here made me think about what I might be missing in the rest of the world. Who else might be letting me down.'

'Were there any girls at home after that?'

'Not at home.'

I smile.

'Here, then?'

'Yes, here. I sort of had my first awakening here,' I say cagily.

'You mean you lost your virginity here,' he says straight out.

I can feel myself blushing. What the hell is a 45-year-old doing blushing when his almost-teenage son starts mentioning sex directly rather than through euphemism? I shake my head at myself. 'Yes, that is what I mean.'

'And?'

'And what?'

'It didn't last, I take it. You and this girl.'

'Till, I was quite a late starter compared to all the blokes and women up here. The girl was just something that happened when she and I were drunk.'

'Safe?' he says, as if he were *my* father.

'No,' I say bluntly. 'We didn't have safe sex in those days. We weren't aware of all the dangers. Not like now. Just remember that when you get to that stage.'

'I will,' he says, placating my protectiveness, 'I will. Promise.'

'There were others, too, but nothing serious, nothing meaningful. Just stuff that happened.'

'But Dad, if you were that busy,' he says seriously, choosing to be euphemistic, 'how could you react so badly to what Mum told you she'd been doing the day before she met you?'

'I didn't get pregnant.' The words are out of my mouth before I know what I'm saying.

'You're a bloke,' he reacts just as quickly. 'That's a stupid thing to say, it really is. What you really mean is that you were a bit of a hypocrite. Probably still are.' He lets the accusation hang in the air.

'I don't know what to say,' I finally mutter. 'You're right, but I couldn't find a way of changing how I felt then, how I still feel sometimes. That's why I feel so guilty about her dying. Because I'm often convinced that it was the way I treated her that killed her.'

'That's silly. Whatever you did wouldn't have killed her.'

Silence.

'If she were dead,' he adds.

'Which she is.'

He ignores me. 'So we're not going in there?' It's a question and an answer at once.

'Correct. Now you think of something else,' I say. 'Like driving home.'

'No chance. You're not getting off that easily. If Mum had run away...'

'Which she didn't.'

'Just assuming she did. Where would she have gone?'

'She didn't have anywhere else. We had a few friends at home, but not really close friends. We three were a bit like a closed community. We never really let anyone in.'

'Bit narrow-sighted, wasn't it? Didn't exactly broaden your horizons, did you?'

'We were a new family. We had other things on our mind.'

'That sounds a bit like an excuse to me. You're always telling me to make sure I've got lots of friends, and not to just stick with people I'm most familiar with.'

'You're young. You need to do that so you don't end up like we did.'

'I won't end up like you did,' he says full of the self-confidence of the young. 'I know I won't.'

'You sound sure of yourself.'

'I've got you, Dad,' he says with something that almost sounds like a compliment. 'And soon I'll have Mum again, too.'

I choose not to disillusion him on either of those points. I just want to get this quest of his over and done with and back to my normal life. Whatever that life is. Maybe Tillmann doesn't really believe what he's saying, and is only trying to help me. Not that I need any help, though, I think. I'm perfectly fine as I am, holding on to one bit of the past that I don't ever want to let go of, that I never wanted to let go of. That God, in His wisdom, chose to steal from me because of my weakness. To punish me for my weakness. I take a deep breath.

'Come on, then,' I say. 'And let me guess, you want us to drive up to see Grandma.'

'I was thinking of it. But slowly, just in case you think of something else I should know, somewhere else we should go, somewhere else Mum could've gone.'

I get up. Time to move on. I'm thinking about something I should tell him.

'Y'know, Tillmann,' I say to him as he's still sitting down. 'I'm just starting to realise how strange it is that I actually know so little about Kate. She's really a stranger to me, always was, the more I think about it. I don't know anything about her parents, nothing of her childhood. I know nothing about her past as a grown-up, except for the job she did in Cambridge, except for the abortion thing. Nothing. How can you marry someone who's such an unknown to you?'

'Perhaps you just loved her so much it wasn't important at the time. So you didn't care who she was. And maybe now's the time to find out.'

*

Of course, the time had to come when all my pent-up rage about what Kate had told me on Tillmann's first birthday had to come out. And so it did. It was the summer after his second birthday. Kate and I were sitting in the garden after he'd gone to sleep. Dusk had not yet deepened into night as we sat out in the warmth of the mid-summer.

We were drinking fizzy white wine and smoking, just chatting about the day that had been. Strange, isn't it, how your level of conversation dips when you get older and have children. Where we used to talk about what was in the books we were reading, or that we'd read, and what they said about our life, life in general, we'd now started talking about everyday things. Things like what Tillmann had said that day, how many teeth he had, how soon he might be out of nappies, what the plan was for tomorrow, and all that sort of banal but vital stuff.

I remember that I complained to her about exactly that as we were sitting out there, surrounded by absolute calm. No wind. No noise. Just a slow summer evening somewhere in England. I'd said that I found it depressing that all we talked about was Till or shopping, and how boring I found it.

'Then talk to me about something interesting,' Kate said, and reached her hand out to me from the chair she was sitting on. 'Tell me something meaningful, and I'll try to make your evening less boring.'

'That a promise?' I say.

She nodded. 'I never break my promises,' she whispered.

'You've changed my life.'

'I know I have. And Tillmann has.'

'You more than him,' I countered. And drew breath.

'This is what I mean,' I suddenly started, raising my voice slightly. 'Whatever I say, whatever we do, you always bring it back to him. Can't we just have a conversation without bringing him in to it?'

'Why are you so angry?' she said, surprised at the venom in my voice. 'He's part of us. Part of the family we've started. Life can never go back to what it was like before he was born.'

'Maybe that's the problem,' I said, unthinking. 'Maybe that's what I miss. Just us two. The way we were. Like when we met. Unburdened.'

'You might've been unburdened,' she hissed, angry at my anger, obviously. 'You might've been without a care in the world, but I wasn't.'

'And whose fault was that, then?' Why was I getting so angry? It was like there was a heat rising up out of the middle of me and nothing I could do would stop it.

'What *do* you mean? What do you mean? Don't tell me you think it was my fault.'

'Well, not exactly. It takes two to tango, doesn't it? Two to make a mistake as big as that.'

She sighed and her lower lip began to quiver. 'I thought you'd been ok with all that, Nairne,' she whispered. 'You didn't say anything when I told you.'

I just grunted.

'You're being unfair, and you know it,' she insisted. 'You made me tell you, even though I warned you that you mightn't like what you'd hear. You got me pissed and made me tell you.' She was almost shouting now.

'You could've controlled yourself and not told me,' I snapped at her. 'Or you could've made something up.'

'You bastard. How could I make something up when I've always been honest with you?'

'So how come you didn't tell me straightaway? How come you waited till I was too drunk to know better?'

'I don't know. I don't know. I'd always sworn to myself that I'd tell you nothing about my past, except for things you'd probably find out yourself. You made me weak. You always have.'

'How, weak?'

'Weak for you,' she said quietly. 'You know I loved you from that day.'

'Sometimes that's not enough.'

'Oh, so I should've known that you'd appear some day and saved myself for you?'

'Maybe,' I said stupidly.

'And what about you? Why didn't you save yourself for me? Don't the same rules apply to you?'

'Sorry. I'm being stupid.' But even as I said this I could feel something in me break, something that stopped me from obeying the rules I'd set for myself.

'Yes, you are,' she insisted. 'I love you. I've never loved anyone truly, not the way I love you. What I thought was love before was nothing but foolishness. I would die for you.'

'Would you?' I said, not realising how prophetic my question was.

'Of course I would.' She squeezed my hand. 'You know I would.'

'But do you regret the past?' I pushed her.

'Yes, I do. You know I do. But nothing I do can change it. Nothing I say can change it. That's all there is to it.'

'But you never show that regret,' I said, letting go of her hand.

'Because I don't want to think about it, because to think about it makes me hurt, because a part of me wishes that I *had* known about you when I was born, that I had been able to save myself for you. Because you're everything I've ever wanted.'

'Then why…' I couldn't think of what else to say that wouldn't hurt her.

'Why d'you think I've never talked about things from way back then? It's because I believe that we should be looking forward. That we should be planning our future. That what's behind us is exactly that – gone and buried. What else can I do? There's nothing else I can do, nothing else I want to do.'

'This is stupid. It's not getting us anywhere.'

'But you started it.'

'No, you started it,' I shouted. 'What else is there you've not told me? What else is there that you've done for other men but not for me? What have you denied me that you never denied another one of your boyfriends?'

She stared at me.

'Nothing,' she said. 'Nothing. But things change when you have a baby. I can't be horny all the time if I'm tired, if he's been difficult, and I'm exhausted down into my bones.'

'If you loved me, you wouldn't get tired.'

'If you loved me, you wouldn't be talking like this.'

'I'm going for a walk.' I got up, walked round the house to the front and went to the pub. It wasn't the last time either one of us would run away from a problem that needed solving. If I'd have stayed, nothing of what happened later on might have happened. Maybe she'd never have died if I'd have stayed with her that night. But it's too late to change that now.

She was asleep when I got home. And I was drunk. I crept into bed beside her, reached over to her curled-up shape and stroked that mass of hair that I loved so much. 'I'm sorry,' I whispered.

She was either asleep or ignoring me, because she didn't answer.

'I *do* love you,' I said, and turned over. I hope she heard me. I can cope with the being ignored bit if she did.

The next morning she acted as if nothing had happened. But I could tell I'd disappointed her. I bought her flowers. Why do we men think that buying flowers will make things better? Nothing changes if we don't make ourselves better. We should try to understand, to change the way we are for those we love. And yet compromise is nothing less than the betrayal of pure love. And now I put flowers on her grave every week.

Later that summer we went on holiday to Brittany. Rented a cottage there. Right out on the northwest coast. A five-minute walk to the beach. We spent eighteen days there. Filled with warmth and laughter. Filled with new adventures for Tillmann, who by now could walk and run and shout and whoop. Sand castles and stone castles, the first built by us, the second by some ancient forgotten knights. And cheap champagne. Kate said she'd always wanted to live like that.

But once we returned home, things started to change. Kate had always liked to go away for days or weekends on her own, but now she started travelling on her own even more. Where to I never knew, because I couldn't ask. Couldn't ask, because I realised that I'd begin to ask her questions in the same vicious tone that had started to colour my soul. Because I understood that I would just start shouting again. Because nothing, no-one, could rid me of the demons that I had released on Tillmann's first birthday. Demons which had flown from me that one summer night, and which just kept on growing and growing until I could no longer control them.

The nights and days I spent on my own with my son were bitter and sweet at once. I played him my favourite music, found new music to share with him, danced across the bare wooden floors in our house with him, laughed with him, cried with him because I missed Kate, because I knew I'd lost her. I always suspected then, when the travels started, that I'd lost her to someone else. Checked her clothes for a foreign scent, for tell-tale marks of infidelity. Pictures that my mind painted for me with the vividness of a pain whose origin we don't understand. There never was anyone else, of course.

Another kind of bitterness came from Tillmann, because I found it so difficult to be with him when he wasn't interesting. When he wasn't interested in the music I was playing. When he wasn't interested in me reading to him from a book I was reading. When he whined. When he woke up too early. When he wouldn't do as he was told. When he couldn't keep quiet. I'd often find myself shouting, and he'd scream back at me, unafraid. He spent a lot of time in the garden then, growing into an almost feral child.

And so he grew up an image of his mother, formed by his father and mother alike. It's not as if we hated each other, Kate and I. We'd just lost something that we'd managed to find and hold on to for a few years after that God-sent coincidence of a meeting on a deserted railway platform in Middle England, desperate for someone to love. Not anyone, but *the* one. Because I was the one for her. And I betrayed her. Because she was the one for me. And now she's gone.

*

Tillmann and I walk back to the car. The sun's skitting

across our faces gently, just as gently as Kate's hands used to touch us and ruffle our hair when she was in love with us. For all our faults she was always there for us. Or am I deluding myself? I have tears in my eyes, and I don't know why. There's a pain in my chest so severe that I think my heart's about to stop. I can hear my breath up through my ears, the sizzling soaring labour of the road towards a death I long for, an end I long for, so that I can be with her again, so that I can be forgiven.

He brings me back to reality, that male imprint of hers onto this world, onto this time. That gift she gave me. That gift she offered to give again and again, through her pain, out of herself. A part of herself for life, for me. Gifts I refused. That boy, almost as tall as me already, with his wayward shock of raven hair, with his blue eyes that make him older than me. He's already wiser than I am. Because he understands, where I can only guess. Because he's certain, where I doubt. He's looking for her, because he loves us both, because he's stronger than me in many ways. Because this is his way of finally making peace with his grief. And it's his way of trying to make me make my peace with Kate and fate – at last. I love him. See what she has made me do. She made me be a father. She made me care.

'How long's this quest of yours going to go on for, then?' I say while we're still walking along the narrow street.

'It's half-term next week, or had you forgotten?' he says. 'No rush, is there?'

'You're lucky you've got a Dad who can do as he pleases.'

'If you say so,' he mutters.

He knows my contracts come and go, that money can be tight as often as not. I'm not a saver. And that all Kate's insurance money went on the nursing. I should've used it for something else and looked after her myself.

I'm not a courageous man. I never have been. I never will be.

We get to the car and jump in. We make our way through the slow-moving traffic as the sun sinks lower. Autumn is here. Maybe they'll be burning leaves where we're going. That smell always makes me feel at home – anywhere.

Twenty minutes later we drive past my old playing fields. There's a hockey match going on. It's Saturday afternoon, after all. I open the window and listen to the players' shouts as we pass by slowly. And the scent is there, that old scent of my long-lost youth. Maybe I should actually stop here on the way back, I think. If we come this way. When I did live here, it was only out there that I was ever happy. So much lost, so much forgotten. We grow old, we grow old.

'That smells good,' Tillmann says, rolling down his window, too.

'It's the only thing you need to remind you that autumn's not such a bad time of the year after all.'

And I tell him about playing mindless meaningful games on those green fields. And of never having taken Kate there because I'd forgotten what it was like.

'She'd 've liked it,' is all he says. He can see into my head, at least that's what it feels like. 'Not the sport, though,' he adds. Yeah, he got his abhorrence for sport from her, for sure.

We leave Cambridge behind and head further north. We won't get to Yorkshire today, not at the speed I'm determined to drive, and not on the roads I'm determined to take. I want to avoid traffic, want to avoid people, be alone with my son. We can always head towards the bigger roads when we need somewhere to sleep.

In the meantime we wind our way along the country lanes, across the big flat expanse of East Anglia, merging into the flatness of Lincolnshire. We don't talk, we don't look at each other. We just listen to the music Tillmann chooses to put on, and watch the countryside grow deeper into the gloom of the autumn evening.

When darkness does come, I find my way to the dual carriageway that runs up England's spine, and we finally stop at a roadhouse motel. We get a twin room. The place looks and feels deserted. There's a café linked to the place that sells beer. I get Tillmann to go in first and find us somewhere to sit while I stand outside in the dark, dragging at a cigarette. I wonder what we'll find tomorrow. How long is it since I've spoken to my mother? Half a year? And seen her? A year, probably. Sorry, Mum.

I grind out the cigarette with my boot. I go in. Order two beers before I sit down. Tillmann's already ordered food. He knows what I like. And, besides, he's always hungry. Doesn't like waiting. I take a big sip of my beer when it arrives. He pulls a face. He's never liked alcohol. Even as a young child, when he was offered a taste of wine or beer, he'd think he liked it, and then grimace as he spat out the thimble of alcohol. Apple juice, that's his staple drink. He scribbles in his notebook while we wait for the food to come.

'What you writing?' I say.

'Just what we've done today.' He closes the book.

'D'you normally keep a diary?' I'm intrigued. I never go into his room when he's not around.

'Naah, haven't got the time.' His tone is slightly dismissive.

'So why this, now?'

'Because even if we don't find Mum, I'm finding out so much about you and her that I don't want to forget it.'

'Have you been planning this? I mean, you seem so organised with everything. The food. The clothes. The book. You even had toothbrushes and a change of clothes.'

'Not really,' he says, and he's not lying. 'I was awake for a long time before I came to your room this morning, and you were so out of it while you were getting dressed that I had plenty of time to put some stuff together. I even had time to drop a note through Fred's letterbox next door asking him to feed the cat.'

'So you reckon we'll be gone for some time, then?'

'As long as it takes.' He starts eating.

'As long as it takes to what?' I'm not sure I'm hungry.

'As long as it takes to find her, or as long as it takes for me to realise that she really is dead.'

Maybe he's coming round to the idea, after all. I'm just worried that he's going to have to start grieving all over again after this journey, when we don't find her, when he realises that he's going to have to keep going back to the cemetery to talk with her, after all. I glance at him over my beer glass.

'Don't worry 'bout me, Dad.' He smiles. 'You've gotta realise that kids are a lot tougher than you think. And you've gotta realise that I'm growing up. I need to do this. And it won't kill me if I'm wrong.'

'Good.' I'm relieved, but not quite convinced.

We eat the rest of our food in silence. When he's finished, he starts leafing through his book again. From where I'm sitting, I can only see a load of indecipherable scribblings.

'Bloody hell, you've written a lot,' I say.

'You were driving so slowly.'

'So what else have you written down there?'

'Questions to ask you that might help you and me both.'

'Like what?'

'Like why you decided to marry Mum and not any of the other girls you'd been out with.'

I laugh. 'Because I'd never thought of getting married

before I met your mother. I'd had massive rows with my dad about the life I was leading. He expected me to get married and settle down quickly. Wanted me to provide him with an heir's heir. There was even a time I didn't talk with him because he said I was betraying the family.'

'Why?' Tillmann's eyes are glittering in the artificial light.

'Because I'd said to him that I didn't want any children ever. That I couldn't see myself ever having kids. Or even getting married.'

'So?'

'Dad was from a different generation, mate. To him it was very important to preserve the family name, to carry it forward. He saw my attitude as endangering what he'd helped maintain.'

'Did you care about that?'

'In a way. Especially after he sent me a letter disowning me. Said he never wanted to see me again if I wasn't going to do the honourable thing. So I didn't go see him for years. Didn't call him. Considered him as dead as he considered me.'

'But you're always telling me what a great man he was, what good friends you were. I'm confused."

'Because, in the end, we did become friends again. Because he did teach me a lot. Because he taught me to be independent.'

'So what changed?'

'Kate came along. As simple as that. Not only did she love me, not only did she say she loved me, but she persuaded me to have a child. And, y'know, they loved each other, those two. Not in any dodgy way. But just that; some sort of ancient love and respect between two people who were totally different from each other, but who made each other laugh, who could have a good laugh. He saw how much she loved me, too. And he loved me more than he'd ever cared to admit. Despite our differences.'

'Was Mum very upset when he died?'

'Yes, she was. Y'know, Kate and I never really found enough time to go up there lots and lots. But when we did, we had a good time. I remember once, we'd been up there for a couple of nights, and Kate got really tearful about having to leave. We started off back down, anyway, but we hadn't even got to the motorway when she decided we ought to go back and stay another night. I think she felt safe there. I don't know exactly why, but she did.'

'What did your mum and dad say when you turned up just after you'd left?' He's fascinated by this story I've never told him before.

'They fed us lots of macaroni cheese, which was just about the only thing Mum could cook, and which Kate loved. I think that's one of the reasons she decided to turn back – because Mum had already said that she was going to be cooking some. Just like you, was your mother. Always out for some food; always eating. And never putting on any weight.'

'Any chance of dessert?'

'Help yourself.'

'Well, ok.' He waves to the guy serving and orders some disgusting sweet cake with cream. 'But seriously, you must've thought about why Mum liked your parents so much.'

'She said she felt at home. She said she'd never been treated so kindly, not even by her own parents.'

He leans across to me. 'But she still didn't go on to say where her parents were, who they were? And you just let it pass?'

'It wasn't any of my business. And, to be honest, I was quite happy with not knowing. I was happy that I didn't have to get involved in more pandering to more parents. Some of the girls I went out with; they had terrible parents with dreadful social demands and obligations. It was great not to have to travel here, there and everywhere to keep another set of parents happy.'

'Didn't you ever wonder, though, what they were like? What they looked like? What they talked like?'

'Not really. Honestly. I've always wanted the quiet life. And that's what I got. My parents never badgered us about anything. They just took us as we were. It was quite strange that, after all the grief he'd given me, Dad never mentioned kids to Kate once. Never called us for anything but a friendly chat. Never asked when we were coming up next. He became laid back, all of a sudden.'

'D'you think he understood that you were so crazy about Mum that you were bound to have a kid sooner or later?'

'I suppose so, yeah. Although I never thought about it.'

'Never thought about much, did you?'

'Sorry. I'm a lazy man, always have been. Could never concentrate much. Never wanted much. Never ambitious. Just music and ball games. If I could've done, the only thing I'd ever wanted to do was to play for England. Preferably cricket. But football or hockey would've done, too. But I was never good enough. No matter how hard I tried. And sport was the only thing I ever worked hard at.'

'Don't apologise to me,' he says without pity. 'Apologise to yourself and to Mum. It seems weird to me that you were lazy in everything but sport and jealousy.'

'Are we conditioned to be like that? That girl you nearly kissed – how d'you feel when you reckon someone else is going to kiss her?'

'Dad, I don't love her,' he protests. 'That's a silly question.'

'But if you did love her,' I push him. 'But if you did, how would you feel?'

'No different to the way I feel now, I guess. But I

haven't got to the sex bit yet, Dad, have I? Isn't it that that causes all this rage and anger? The possession bit? The having and holding bit?'

'Of course it is. But doesn't that start with a kiss? Isn't a stolen illicit kiss just as bad as having sex with someone else?'

'Depends on the context.' He's starting to look uncomfortable. 'But, Dad, you know about these things. I don't. I've not even started kissing yet. Or holding hands.'

'Mmm. I forget that you're only a twelve-year-old who talks like a twenty-year-old.'

'That's your fault.'

'How's that?'

'Because you've always only ever spoken to me like an adult. One of the first things I remember is you trying to explain something to me in a grown-up way rather than explaining it simply. When I was throwing a tantrum, I think. I couldn't really understand what you were on about.'

'I could never speak to kids like kids. I always thought it was disrespectful. Just like pandering to their whims was dishonest. And look what I ended up with – a kid who never listens to me when I tell him to stop playing video games.'

'But a kid who's gonna help you get your life back.' He smiles.

Chapter 5

What do you say about a marriage when all you can really remember is its end? There are all the obvious staging posts, of course, like the wedding, the anniversaries, the pregnancy, the child, but they all get lost in the noise and grief of the final act, the dying of joy, death. But when Tillmann started school, that was still a long way away.

What would be do with our lives if we knew how we were going to die? What would we do to avoid the inevitable? And how would we try to change our lives so that we never arrived at that final point? How could we make sure that we weren't where we were supposed to be when the time came for us to go? I don't believe there's anything we could do. Our fates were carved into our genes ages ago, and all we have to cling to are those few seconds of free will between birth and death.

I suppose I could measure our life together in cigarettes and cups of coffee and glasses of wine. Or in nights and days and weeks and months and years together. The sums wouldn't be difficult to do. And they wouldn't add up to much, either. They'd come to nothing, in fact. And I could measure my life since then in the number of times I thought I'd heard her laughter, the number of times I'd woken up thinking she was still lying there, next to me. Or in cigarettes and cups of coffee and glasses of wine. But let's face it, I killed her before she even died, killed what we'd had.

I remember Tillmann's first day at school, because, like all of his life, it's down there on paper, in the photo albums. He looked so cute in his uniform, in his grey trousers, his white shirt, his tie. He was only three and a half when he started nursery school. We were lucky that it was just across the road from the house. Kate walked him there while I watched from the window. I saw her bend down to place a chaste mother's kiss on his cheek, and then turn around and walk away. When she got back inside the house she cried.

'Oh, Nairne,' she sobbed. 'I miss him so much already. D'you think he'll be alright? He will be alright, won't he?'

I just stood there and held her in my arms, felt the sobs ooze out from under her skin like hot sharp beads of molten lead burning themselves into me. I'd thought she'd be glad of the peace and quiet she'd have, winning back whole big swathes of the day, where before she'd only had slivers of hours while he was at a part-time playgroup.

'I feel incomplete,' she spoke into my neck. 'As simple as that. He's a part of me, and now I feel all alone.'

'And me?' I said. 'Don't you feel happy to have me all to yourself?'

'That's different. We're grown-ups. We can try to make sense of the world, can explain it to ourselves, but he's still a baby, really, just a dressed-up baby of an office boy in his suit and tie.'

I tried to kiss her, but she pushed me away.

'And you're a spoiled and oversexed homeworker who doesn't know his place.' She smiled. 'Cup of coffee now, servant.'

But after that brief laughter, she lapsed back into the dark thoughtful Kate for most of the day. The mother bereft of her child, looking at the clock every five minutes, wishing for time to move more quickly so she could wander across the road and pull her precious boy in to her self again. And the next day and the next. He started crying every morning when he went to school, too. I told her I thought this was dangerous, that it was threatening his ability to stand up for himself, to become independent, his own boy.

'But he's not even four,' she shouted at me one morning after we'd had another one of those arguments that no-one's ever going to win because they're not actually really talking about the same thing. She was talking about her feelings, the need to protect, while I was talking about practicalities, the need to be a man. Too soon, too soon.

There were upsides, too, though. She'd been so proud that she'd managed to teach him to write his name in block capitals, and she was even prouder when he came home one day and showed her a piece of paper with his name on it – in joined-up writing. For her it was a huge step; for me it was just something I'd expected anyway.

Would men and women ever find a path to each other if they weren't so different? Or would it be easier if we were more similar? Our words drift past each other as we speak them, because, although we often mean the same thing, we say that thing in such different ways. We don't just misunderstand each other. We don't understand each other at all. And the heritage of our sexes has given us differing priorities, no matter how hard we try to be softer or harder.

It would be wrong to pretend that I missed Tillmann as much as Kate missed him when he was at school, but I did miss him, and I didn't just judge him on what he was achieving. He became more outgoing, more interesting to me than the little boy who'd looked at me bemused when I'd been dancing around the room to some loud music. He started to talk more and make more sense. He became easier to love, exactly because he wasn't around all the time. And when I used to pick him up from school his big grin and cuddle were enough to bring tears even to my eyes.

How do you write about life when life is nothing? Because that *is* what it is. How do you make a life when you know that there's an end to it? How do you make sense of the boredom of each day when that's all there is, because all you're doing is waiting to die? I guess you don't think about it, but you don't write it down either, because while you're waiting to die, you're too busy doing things that'll take your mind off dying.

Some days, when Tillmann was at school, we'd walk out of our town into the fields behind and watch the flowers sway in the wind. Some days we'd go back to bed after he'd gone off on his smiling way. Once he'd got used to going to school. Once Kate had got used to him going to school. Got used to losing her influence. Used to losing her baby. And so she wanted another.

'Nairne,' she said one day just after Tillmann's fourth birthday. We'd just spent an hour in bed in the middle of the day. Bliss. I was breathless with her beauty as always. Little did I know what was coming.

'I know that you've always said one child is enough,' she went on, 'but I really want another. I feel like my life's nothing without a baby around.'

I sighed. I suppose I should've been expecting this. At that point I wasn't too disinclined, to be honest, but I couldn't bring myself to say so. Instead I stroked her naked back and pretended to be thinking.

'Wouldn't it be wonderful to be making love knowing we'd be making another baby?' she crooned, making those blue eyes huge with a wistful hopeful smile. I grabbed the camera from the bedside table and took a picture of her with that look on her face. And grunted.

'Haven't we got our hands full with Till?' I said. 'Wouldn't we be better off getting him to fulfil his potential?'

She said nothing, but I guess she must've been thinking that if she could just push me a bit further, just get me to feel that cosy four-person family feeling, I'd say it was ok. That we should start making babies again. Or did she hear nothing but the voice of a man ambitious for his child and desperate for the quiet life?

I loved to feel her weight on my chest, to feel her warm skin moving against me with her angel's breath. Loved to bury my face in her hair while she slept. I loved having her to myself. I didn't want more disrupted nights, smelly nappies, screams and whines. Didn't want to go through the whole cycle again. Didn't want the same things she wanted. I'd missed her enough when Tillmann had been younger, missed her enough when she went off on her travels. Didn't want to start missing her even more – again.

'Why don't we think about it a bit more?' I said. 'Ask Tillmann what he thinks.'

'We can't ask him what he thinks. First off, what if he really doesn't want a younger sibling and we go ahead anyway? And what if he does really want one and we can't make one? That'd be so unfair. Both those things. We can't rely on a four-year-old to make our minds up for us.'

'But your mind's obviously made up already,' I said gently. 'Why ask me?'

'Because you're the one who wears the condoms in this house.' She laughed.

'And you're obviously the one who wears the trousers.' I laughed with her.

'Grrr!' She growled again and forgot her question for another hour.

You can never go back to those moments when you had a choice and made the wrong one. You can never undo the past. Never have that choice again, and choose the way you should've gone. Because even one second after that juncture, it's too late. One simple word, one breath, one simple gesture. They all change your life beyond recognition. And there you are, hurtling along a road too much travelled. Because we all make the wrong decisions. We all choose the wrong way to turn, the wrong things to do. The disastrous, the painful, the deadly choices. Because those choices are so easy. So easy on us, choosing only ever to satisfy the selfish and smug demons that possess us from the moment we begin to think.

I don't live one day without thinking back to that startled feeling inside me, that I wouldn't mind another kid, that it'd be quite cool to have another kid. Thinking back to the lies I told her, to that stupid male selfish pride. That, even in front of the person I loved most, in front of the woman who had made my life complete, I thought I couldn't afford to lose face. That's where all of this started and ended. That's where all the jealousy began, where life went wrong. Because I couldn't trust myself, wouldn't trust myself. Because I didn't think I could do the difficult things in life. Because I always thought everyone else was better than me at everything. Because I never could love myself.

Every day I ask myself why I didn't admit to her that I wasn't frightened by the prospect of having another child. That, despite my black temper, that despite my occasional furies, to be with her, to make another child with her would have been the most wonderful gift she could make to me. But it was the easy way out, not to say anything, not to change my mind, to play for time, to keep up this pretence of never having changed in all the time she'd spent with me. Because women are always trying to change you, aren't they? Except, looking back, I realise she never did try to change me. She just tried to bring out of me the goodness she saw in me. And I denied her that.

When I showered later the moment had passed. What I'd felt when she'd asked me about making more babies had evaporated. After Tillmann had gone to bed that night, I went out shopping as usual and stocked up on condoms.

*

It's morning again. I'd chosen the bed nearest the window in our ground floor room so I could smoke out of the window. I'd sat in the dark with a half bottle of red wine and a packet of cigarettes after Tillmann had gone to sleep. There'd been too many thoughts in my head for me to go straight to bed. But the wine and the fresh air and the nicotine had slowed me down. In the end, I slept better than I'd slept for a long time.

I've woken up before Tillmann. It's eight o'clock. Sunday. Time to move on. But I haven't the heart to wake him yet. Emotions can be so much more wearing than physical exercise, and he's going through a lot right now. Even though he denies it. Even though he's much more cool and calm than any thirteen-year-old should be.

We're on the road again two hours later. We've showered, had breakfast, put on clean clothes. Done everything civilised people are supposed to do. The sun's shining. The world seems ok. Until my mobile rings.

Tillmann answers the phone, as he always does when I'm driving. As usual I can only hear one half of the conversation.

'Hello? Yes, this is Tillmann, Nairne's son. My dad's driving and can't talk right now. I can take a message.'

There's a pause while he listens to the tinny voice in his ear.

'Ok. We're on our way, anyway. We should be there in a couple of hours. See you then.' He puts the phone back on the dashboard.

'And?' I say.

'That was one of the ladies at Dorset House,' he says. That's where my mother lives, surrounded by people who are just as senile as she is. 'Nothing to worry about, but apparently Grandma's been asking after you. She's insisting that you visit her, so they say. They just wanted you to know.'

'Your timing's good this weekend, isn't it?' I say. 'Just think, if we hadn't started out on this crusade of yours yesterday, we'd have had a long trip in front of us.'

'Some of us have it, some of us don't,' he says.

I wonder what's wrong with my mother. She doesn't normally ask after me. Probably doesn't even know who I am most of the time. Maybe it's coming towards the end with her. She's about eighty, and she's been without Dad for nearly twelve years. She started living at Dorset House when Tillmann was about three. It took a lot of talking by Kate and me to get her to make the move.

Robert Palmer's singing about Johnny and Mary now. I used to play that song every Sunday when I was about twenty, because it was the only day of the week I shaved, and I'd always thought it was great song for wet shaving. On a tape, I used to have it. Found it on the Internet a year or so ago and downloaded it. Tillmann's obviously nabbed some of my CDs as well.

Two hours later, we're where we want to be. South Yorkshire. Dorset House is an old building set back from a long straight road that's become a council estate. The only reason Mum finally accepted going into the place was because her sister was already there. And because we managed to convince her that she really was starting to be a danger to herself left on her own. Will I be like that when I grow old? I hope not. Hope not to get that old. It's lonely enough already. At night.

We pull off the road and follow the drive down to the house. I'm always surprised there are so few cars here. No-one ever seems to get any visitors. But then who am I to judge? I'm here about once a year, no more often. And I don't phone her much more frequently, either.

I ring the bell for someone to let us in. We wait for about five minutes before one of the ladies comes to the door. Always busy, these women. Do they take any time off? They actually enjoy their work, they always tell me.

Love the old dears to bits, they say. And so it seems.

This is one of the better places I've been to. It smells of old people, but it doesn't smell of piss or worse, like some others. It must have been a wonderful house to be in when it wasn't an old people's home. We follow Ida down the corridor through the rabbit warren they created when they converted it. Mum's sitting in her usual chair in the TV lounge. I walk across to her. She still likes it here, although her sister died a couple of years ago.

'Hello, Mum,' I say, as I bend down to kiss her on her white hair.

'Oh, hello,' she half shouts. 'What a lovely surprise! I wasn't expecting to see you! Ooh, and there's your son!' she calls out when Tillmann steps out from behind me. This is remarkably lucid for my mother.

I take her hand and she shakily gets up. Gives me a big hug. Tells me again what a lovely surprise it is to see me. I tend to take her up to her room when I see her because it's more private. We walk back along the corridor to the lift.

'Who are you, again?' she says, as she always does. 'Are you my brother or my son?'

'I'm your son,' I remind her, as always. 'My birthday's two days after yours.'

'Oh yes. I remember now. It's so nice to see you. I wish you'd come to see me more often.'

'Sorry,' I say. And I mean it. I just can't face the trip, and I just can't face the old lonely faces, and the sound of the woman screaming 'I'm DYING; Lynn, I'm DYING!' every five minutes.

'Ach,' she says, 'you've got your own family to look after. That's the most important thing. How is that lovely wife of yours?'

'She's dead, Mum. She's been dead for a long time.'

'As long as you're all well, that's all that matters,' she

says, ignoring what I say.

We get into the lift. Tillmann's got a funny look on his face. I'll have to ask him later what he's thinking.

We've borrowed the key to Mum's room from Ida. I always think Mum's got the nicest room in the place, although it hasn't got its own toilet. It's on the first floor. It's got a bay window. And it looks out over the garden. And next to the window there's a tall cherry tree which blossoms and scents when spring comes. Mum's favourite time of the year.

She plumps down into her reclining armchair which is one of the few things we brought here from her old house. Along with a wardrobe and an old book case. Tillmann and I bought her a new TV with a DVD player two or three years ago. And a mobile phone. She's never used the phone or the DVD player. No surprise there, I guess.

Tillmann and I sit down on her bed. If there's one thing my mother likes better than most things it's chocolates, despite not having any of her own teeth anymore. We stopped on the way up here to buy a big bag of the things. Tillmann gets them out of the shoulder bag he carries everywhere with him.

'Here y'go, Granma,' he says.

'Oooh, thank you. What's your name again?'

'Tillmann,' he says. 'Should I open them for you?'

'Yes, please.' She takes the open bag, takes a chocolate for herself and offers us the bag. We take one each.

'So, how are you?' I say. Always the same questions. Always the same answers.

'I'm fine,' she says. 'It's nice to have so many people in the house to keep me company. And I'm well looked after. I can't complain.' She takes another chocolate, although she's not finished chewing the first one – which she does with difficulty.

'Ida called me to say you wanted to see me.' I try to

start a new conversation. 'Was there anything in particular you wanted to talk to me about?'

'How are you and your family?' she says, oblivious to my question. 'As long as you're all fine, that's all that matters. As long as you've got your health, that's all you need.'

Maybe one of the reasons I don't come up here much is because it's always like this. She can't help it, of course, that she's senile. That she's lost her reasoning. Dad did everything for her. So maybe it's his fault. That she got lost so quickly after he died. That she had no clue about looking after her money or herself.

'We're all fine, as you can see,' I say.

'And Nairne, how are you?' she asks Tillmann. 'You are Nairne, aren't you? My son?'

'I'm Tillmann,' he says, patiently. 'And I'm your grandson. I'll be thirteen the week after next.'

'They grow so fast, don't they, Sonny?' she says to me. She turns back to Tillmann. 'I can remember when you were a little boy, getting under everyone's feet. And now you're nearly as tall as your Dad. You'll be as big as him by Christmas, won't you?'

'Maybe, Granma, maybe,' he says, smiling.

'And how's that wife of yours?' she says. 'Pat, wasn't it?'

'Kate,' I say. 'And she's dead.'

'Ooh, is she? And such a lovely girl, too. I'm sorry.' She looks me in the eye with that wavering old woman smile, that lost and forgetful look. 'Was it recent, then?'

'Mum, it was eight years ago.' I try not to sound exasperated or sad. I don't want to set Mum off.

'Oh dear, I am sorry. You know, my memory's not what it was. I feel bad now. I'm sorry, son.'

'Mum, it's ok, it really is. It's not your fault. I should come more often.'

'As long as you're healthy that's all that matters,' she

says, drifting off again. 'And your family comes first, of course it does.'

She takes another chocolate. So do we. And we're all quiet for a few minutes, watch the sun out of the window. It's another beautiful day.

'So do you ever get out into the garden, Mum?'

'Sometimes,' she says. 'But it's a bit cold this time of year, isn't it? Best off indoors.'

She probably doesn't get out at all, I think.

'Of course, I still get to church every Sunday, and the occasional day trip.'

How does she remember unimportant stuff like this, but not the fact that her daughter-in-law, her only daughter-in-law, died eight years ago? Lord, I'm scared of old age. I look at my son. Will he desert me like I've deserted my mother? Like I deserted my wife?

There's a knock on the door.

'Come in," I call.

It's Ida.

'Have you shown him, then, dear?" she says to Mum.

'What's that?' Mum says.

'The envelope, luv,' Ida says. 'That's why you asked us to call him.'

'Oh,' Mum says. 'I almost forgot.' She reaches behind her chair and pulls out a brown padded envelope. 'This came today.'

'A few days ago,' Ida says. 'I'll leave you to it.'

Mum looks at the envelope as if she doesn't know what to do with it, then empties its contents onto the bed. There are about seven or eight notebooks. They look like school exercise books. I pick up one of them. On the front of it, in writing I recognise, are two black ink words. *Kate's Journals.*

*

Kate didn't say anything when she saw that I'd been out and bought more condoms. It wasn't her way. Over the next few weeks she wanted to make love less and less. It made me impatient and frustrated. By now I'd totally forgotten any subconscious desire I might have had about having more kids. I was just irritated and angry. I thought my rights were being denied me. As if I'd had any rights over her. We spent more and more time apart in the house, me in the living room watching TV or reading, she in the bedroom reading on the bed. And sleeping. More and more sleeping. Tired all the time.

Things came to a head on Christmas Eve. It was Tillmann's first big school holiday. He'd been overwhelmed by everything leading up to Christmas. The cards that parents habitually made their kids swap with each other, greetings hurriedly written by mums and dads, names scrawled hugely across the entire inside by the children themselves. Overwhelmed, too, by taking part in the school's annual Christmas entertainment and carol singing, nervous and excited at once at the prospect of performing his little bit in front of a hundred people including his parents. Kate and I had both cried, naturally, when we'd seen our tiny boy standing on stage mumbling his way through a sentence or two of a Christmas poem. Such is the sadness and gladness of parents. Everything else goes out the window; ideals, promises, our selves. If you're strong enough. She was. I wasn't.

My family had always had this tradition of giving some presents out on Christmas Eve, and leaving Father Christmas to deliver the big presents during the night, ready to be opened on Christmas Day morning. It was a tradition that Kate and I gladly continued. Much more romantic to give and receive presents by candle light with the curtains closed than to do so on grey and damp and dank English winter mornings.

Tillmann was kneeling in front of our small Christmas tree, gazing with amazement at the pile of presents under it. He'd grown more aware of Christmas every year, but this was the first year that it had really clicked for him, I think. We had the Christmas song CD on, and he was humming along with it. Kate and I were sitting on the sofa watching him. We'd already found our presents and retrieved them from under the tree, but were waiting for Tillmann to unwrap all his before we opened ours. We were really as contented as we could have been. Life wasn't making a noise. It was just there.

Suddenly Tillmann stopped humming. Stopped moving. Just sat there, with his hands in his lap. Just as quickly turned round and looked at us, his eyes ablaze. 'Will I get a baby sister for Christmas?' he said in his thin voice.

I nearly choked. I looked at Kate. She was transfixed by this suddenly alert angel boy asking a question she'd always wanted him to ask. Her face, which seemed to have grown harder and thinner these last few months, softened and flushed. I wish she'd have looked at me like that. She took a deep breath and swept her hair back with her hand.

'Babies aren't really something Father Christmas brings,' she said to him, holding out a skinny arm to him. He grabbed her hand and wound himself into her embrace. He loved the feeling of her long hair tickling his little face, and he giggled. If Kate'd been a cat, she would've been purring.

'Why?' he said. 'Sam at school says he got his little sister at Christmas.'

'I think that might just've been a coincidence, big man,' I said. 'Babies come into the world all year round.'

Kate wasn't saying anything, just playing her hair games with her one and only son.

'But I asked Father Christmas for a sister,' he said.

I hadn't seen anything about that when I'd helped him write his letter that we'd posted to Lapland.

'Did you?' Kate said, her head still moving across Tillmann's face.

'Yes, I did.' He shouted his little boy's shout and pushed his way out of her hair and out of her embrace. He stamped his foot. 'I want a little sister.'

'Well, Tilly,' Kate said, 'We'll have to see what we can do about that. You know it's not all that simple, because Mummy and Daddy have to want another baby to look after, too.'

She looked at me when she said that and smiled at me. I think she thought she had me where she wanted. Because, whatever I am, however I might behave, she knew I loved Tillmann. So she thought I'd not be able to refuse him his wish. I managed to produce a smile back at her, but I wasn't smiling inside.

'Ok,' he said and went back to unwrapping his presents.

Children have this wonderful gift of being able to jump from one thought to another without transition. Of switching off from one thing without any noticeable pause, just to carry on with something else that's grabbed them. Kate understood this better than I did. Possibly because she was less confrontational than me. Most probably because she was kinder than me. And gentler. Inside and out.

Much later that night, as we were getting ready for Father Christmas, Tillmann already fast asleep after having stayed up much later than normal, Kate turned to me with that unmistakable glimmer in her eye.

'So, are you going to give me a special Christmas present?' she said. 'I've got my stockings all ready.'

To this day I still don't understand why I reacted as violently as I did. Maybe it was the drink, maybe the frustrations that had been building up ever since I'd almost given in to her wish. There is no explanation, not in the now, nor in the then. Not in my own past. Not for my outburst of unjustified anger. Being an only child probably coloured my view on children. Having a mother who was ineffectual probably did as well. But those things couldn't explain away my angry temper.

'You put him up to this, didn't you?' I hissed at her. 'You thought you'd get at me through him, didn't you? It's always you, you, you, isn't it? No thoughts about me, what I feel, what I might want.' I started to shake.

She stared at me long and hard before she said anything.

'Are you really the man I married, Nairne? That kind, slightly confused, jinxed and shy man who could hardly talk to me that day we met?'

'Jinxed with a selfish wife,' I said, sat down heavily on the sofa.

'How can you say that?' she said, sitting as far at the opposite end of the sofa as she could. 'I try to make a happy end to a happy evening, and you scream at me. I can't help what my four-year-old son says.'

'But he said what you wanted him to say. So you're happy. Bully for you.'

'Nairne, I didn't ask him to say what he did. I haven't mentioned anything about how I feel about more children to him.' She took a deep breath because she wanted to control what she was feeling and saying. 'Just in case you've forgotten, it was you who suggested that we should ask Tillmann what he thought. And it was me who said that we couldn't, shouldn't, involve him in this because he's too young to know what he's saying.' She folded her arms abruptly across her chest and slumped into the cushions, her eyes closed.

'So that's alright then, is it?' I said, hurtling towards self-destruction. 'Who says you haven't changed your mind since then? And decided to manipulate your precious little son anyway, just so you can get your way about having more kids? Why should I believe you?'

'Because you love me,' she said softly without opening her eyes. 'At least I thought you did. But now I'm not so sure.'

I could feel a secure rug being pulled from under me. Had that horrible feeling of hovering above the abyss just before I was about to fall. Because there was no way back from here.

'I *do* love you,' I said, trying to make my voice sound soft. 'I just don't understand why you keep going on about this when I thought we'd decided not to have any more kids ages ago.'

'It's a bit late to try and placate me now, Nairne,' she said and opened her eyes. Sat up straighter. 'You've no right to shout at me for what our son says. You've no right to judge me because of the feelings I have, or because of the physical needs I have. No right whatsoever. You're not a woman, and you don't understand us one little bit.'

'Oh, so now it's a sisterhood thing, is it?' I sneered. 'You women have always been better than us, haven't you? Always wanted everything and tried to get it the easiest way you could think of. And us men? Oh, we're the toughies. We'll always come out on top. Because we've got no feelings or needs ourselves, have we? I forgot about that. I *do* apologise. How should I beg the great sister in the sky for forgiveness? Or am I forever damned, mere man that I am?'

'You're pathetic. Ridiculous and pathetic. I thought we'd be able to talk about this like adults, but you've obviously forgotten that you're a grown-up.'

'But we *have* talked about it, Kate! And you've never been able to accept that you married someone who doesn't want a houseful of kids. Someone who wants a quiet life; just a house to hide in and a wife to be with.'

'I don't think we've ever talked about it properly,' she

said calmly.

She could always control her temper, could Kate, until towards the end. The only times I saw her angry were when she'd been reading a book she discovered she hated and hurled it at the wall accompanied with a torrent of Anglo-Saxon abuse.

'We've talked about it forever and a day,' I said. 'What more is there to say? I hate wearing condoms, but I don't want any more kids. It's bad enough with one.'

'Ha,' she snorted. 'As if you've done so much with Tillmann.'

'You bitch!' I got up. My sick mind was telling me I'd had enough. 'So who's looking after him when you're out with all your fancy men, eh? Me, that's who. So why don't you go and get one of them to give you a baby? Go on. Go. I'm sure you'll be able to fix yourself up with one of your mates at this time of night, any night.'

'You're mad,' she said. Her eyes were sad, disappointed pools of glistening blue. She was crying. She walked to our bedroom door, crossed the threshold, turned and looked back at me. 'I don't want you in my bed again, ever.'

Chapter 6

I stare disbelievingly at the notebooks.

'When did you say you got these?' I ask my mother, my heart racing.

'What?' she says. 'Oh, yesterday, was it?'

'There must be some mistake,' I say. 'It's impossible. They must've come ages ago. When Kate was still alive. Who'd have sent them now?'

Tillmann's got the envelope in his hands. 'The postmark's from a week ago,' he says.

'Does it say anything else?' I say.

'It's a bit difficult to make out,' he says. 'Sod's law. Here, see if you can make it out.' He passes me the envelope.

We both walk over to the window for better light. I can make out the first two letters of the postmark quite easily. N and A. The rest is smudged quite badly. My mother's sitting passively in her chair, looking bemused.

'How can we make this more legible?' I ask Tillmann. 'I think I remember using a biro to trace postmarks when I was young, just sort of following the lines by intuition rather than trying to make them into anything. But I'm not sure it'll work with this.'

'Here, bring it over here,' he says, switching on my mother's bedside light. He gets a pencil out of his bag. 'Means we can always rub it out if it looks like it's turning into nothing,' he says. 'This is exciting.'

Mum gets herself another chocolate. She's always liked just sitting and watching people do things, even before her mind starting leaving her. She used to sit in the shopping centre in town for hours, just watching. And talking to anyone who happened to sit down next to her. I think it's when she stopped going into town that she started losing it, gave up and stopped resisting the senility.

Tillmann and I clear everything except the light off Mum's bedside table. We flatten out the corner of the envelope. He sharpens the pencil until its end is thinner than a pin's.

'D'you want to do it?' he says. 'Or should I?'

'I'm shaking too much to do it. And you're more arty than me.'

He leans over the envelope, half closes his eyes. 'It's like picking at bee bones,' he mutters.

'Eh?'

'It's like taking the bones of a bee and trying to put it back together. Such tiny fragile things, bees, just like letters and broken words.'

I think I'll have to stop him reading so much when we get back home. And playing so many fantasy video games.

'Did you know,' I say, totally unrelated to what he's trying to do, 'that people still don't know how a queen bee is chosen by her hive when the old one dies? All they know is that some eggs are chosen by the worker bees for special feeding. But they don't know how.'

'Just like we don't know why people fall in love,' he says. 'How did *you* choose *your* queen?'

'I think she was chosen for me. And I think I wasted that gift.'

'We'll see,' he says. 'We'll see.' He sets about his task again. Frowns. 'Granma, have you still got that magnifying glass you used to have to read?'

'Oh, yes,' she says eagerly. 'It's over in that chest of drawers under the telly.' She starts getting up.

'It's alright, Gran.' He stops her. 'I'll find it.' He rummages around in the bottom drawer first and finds it. 'I reckon she hardly ever reads,' he whispers to me, 'so it wasn't going to be anywhere handy. And the top drawer was full of chocolates the last time we were here.'

He bends over the envelope again, holding the

magnifying glass in his left hand while he tries to trace the black blotches on the envelope back into their original shape.

'I,' he says.

'You what?'

'It's the letter I,' he repeats. 'So we've got NAI so far.'

'Spooky,' I say. Lapse back into silence. Listen to my mother's breathing. Listen to Tillmann's breathing. Enjoy the contented sound of activity. The sound the pencil makes as it scratches the paper. Look at the little finger on my left hand, and the ring on it that has one tiny sliver of diamond in it. That'd been my Christmas present for Kate that last Christmas together, that dreadful destructive Christmas Eve. I never gave it to her, and I never got my present from her, either.

'It gets spookier, Dad. Have a look at this. Is that an R, or am I just imagining things?'

I take the magnifying glass from him and look down at the enlarged pencil lines on the envelope, drawn across the ragged stamps. He's right. It is an R. NAIR... No, that's impossible.

'Someone's making fun of us,' I say, standing up straight again.

'There's only one more letter to guess, by the look of it.'

'Let me guess it,' I say. 'It's an N.'

'Looks like it.'

'And there's not another letter?'

'Nope.'

'Are you sure?'

'Just about. Have another look.'

I do. And there's just a blank space after that last letter. A vast expanse of stamp and space, but nothing black until my eye reaches the outer circle of the post mark.

'It can't be someone making fun of you, Dad,' Tillmann insists. 'If it had been, they'd have put your proper name on there, with the E at the end. This just says Nairn. It's got to be genuine.'

'Let's have a look at the envelope. Who's it addressed to?'

'Mrs Naomi Watt, care of Dorset House, blah, blah,' he answers. 'So that's right. Nothing strange there.'

'What about inside?'

He pulls the opened end of the envelope open wider. Peers into it under the bright light. 'Nothing,' he says.

I turn to the pile of notebooks on the bed. Put them carefully into a pile and lift them off the bed. 'Nothing came out of it except the books, either,' I say.

'Have a quick leaf through each one.'

I take one of the books after the other from my knee, hold them by their spine, and shake them out over the bed. Nothing.

'Hmm,' he grunts.

'Where the hell is Nairn?' I think out loud. 'I never knew such a place existed.' I look at Mum who's looking straight back at me.

'What's that about Nairne?' she says. 'I've got a son called Nairne.'

'I know, Mum,' I say with a heavy heart. 'That's me.'

'I knew that,' she says calmly.

'Why did you call me Nairne?'

'It's a nice name. And it starts with the same two letters as my name.'

'And Dad's name,' I add.

'And Nathaniel's name, yes. Oh, Nat, I miss you so. I wish he was still here.'

'We all do,' I say. 'We all do.' Does it mean anything? 'D'you know what the name means, Mum?'

'I used to,' she starts. 'Let me think. We found it in some book somewhere, something to do with rivers and valleys, I think.' She's exhausted her emptying brain.

'Hang on, I remember now,' I say. 'It's from the narrow

river glade. That's what it means, I mean. I remember now from when Kate and I were looking for names for you. Till she came up with Tillmann from nowhere.'

'To be honest, Dad,' Tillmann suggests. 'I think an atlas would be more help than what your name means. It's not your name that's on the postmark. A similar name, but not exactly the same.'

'What's one letter?' I say. 'One hell of a coincidence, mate. And there's no such thing as coincidence, anyway.'

'What d'you want to do, Dad?'

'I've not come all this way to spend only an hour with my mum. Why don't we take her down the pub for lunch and then find ourselves somewhere to stay so we can read those notebooks? I can have these notebooks, can't I, Mum?'

'Of course you can,' she smiles at me. 'That's why I wanted to see you.' Spoken as if she's always been lucid.

'Get your coat on then, Mum,' I say. 'We're taking you out to lunch.'

'Oooh, that's nice,' she chuckles. 'Anywhere nice? Must make sure I go to the loo first.'

'No rush,' I say, 'No rush.' And I mean it.

We get Mum back to her home just before her tea-time. Although she gets very confused when she's on the outside, it's nice to take her somewhere that changes her scenery for her a little. And she eats like a horse. She'd become a rake before she'd moved into Dorset House because she'd either not eat, or because she'd eat out of date food that made her sick.

I resolve to try to visit her more. To try to learn to love motorways and dual carriageways. It would be a shame not to see her more before she dies. Am I just trying to rid myself of guilt?

We leave Mum sitting in the chair we first saw her in this morning. She'll not have long to wait before she gets her favourite sandwich. She's always hungry. Thankfully, still. We wave goodbye to her from the door out into the corridor.

'See you tomorrow, Mum,' I call and blow her a kiss.

Whatever happens, whatever we plan to do, we'll call in on her before we move on.

Ida lets us out and locks the door behind us. It's getting colder, although it's still light.

'Looks like you've struck gold, son,' I say to him as we get into the car. 'Sure it's not you who's setting me up?'

'Dad,' he says, strapping himself in. 'Firstly, I don't think you're being set up. Secondly, why would *I* want to set *you* up? This hurts me as much as it does you, this never-ending grieving. I just want it to be over. Which it will be by the end of this trip, one way or another. Come on, let's go.'

I drive across town, to a hotel we always stay in when we come up here. I used to stay there before I met Kate, sometimes, when I was playing cricket up here and didn't want to go back to Mum's and Dad's house drunk. On the way we stop at a petrol station and buy an atlas. I know I should have one in the car, but I kept losing the ones I bought, so I stopped buying them. And I never drive anywhere anyway.

Once we've got to our room, we lie down next to each other and get Kate's journals out of Tillmann's bag. And start reading.

*

1981

Caitlin said I should write a diary. She says she *knows everything best. I can't face writing something every day. I'd give up. There are more important things for me to do. Like find a job to save up enough to get out of this hell hole of a home. I can't write, anyway. Everything comes out sounding posh, and when I read it back to myself I think it sounds stupid.*

Father hit Mother today. Again. On my birthday of all days. He came home drunk and shouted at her. They're shouting now. And there's screaming. I've locked my bedroom door. It's quiet now.

I hope Father doesn't find this notebook. I haven't told Caitlin that I followed her advice. Mother mustn't find it either. If she does, she'll tell Father about it when he's beating her. So I've cut a hole in the wooden wall behind my bedside table to hide it in.

Happy 16th birthday! It's the fifteenth of August, and I'm starting a new life.

I've got a job! I'm working in one of the caffs the other side of town. Weekday evenings and Saturdays. They asked me how much holiday I wanted. None, I said. I just want to earn enough money to get away. I didn't tell them that, though.

Mother and Father know that I've got this job. So does Caitlin. But none of them know how much I'll get paid. Or that I'll get tips as well, which means that I'm getting a lot of money for a girl my age.

I've opened a Post Office savings account as well. That means I'll be able to put my money away every week when I get paid. And because I've got a book for it, I don't get anything in the post, which means Mother and Father and Caitlin won't know that I'm saving to get away from here. I'll be getting fifty pounds a week plus tips. If they do ask me how much I'm getting, I'll tell them twenty-five a week.

I held hands with a boy from school today. He's called Tillmann and I think I love him. He's seventeen, and we'd been looking at each other in that funny way a lot lately.

The job's fun, and I don't get too tired. It does get a bit much in the evenings sometimes, when drunk boys start coming into the caff, because they want to try and chat up the three of us who work there as waitresses. We just try to ignore them, although we can't help giggling when they do stupid things like singing us songs from outside the door.

I felt really proud of myself when I put my first money in my account. One of the girls who's been working here for six months said that she gets over ten pounds in tips every week!

Father made me cut off most of my hair yesterday. He said it looked slutty to have such long curly hair. He said I looked like Mother when she was young, before she had the sense to marry him. Before he made a decent woman of her, he said. He doesn't want me to be a slut like Mother, he said. One of these days I think he's going to try to hit me. I hate him. Caitlin says he's only doing what's best for us.

I've decided to keep a knife in my hole in the wall.

I hope my hair grows again quickly. I hate Father. He's evil. Caitlin says he's just making sure that we don't turn out bad. Like him, does she mean?

Tillmann says my hair looks great. He thinks it's punky like this. And he says girls with short hair are cool. I'll still grow it long again, though. I liked the feel of it on my neck. And it kept me warm. I'll feel cold with it short.

Tillmann's bought me a woolly hat. I laughed when I saw it, but he says it will keep my head warm when it does get cold. And he says all the best people wear them. It's black, like my hair. Tillmann has one, too.

The weather's awful. October must be the worst month of all. It's not properly winter yet. We're just waiting for it to be. I fell over on the way home when I slipped on some wet leaves. It was just after Tillmann asked me to kiss him for the first time.

Kissing Tillmann was nice. He's gentle. I think it's good to have a boyfriend who's not much older than me. That means he can't bully me like Father bullies Mother. I wonder if he loves me. At least I'll remember my first kiss really well. Because of falling over afterwards, I mean.

Christmas Day was as miserable as ever. None of us got any presents. Just a bit of money from Mother. And cards from Father. He'd written into them about how only good girls get things for Christmas. Not sluts. Mother didn't get anything either. Father gave himself a couple of bottles of whisky and a box of cigars.

Less than two years until I can get out of this place. I could run away now, but I haven't got enough money yet. I don't want to be one of those homeless girls in London. Or a prostitute. I need to know that I've got enough money to look after myself. No-one else will. And I don't want to have to rely on anyone else.

That's why Mother doesn't leave Father. She's dependent on him and his money. She only worked for six months before she married him, and she hasn't worked since. She understands nothing about anything. She's weak. I don't want to be like her. I won't be like her. Caitlin says she's like all women should be. Just that she isn't obedient enough. Not like Caitlin. Father's favourite.

I can't wait for time to pass. I'll have a whole new life then, not just inside my head.

Tillmann gave me a gold chain with a pendant for Christmas. He had it engraved. On one side it says pure *because that's what Katherine means, and because that's what Tillmann says his love for me is. On the other side it says* people's rule*, because that's what the name Tillmann means. And he says he thinks that's why he's a socialist, because of what his name means. I don't care about politics, actually, but if it means he'll carry on being kind, then that's ok.*

I'm not telling anyone about Tillmann, least of all Caitlin. He doesn't mind being kept secret. He says it makes him feel more important and our love more special.

1982

Happy New Year! I wonder what it will bring. Everyone always hopes that things will change with the New Year, but for some they never do. I hope they change for me. Only just over a year and a half until I get out of this place.

Time is going too quickly, and not quickly enough. Tillmann says he's got into university at Cambridge. He says I should move there when I'm eighteen. He's sure I'd be able to get a job there. It's quite a scary thought, but not as scary as not being able to see him every day. Still, it's over half a year until then.

Caitlin says we should make sure we stick to our New Year's resolutions. She says she's resolved to lose weight. She needs to, too. I told her I hadn't made any New Year's resolutions. I didn't tell her that my one and only resolution is to get away from her and Mother and Father. Why Caitlin likes it here so much I don't know. I can't understand her.

Are sisters supposed to be really good friends? Because we aren't. I don't think we ever have been. All I can remember is fighting all the time. And her being bitchy and bossy. Maybe we'll discover each other when we're older. Or maybe we'll never see each other again after I've gone. I certainly don't want to see Mother or Father again.

We had a couple of inches of snow yesterday. It was fun running around in it while it was coming down out of the grey sky. My woolly hat came in handy.

Caitlin and I had a snowball fight. I think it's the first time I've seen her laugh. She usually doesn't show anything on her face at all. Or she just sneers at me. She thinks she's better-looking than me. But I know that's not true. Otherwise Tillmann would be going out with her. And he's going out with me.

I'm happy in my own little way. I like kissing Tillmann, and I like it, that that's all we do do. *I don't want to lose my virginity while I'm still here in this house. I want to be my own person first. I wonder if Caitlin's still a virgin. She must be. She's Father's little darling, because she does as she's told. Won't she ever leave home?*

Nothing ever happens. That's why the waiting gets very boring.

Even though I know that I'm doing my best. But I need to wait.

School. I just realised that I've not written everything down about school. It's not that it's boring. Because, actually, it isn't. I'm looking forward to doing my exams in June. I chose to do German and French, because I enjoy learning different ways to say things. And I chose History because it lets me escape into another world. I always read lots of history books. Even ones we're not told to read. That way I can just lie on my bed up here and keep out of everyone's way.

The exams won't mean anything, of course. The really important ones happen next year. All the studying is just a means to an end. I know I won't go to university, because I won't have the money to when I run away. But I want at least to be able to say that I'm clever. Because I am clever. Cleverer than Caitlin.

And of course I need to fit in all my studying into small bits of time because I'm working all the time. Sunday is the best day. I get up early while they're all still asleep, while Father is sleeping off his Saturday night binges and Mother's nursing her bruises. I listen to the radio while I'm doing all my translation work, and while I'm doing all my reading.

I need to do well.

It's the end of February now. It's a bit like October, really, just the other way round. You can tell that winter's going to come to an end, but you're still just waiting for it to go. Because the dampness goes all the way through March in bad years.

I'm still wearing my woolly hat. I got my ears pierced – again! – last week. I've three ear-rings in my left ear and two in my right ear. Tillmann says they go well with my hair. But it's still too short, although he says it looks great so spiky. The gel I bought helps. Tillmann says I look like Nina Hagen. I wish!

Caitlin says I've copied her, because she's got five ear-rings, too. I didn't even think about that. But I'm not taking them out. She can take hers out if she's that worried about it.

Tillmann says he'll take a lot of my tapes to Cambridge with him. That way I'll have less to carry when I do run away. I think it's a cool idea. And he says when he comes home for the holidays he'll take more with him. I've started giving him a few tapes every time I see him. Because I've got over 300 tapes. It's the only thing I spend money on. So I can tape good music from the radio. So I don't get tempted to buy records.

Why is time passing so slowly? I'm getting impatient, and that's dangerous.

The trees are starting to blossom. I realise I miss out on a lot of life because I work so much, but I don't have a choice. I'm surprised Tillmann puts up with it, actually. I think we've only been out together two or three times. When he goes to Cambridge at least we won't have to worry about keeping it a secret anymore. He's told me lots of the boys and girls in his year think he's gay because he hasn't got a girlfriend. Ha!

Caitlin's being moody for some reason. Maybe it's her time of the month. She's always complaining about not feeling well. I think it's her excuse for not doing anything. Because, of course, Father's darling doesn't actually have to help around the house!

I've been thinking about asking Mother to run away with me. Although I don't like her, I feel really sorry for her. How she gets away with claiming she's fallen over when actually Father has hit her, I don't know. Why does she stay? Maybe it's really Father who gets away with everything.

I've changed my mind about talking to Mother. Father hit her really hard last night, and I could hear her thanking him for showing her how bad she'd been. That's not normal, is it? Does he hit Caitlin, too? But where none of us can see it? I'm worried now.

Caitlin told me not to be so stupid. She also called me a nosey old cow. Whatever Father does, he does it for all the right reasons, she said. It's Father who pays for everything, she said, so he has a right to be in charge, she said. I think she's stupid and blind and fat. I wish she was dead. And Father. I'm not sure about Mother, but I probably wish she was dead, too. So that I'd have no past.

Tillmann played a silly April Fool's joke on me today. We met in our secret place behind the squash courts at school in the long morning break. I kissed him very gently and he held me close. Then he got down on one knee, with his hand in his blazer pocket and asked me to marry him. I was about to say yes when I saw the look in his eyes. And then he jumped up and whispered 'April Fool!' because he couldn't risk being heard.

I was a bit annoyed with him, because I'm sure it's bad luck to ask someone to marry you if you don't mean it. He apologised, but said he did mean it, just that we couldn't actually get married yet, because I wasn't eighteen yet, and because we didn't have any money. So maybe it does still count as a proposal, and we'll get married when I'm eighteen. When I move to Cambridge.

Or maybe not. It doesn't matter, anyway, as long as we'll be together.

I've been busy because exam time will be here sooner than we all think. Caitlin says I'm stupid starting to revise so soon. I don't care what she thinks. For once Father said something good about what I'm doing. It's wise to start revising early, he said. The more you revise the more you'll remember. But then he brought me down by saying that clever girls like Caitlin don't need to revise. If she's so clever, then why does she think he's so great? I wish it was next year already.

I'm going mad here. I'll try to calm down.

I did well in my exams. I got a good report. Father gave me five pounds and a sort of cuddle. Big deal. He's a creep. Caitlin says I should be grateful. And thankful. And that I should have done better.

Mother and Father and Caitlin have gone on holiday. I've used my job as an excuse not to go with them. I can earn extra money in the summer holidays, I say. Fine, they say. They lock their rooms before they go and take the keys with them. I don't care.

Tillmann was here yesterday for the first time ever. In the house, that is. In my bedroom. We got a bit carried away, but nothing stupid happened. I think he respects me. He came to the house up the back lane so no-one would see him.

Father and Mother and Caitlin are back. Just in time for my seventeenth birthday. How sweet. Caitlin's bought me a record by The Jam. Now that's a surprise. Why? What does she want? Nothing, she tells me. She just thought it would be nice. Father gives me another five pounds, another creepy cuddle, and Mother gives me a dirty look. The bags under her eyes look yellow.

I went to the Post Office to get my book updated. I've got two thousand pounds now! Yippee!

Tillmann goes tomorrow. His parents are driving him down to Cambridge. I'm going to miss him. He says I should write to him every week, but that he'll not write back because he doesn't want anyone to intercept the letters.

I've been trying not to think about Tillmann. That's why I've not been writing anything in this diary. Just keeping all my thoughts in my head. Or not trying to think. Not trying to think, actually, because it hurts to think. It really does.

Tillmann came home last weekend unexpectedly. He's given me the number of a phone box in Cambridge so that I can call him once a week. He'll call me back. His parents are giving him plenty of money.

It's November already. Less than a year before I can escape.

Caitlin comes into the restaurant one night. I let her have her food for free and don't remind her of her New Year's resolution. She looks tired. And she's even fatter than before. Why haven't I noticed before?

I woke up this morning and wondered what was different. It's Christmas Day and there's no shouting. I went downstairs. Mother and Father were sitting in the living room in front of the ashes of last night's fire. It smelt of coal down there.

Caitlin's gone.

*

I close the first book and look at Tillmann.

'Well,' I say, scratching my head. 'We know now where the idea for your name came from.'

'I'm not sure I'm happy about that,' he says. 'Being called after my mother's first boyfriend.'

'Quite serious about each other, they were, by the sound of it.'

'You're not jealous, are you?'

'Not really. It was me she married, after all.'

'Yup. How about listening to some Jam while we read more?'

'Ok. And we'll have some pizza in our next break.'

'Piizzaaaaa! Yeaaaaaah!' He waves his hands above his head, mocking me.

'Oh shut up and read.' I laugh. I do love my son.

Chapter 7

1983

It's weird without Caitlin. I know I hated her, but now I'm not so sure anymore. I don't like being here on my own with Father and Mother. They've locked Caitlin's room and kept the key. I don't know why. Are there secrets in there that I mustn't know about? It's probably my imagination running wild with me. Because I'm so bored and have no life. Except for the letters I write to Tillmann, and the once-a-week phone call. I love the sound of his voice.

I've changed the lock on my door. I don't want Father or Mother in here snooping around, and I don't want Father coming in here when I'm asleep. I'm sure he used to do that with Caitlin. But I don't know for certain.

Eight months to go before I run away.

I wonder where Caitlin is.

Father and Mother can't be that worried about her, because they haven't told the police. Maybe they got rid of her. But it doesn't make sense – Father getting rid of his darling. Naturally I can't ask them. We hardly talk anymore, anyway.

Tillmann took the rest of my tapes to Cambridge yesterday. I'll only need to pack a small case when I go then. All that's left now is to revise for my final exams in June, wait for my birthday in August, and then I'll be free. Tillmann says he's looking around for somewhere for me to live already, because unfortunately I won't be able to live in his college with him. Maybe he'll come and live with me. I can hope, can't I?

Where's Caitlin? No-one seems to know. I've asked round at school and in town, but no-one's seen her since last year. People keep telling me not to worry, that she's able to look after herself.

Tillmann says I should leave it and just concentrate on passing these exams. He says he's going to go back to Cambridge early in August to help me settle in.

I was going to try to pick the lock on Caitlin's door, but Father or Mother have put some padlocks on it. I can't afford to cause any problems with only two months to go before I pass my exams. I thought I heard someone trying to open my door last night, but I may just have been dreaming. Would Father risk breaking the door down?

Caitlin was in my dreams last night, for the first time since she disappeared. The first time I can remember, anyway. She was thin again, and her hair was flowing behind her as she was running across a field. She didn't keep turning round, so I don't think she was being chased. But she was running to me. I think I'll start looking for her when I get to Cambridge. I don't know how, but I'll think of something. I don't know why, but I think she needs me. Even though she's older than me.

A month to go to the exams. I keep thinking I won't make it. I keep worrying that I'll oversleep on exam day. Or that Father or Mother will stop me from leaving the house. I'm shaking with fear and excitement all the time. I'm not sleeping very well. Tillmann says it's natural for me to be nervous. I suppose he's right. I miss him. I can't wait to see him.

I'm finding it difficult to concentrate for long enough to write anything down. Two weeks before the exams start. I'm frightened now, because I don't want to fail. I don't want to let myself or Tillmann down. I can hardly eat. I've lost a lot of weight since the beginning of the year. My hair is almost down to the nape of my neck now. I wear hats a lot, even in the house, so Father won't notice.

I've just got up. It's light outside, but very early. Today's the first exam. I think I'm going to throw up.

The two exams today weren't as difficult as I thought they'd be. Another week and a half before they're over. I hope I don't throw up every morning.

I did throw up again this morning, although I didn't really have anything in my stomach to throw up. Just bile. I shouldn't be this nervous, should I? About exams.

My final exam's tomorrow. Life won't change, though, because I need to wait till my eighteenth birthday before I can go.

What can I while the summer away with? The odd minute now and then with Tillmann?

Work goes on as normal. There's nothing to write about.

Tillmann and I talk about the future, but all we're doing right now is waiting.

Tomorrow's my eighteenth birthday. I'll go to work this evening, come back here afterwards and go to bed as normal. I'll set my alarm for five in the morning, and then I'll leave the house. I've already got my bus ticket for Cambridge.

Father was waiting for me when I left my room this morning. He asked me what I was doing with my small case in my hand. I told him I was leaving. He tried to grab me, but all those days standing on my feet at the restaurant have made me strong. And losing weight has made me fast. When I got to the front door he made a last effort to catch me. I hit him in the face with my case.

I'm on the bus now. That's why the writing's so wobbly. The sun is warm on my face, and the rhythm of the bus makes me feel safe. Did Mother love me when I was born? It doesn't matter, does it, because she doesn't love me now.

Tillmann went back to Cambridge last weekend. He said it wasn't a good idea for us to catch a bus together. We might be seen, he said, and that would be a disaster. He's right, of course.

Only a few more hours and I'll be there.

Tillmann met me at the bus station yesterday. He had sorted out a bedsit for me about half an hour's walk from where he lives. I went there with him straightaway. He kissed me when we got there, but we agreed that we should wait a few more days to do what we've been waiting to do for almost two years. I want to find a job first, and once I find a job I want to find a flat, not just a dingy room. I want to feel ready for him before we do it. He understands. He says I should try his college for waitressing jobs.

I sent a letter to school telling them about my new address. They'll send my exam results to my bedsit.

I'm a waitress again. Oh well. It's a beginning. I start work at Tillmann's college tomorrow. It'll be weird, but I'll manage.

I got my results today after I got back to the bedsit from work. I managed to get top marks in German and French, but only a B in History. But that's not too bad. Once I get my certificates, I might be able to get a better job. I don't want to be a waitress all my life.

I've found myself a one-bedroomed flat a bit closer to Tillmann. It's a bit more expensive, but I've still got three and a half thousand pounds in the bank, and I'm earning almost a hundred pounds a week before tax.

It's November now, and Cambridge is very cold and wet. An insidious wet that gets inside you. At least I've a gas fire in the flat. Tillmann and I have agreed that we'll do it next week when I've got a weekend off, and he's not playing hockey.

I'm more nervous than before my exams. I threw up twice this morning. It's two o'clock now, and Tillmann's going to be here at five. I've bought some nice wine and some nice food to make for us. I want this to be romantic. That's why I've bought some candles, too.

Tillmann's still asleep in my bed. I can't describe what it was like to lose my virginity. I've never felt so full and satisfied before. It's a strange feeling, having a man inside me, but it didn't hurt like I thought it would. Tillmann was very understanding about using a condom. He loves me, I'm sure.

The sun is shining and November suddenly has a friendly face.

It's Monday afternoon, and I'm getting ready for work. Tillmann stayed here last night, too. I've told him he can move in with me if he wants to. He said he'd think about it.

Tillmann says he'll move in after Christmas. I'm so happy. Better still, I met a nice old man called Bill in the Heffer's bookshop just down the road from Tillmann's college, and he said I could start a trial period at his shop in the run-up to Christmas. I'm so happy!

I met Tillmann's parents for the first time today. They came down because he told them he wanted to stay in Cambridge for Christmas. To be with me, And after they'd gone again he asked me to marry him! I said yes, of course. Can it get any better?

It's Tillmann's last game of the year today. I've taken the afternoon off to watch him. I'm so excited. After the game we're going to pack up his stuff and take it to mine.

NO! NO! NO! Tillmann's in hospital. He got hit really hard on his head by a hockey ball. I heard it hit him. I saw him fall. I ran to him, all across the muddy field. But he didn't move.

I was allowed to drive to the hospital with him in the ambulance. But he didn't open his eyes for me. His skull's fractured. I don't know what to do.

Tillmann still hasn't woken up. His parents have come back down. They blame themselves for letting him play such a dangerous sport. We all go to see him every day.

It's Christmas Day. Why are they always so sad?

Tillmann stopped breathing this morning. He's dead. Where are my dreams? His parents have said I can come to the funeral, but I don't think I can. Father and Mother will be too close. I don't want them to know where I am. I hope Tillmann's parents can understand. I'll write them a letter tomorrow.

It's Boxing Day. I haven't slept. I walked my letter down to the hotel Tillmann's parents are staying at. I wasn't brave enough to see them again. Why me?

Bill has offered me a full-time job at his shop. I said yes. What else can I do? I can't think of anywhere else to go. I haven't even got any photos of Tillmann. I'm still not sleeping properly. The bed's so empty, and he keeps talking to me in my dreams.

It's New Year's Eve and I don't want to be on my own.

*

'Bloody hell!' Tillmann says.

'He'd be forty-one now. Jesus wept. Poor Kate.'

'And you? What about you?'

'What about me? I'm still alive, at least. And now I understand why she had to call you what you're called.'

'A dead man's name.'

'We've all got dead men's names.'

'Dead people's names.'

'Whatever,' I say. I'm tired and hungry.

'What about the necklace and pendant? Didn't you ever find them?'

'No. But then there's lots of stuff I didn't find after she'd died.' And lots of things in my head I'm finding. Thinking. Like, where was I when all this was happening? Nowhere near her, that's where.

The pizza arrives with some red wine for me. Apple juice for Tillmann. We drink and eat. I go outside for a cigarette. We go to bed. I watch my memories while I listen to the sleeping boy's breath. And then I dream, too.

*

'I don't want you in my bed again, ever,' Kate said quietly and closed the door.

And I never slept with her in our bed again.

The next morning, Christmas Day, I woke up on the sofa. I was hung over. I'd got so drunk after our argument that I just about drank the house dry. The present I'd bought for her was still on the floor. I put it into one of the drawers in my desk. The present she'd bought for me had disappeared. I lay there, looking at the ceiling, asking myself what I was supposed to do now.

'Morning!' Her voice came into my sickness. She kissed the top of my head. I was confused.

'I'm sorry 'bout last night,' I mumbled. I got out of the messed-up sheets and duvet on the sofa. Tried to put my arms around her bathrobed waist.

'I don't mind being friends with you, Nairne,' she said, pushing me away. 'I do still love you, but I don't want anything more than platonic love from you from now on. Kisses on tops of heads and cheeks are fine. But that's it.' She walked through to the kitchen. 'Tillmann's been up for hours playing with his presents. Shame you missed it.'

Except for the sleeping arrangements and the lack of

sex, things didn't change much. I didn't want to move into Tillmann's room, because I didn't want to share with a baby, and because I didn't want to accept that things with Kate had gotten so low. If I slept on the sofa-bed outside our bedroom door (I suppose it was really her bedroom door now), there was always the chance that, one night, she'd slip in beside me, or open the door and call me in. Neither happened.

'Can't we work this out?' I said a few days later. 'Isn't there something we can do? Marriage counselling or something like that? To make things better again?'

'The only thing that can make it better again is you saying you'll have more children. And you stopping this ridiculous jealousy thing.'

'I can't help it. It's like an illness inside me. I need to have everything black and white. If I don't care what you're doing, if I don't worry about you, that means I don't love you. So I either love you or I don't.'

'And which is it now? Come on, Nairne, which is it now? If you really really loved me, you'd say we'd have more children. If you didn't love me, you'd go.'

'I can't go. I can't leave you or Tillmann. It's impossible. I love him, but I don't like him. But because I love him I have to stay. Although he wakes me up at stupid times.'

'But do you love me? Do you? Because I don't think you do. Not the way I want you to love me. I've always wanted lots of children, and you're denying me that chance.'

'You denied yourself that chance when you had that abortion. Why didn't you have that child? I'd 've accepted it as if it was mine.'

'Would you? Would you really? I don't think so, not after all the hurt you've caused me since I told you about it.'

There was no answer to that. Because she was right.

Although she'd slept with that man before I knew her, I took it personally. As if she'd slept with him after meeting me.

A week later, she went away for a few days. She'd been getting quite a lot of phone calls since our row. I looked after Tillmann as I'd always done when we'd been alone. Lots of music, lots of shouting. But I didn't dare sleep in our bed. It was a no-go zone now. And she'd locked all her drawers and taken the keys.

When she got back, all her lovely wonderful hair had gone. Tillmann noticed it, of course. She just smiled at him and said she'd got it cut to look younger. At thirty-one. He believed her, of course. And told her how lovely she was.

'I've got a kind of cancer they don't understand,' she said to me later, after Tillmann had gone to bed. 'There's nothing they can do about it. The doctors reckon I've got a year at the most. Probably less.'

I couldn't grasp this. And she was so emotionless about it. I cried and I cried and I cried. She just told me to stop it. To stop being so silly. These things happened. There was nothing any of us could do about it. All she wanted was to die in peace.

'I have always loved you,' she said.

It was almost morning again. She'd hugged me and kissed me on the cheek. As if she needed to comfort me. I could find no way to comfort her. I didn't even feel close to her anymore. Despite that familiar perfume of hers. The thought of her death disgusted me. The thought of having to look after her dying body and the mess it would leave.

'Can't we get a second opinion?' I said.

'Been there. Done that,' was all she said. 'It's a fact.' She looked at me as if she'd never been this close to me before. 'And it's fine with me if you get someone in to look after me when it gets really bad. I know that you're not very good with mess. Just, please, let me die here, with you and Tillmann. Don't let them take me away. Despite everything, because of everything, this is where I want to be.'

I couldn't contradict her. I didn't have the strength. Life went on. She didn't actually seem particularly ill at first, except for the increased frequency of her headaches. The she started to get tired. Tired all the time. She told me it was because of her medicines. Because of her radiotherapy. Not that these treatments were giving her any more of a chance to survive.

But she wouldn't allow me to go to the doctor with her. She wouldn't allow me to go to the hospital with her. She wouldn't let me look at her notes. She refused to talk about her illness. And as spring came, she grew weaker and weaker. But she refused to give in. Refused to just sit indoors. Walked as much and as hard as she could. Took Tillmann across the road every school day. Didn't stop reading. Didn't stop throwing books at the wall.

The only thing she stopped doing was asking me for another baby.

*

I don't know where I am when I first wake up. For a minute I think that Kate's back in bed next to me. But it's only a pillow. And it's Tillmann's breathing I can hear from the other bed in the room. It's late and I feel hung over. It's Monday and it feels strange that we should be here in a hotel and not at home.

I swing my feet out of bed and bring them down to the floor. I face the sleeping child, my sleeping son. And despite all that I've understood these last couple of days, despite recognising my selfishness, my need to be acknowledged and understood, and knowing that these things count for nothing; despite all this I wonder how he'll remember me when I've gone, too.

Time stops, somehow. It's the memories that stop time, that hold time back, that give us the immortality we crave. I recall lying awake one night in my bed, waiting for a girlfriend to come home to me when she had promised to, only to find the next morning, when I woke, that the empty space next to me in bed was still empty. Because she was with someone else. But it didn't matter then, and it doesn't matter now, because *he's* here, and we're on this journey together. Not just this weekend, not just here and now, but forever.

I see Kate in all her willowy wildness, and I understand at last that the past counts for nothing, that it has no bearing on our present. That everything that lies behind us lies behind us forever, because it's the future that matters; it's the future that changes us, not the past. And everything that's been has been, and everything that will be will be, not because it's preordained, not because it's there waiting for us regardless of what we do. But because it's there, hidden, secret, silent, waiting for us to make the effort to grasp it. Waiting for us to make the choices that will make all things possible. Because *we* have the power to make it real.

Tillmann snorts. He's awake now, and all the images in my head fade. 'Hey, Dad,' he mumbles and sits up.

'Morning, son. It's time we decided what to do.'

'I'll get that atlas,' he says, and reaches down into his bag. 'Nairn's in Scotland,' he reveals when he's finished leafing through it. 'And it's time we started driving up there. It's over 400 miles north.'

'Let's go see Mum first. Let's have lunch with her before we leave.'

'What about the journals?'

'You can read 'em to me on the way. And let's have some Eighties music to go with the reading.'

It'll take us two days to get up there, I think. I'm not

driving ten hours in a single day, because that'll take us to midnight if we have lunch with Mum. And anyway, Tillmann's right, there's no hurry. And I want to know what's in the rest of those books before I get to where they were sent from.

Lunch with Mum is fun. She's still as senile as yesterday. Can't remember us going to see her yesterday. Can't remember giving us Kate's journals, either. But she's alive and she's talking and she's smiling. Good. As long as she's happy. One day soon she'll be dying, and I just hope that she'll remember then how much difference she's made to our lives, mistakes or not, madness or not. She has no god-given right to my affection, but I owe her my life.

Once we've left Dorset House, we head back in the direction of the hotel. Just before we get there, we take the last exit off a roundabout and onto the main road up to Scotland. Tillmann puts in a CD, and the first thing I hear is that tune *Pickin' The Blues* by Grinderswitch which John Peel always used as the start of his radio shows. And then Tillmann starts reading.

*

1984

I feel old. I feel like a widow. I am *a widow, in all but name. I didn't go to the funeral. I stayed here and worked. Tillmann's parents sent me a letter and asked me if I'd mind keeping all Tillmann's things that he'd already moved into my flat. I sent a letter back thanking them for being so kind. There's a shirt here that still smells of him. I can't sleep without him. So I sit up and read. More and more books. In my head. I feel like dying. Something inside me has died.*

The couple of bottles of red wine Tillmann and I had bought for special occasions have gone. The bottle of champagne we were going to drink when he finally moved in 'properly' has gone. I could have saved it for something else, I suppose, but I don't feel like there will ever be anything special again. Not now that I'm alone.

Nine months since I've written anything here. I'm nineteen now, and I'm an old woman. My birthday passed with only Bill, my boss, remembering it. He gave me some flowers. He said his wife had said they might be the best thing. He's a nice old man. He seems to understand. He met Tillmann a couple of times. He was happy for me, for us. I'm full-time now. Bill promoted me to Head of the History section. Thank God for good exam results. Thank God for such small mercies that keep me alive. My hair is touching my shoulders now, and it's thicker than ever.

I finally sorted through Tillmann's things last night. My tapes I'd already got back from him, of course. I just wanted to find something more than a shirt that now smells more of me than of him, I suppose. Although I imagine I can still smell him on it. Scent is memory, isn't it?

There was a small box of things that I'd never seen before. I had *to look through it. I couldn't imagine that he'd ever keep secrets from me. I knew he had no secrets from me. Yet I discovered a secret, and it gave me back my will to live. Because I'd forgotten about her amidst all this grief. Forgotten about my older sister.*

I found a letter. To Tillmann. From Caitlin. I suppose he'd been planning on telling me about it when he moved in. I'm sure he'd 've told me about it, because he knew how much I wanted to find her.

The letter was headed with a phone number, no address. It was a short letter, scribbled in a hurry, judging by the writing. She explained that she'd known about Tillmann and me, that she'd not had the courage to talk with us before, and that she wanted to get in touch with me. Could he tell me about this when he knew for sure that I would be staying in Cambridge? It was actually dated two weeks before he died.

I called the number as soon as I'd read the letter. Of course I didn't know if she'd still be there, but I had to try. She actually answered the phone. It was like talking to myself. She's somewhere in Scotland. Working as a shop assistant in some place near the sea. Tourists and all that. I told her that Tillmann was dead and that I wanted her to come and live down here with me. She said she'd think about it.

I went to meet Caitlin at the bus station. She looked a lot thinner than when I last saw her. And very very tired. The first thing I did was cook her some tea. She wolfed it down like she'd not eaten for months. Then she had one of her headaches. She's asleep now, but we'll talk tomorrow.

Caitlin has told me all about Father and Mother. I'd thought she'd been getting fat because of something that Father had done to her, but she told me that she'd deliberately made herself fat so that Father would stop pestering her. Told me that he'd been creeping into her bedroom for years, and that there was nothing she could do about it. That Mother had accused her of stealing Father from her. That Mother had deliberately ignored what was going on.

I asked her why she'd been so nasty to me. Because she'd wanted to protect me, she said. Because as long as she was Father's favourite, she knew he wouldn't touch me. And that she'd known about Tillmann from the start, because she'd once seen us together. And that was why she'd bought me that Jam record, because she'd wanted me to understand that she actually knew and cared.

Why didn't she go to the police about Father? I don't know. She *doesn't know. So why didn't she try to escape sooner? She didn't feel she could. She'd had an inkling that I was thinking of running away, and she hadn't wanted to expose me to Father.*

So why had she run away that Christmas Eve? Because Mother had held her down when Father tried to rape her instead of just touch her. Because she'd suddenly seen the pathetic self-pity in Father's eyes when he'd been leaning over her, panting his foul drunk breath into her nose. Because she'd seen Mother grinning like a maniac when her husband tried to pull down her oldest daughter's knickers in the front room.

She'd bitten Mother, kneed Father in his balls, and run upstairs where she'd just thrown all her money and some clothes into a supermarket carrier bag. Then she'd shinned down the drainpipe next to her window and run down the hill to the railway station. She'd just picked a town name from the timetable by chance and bought a single to the place. Never mind how much it cost. I don't know why I'd not heard the noise they must have made. Probably because I'd been dreaming of Tillmann and of escape.

Once she'd got off the train, she'd been on the streets for a couple of nights in the middle of winter until she'd found someone to look after her. Someone who had become a friend, not a lover. Because she didn't want lovers, not yet, not ever, not after what Father and Mother had done to her. And then she'd managed to build a small life for herself up there. Some place called Nairn. In the Scottish Highlands. Far away from anyone or anything that could hurt her.

But now she's here. We've always belonged together.

*

Tillmann stops reading and pauses the music. I stare at the traffic and try to take in what I've just heard.

'Well, Dad, looks like this Caitlin woman must've sent Gran these notebooks. Did Mum really never mention her to you?'

'No; never ever. When I met Kate, it was like she'd just appeared out of nowhere, like she had no baggage, nothing.'

'But if she thought that her and Caitlin had always belonged together, why did she never talk about her? Why didn't she let you meet her?'

I shrug. 'I haven't got a clue. Mind you, who's to say that Caitlin did send those notebooks? She could be dead by now, too. Cancer's in the genes, isn't it, runs in families.'

'But who then? And how did whoever sent those books know Gran's name and the Dorset House address? Whoever it was must've known about you and Mum.

Whoever it was must've known Mum *after* you met her.'

'Whoever it was, what I'm wondering is why those books were sent now, or a week ago, anyway, so close to the anniversary of Kate's death, so close to the anniversary of when we first met, and so close to your birthday.'

I can't look at him; the Monday afternoon traffic's too heavy. I hate these bloody roads.

'I suppose we'll find out when we get there,' he says, curiously patient. 'Although how we're gonna find whoever sent the books, I don't know, because there's only the postmark to go by.'

'How about finding the main post office in Nairn and asking some questions?'

'And show them the picture of Mum. If this Caitlin is still alive, and if she is the sender, then surely there'll be some family resemblance.'

'But this woman's older than Kate would be now; at least that's what I understand from the journal. Would she look similar, still?'

'Possibly. ... Dad? Don't you feel a bit betrayed, even more than when Mum was alive?'

'Not really. I always knew your mum was full of secrets, always guessed, I suppose, that she'd had a really crap childhood, which was why she never talked about it, never really mentioned her parents or family. I'm surprised it's turning out quite so intriguing, though.'

'But that doesn't make sense, Dad. How could you get so jealous over her and that bloke before you met, but not really care about what we've found out this weekend?'

'I guess it's because jealousy is fundamentally sexual. At least mine is, was. Sexual and physical. All about power. And I think we men measure ourselves against other men in very physical ways. Things men think are like, does he earn more than me, is he taller than me, is he thinner, has he got a six-pack stomach, has he got more hair than me, is his knob bigger than mine, is he funnier, cleverer, and so on. And I've always seen myself as a loser in all those things, because of the way I led my life, have always felt threatened by most other men, because I've never seen myself as much of a man, basically.'

'But Mum married *you*.'

'True, but when you're in that mind-set, you're always afraid that things will change, that the smallest mistake you make in anything, work, sex, conversation, will lead to you being left behind. It's not necessarily even the fear of losing someone you love that scares you, but it's the idea of being made to look a fool, being proven to be inferior to everyone else, just like you've always known you are. And then there's the plain fear that people have pretended they love you just so that, in the end, they can turn round and tell you they were lying and make you feel bad. That they've just been stringing you along the whole time, that it's all just been one big game, and that you've been had.'

'But that's ridiculous. I've never even thought of you acting like that, being like that. As a kid I always thought nothing could scare you.'

I laugh. 'Tillmann, everything scares me.'

He shakes his head. 'But you've never brought me up to think like that, the way you just said.'

'I should hope not, mate. It's a terrible way to be, and there's a terrible price to pay. It's an illness, really, and nothing anyone tells you can make it better.'

'Not even therapy?'

'I never tried it, because I thought it would dig up too many other skeletons in my head, to be honest. That it would make the past too important again. And I reckoned I should deal with it myself. Never really got the chance, though, did I?'

'And if you got a second chance, could you deal with

it? Now?'

'That's a hypothetical question. If you're right and Kate is still alive – which I don't believe, just for the sake of completeness – then I don't think she'd give me another chance. And I don't know if I'd like another chance.'

'Although you still love her?'

'What is it I still love, Till? Her or the memory of her?'

'Both, I think.'

'Who knows? And who cares?'

'You should care, Dad, because you're killing yourself.'

'I know,' I say, 'I know.'

'Whatever happens, Dad, I think it's about time you kissed a girl again.'

'Not me, mate. I'm past it. But maybe I'll try, maybe I will. Just one more time.'

'I hope you do.'

He turns the music back on and we carry on driving. He doesn't start reading again, because I think he can tell I want to be alone with my thoughts for a moment or two.

It's the Cocteau Twins' version of *Song to the Siren.* Although they released this ages before Kate and I met, it was one of the songs that bound us. Its ethereal sound always seemed to me like her voice, like her whole being. And she was a siren, she really was. A mysterious woman whom I couldn't resist, who drew me to her like no-one I'd ever met. She was too good for this life, too good for the earth we wear under our feet. Why I had to force her into destroying part of that mystery I shall never know.

Chapter 8

The day Kate told me of her cancer was the last day we were really close. Although she kept fighting, although she never seemed to even think of giving in, she grew ever more distant from me. We didn't kiss again after that day, not until the day she died. We hardly even touched each other after that day, not even accidentally, not even in the daily run of things. She'd begun her withdrawal.

In the March of that year eight years ago, her treatment stopped. Not because she was in remission, not because there was any hope. But because there was no hope. Her body had started to swell, her hair was almost totally gone, bald patches scarring her head. Her eyesight was leaving her, too, and she took to wearing half-spectacle, half-binocular glasses to allow her to see things in focus at all. If it hadn't been so tragic, it would have been funny.

How Tillmann coped with all this, I don't know, but children are resilient. The nurse began to come every day, and I thought it would now only be weeks until we would lose Kate. But she was strong, she really was, and as time passed, I thought that maybe that myth was true, about dying people saving themselves, with one last effort, for a special occasion. There were only just over 6 months until her son's fifth birthday, after all.

Naturally, I was the main carer for Tillmann now, but if he was sad or if he'd hurt himself, it was still always Kate that he'd go to. He would spend hours with her in her room, often with the door shut. I think he understood that he'd have to say farewell sooner rather than later, to this wonderful creature who had given him life. To this wonderful woman whose vanished looks he had inherited.

I tried to spend time alone with her in what had been

our bedroom, too, but often she was too tired to even look at me. Sometimes, though, very rarely, as she would be lying there without her binoculars on her face, she'd open her eyes, and I would detect, still, that electric blue burning in them with an unbendable will for life that I couldn't understand. Not at this late stage of the illness. I'd have been dead long ago, I think, because I never had the same willpower that she did. And I blame myself for having destroyed some of her strength by making her take herself away from me because I didn't want any more children.

My guilt, my fault, mine the blame. I still feel that. I'm sure, deep down, that I hurt her so much with my forceful entry into her past, with my refusal to compromise over the child issue, that her body threw an internal switch that made her ill. That I directly caused the cancer to grow in every single part of her body because I was the way I was. I know that I killed her. I think she would have lived to be older than me if we'd had all the children she wanted. Her strength in her dying threw my weakness in my living into a stark, painful and accusatory relief.

Occasionally she would get phone calls which led to her having her bedroom door closed. I never fathomed who these calls were from, and by that time I was bathing so much in my own guilt that I didn't have the energy to even worry about them, or ask about them. Maybe that was for the best.

What was strange was how normal life went on, outside her bedroom door, outside the house. Tillmann still had to go to school. I still had to work on my contracts. And the nurse would come and go with her own key to look after a dying woman who was growing paler by the day.

When the summer holidays came along, Kate tried to insist that Tillmann and I should go away for a couple of weeks, just so that we'd get a break from sharing her dying. But neither of us wanted to leave her. Although she'd become a stranger to me, just about, I didn't want her to be on her own. I didn't count the nurse as being part of our family. That's probably why I can't remember her name.

That summer was quite hot, and it took its toll on Kate. We hired an air conditioning unit to try to keep her room at a steady temperature, but I believe she still suffered. And she still refused to take more painkillers than she thought were necessary. She said to me once that she was trying to love her disease, because that way, she could either love it away and get better, or she would grow to love it so much that she wouldn't be bitter about it taking her. That, I thought, was very strange, but I couldn't argue with her.

Midway through the summer she became finally permanently bound to her bed. Her body stopped swelling. Instead it began to shrink. It went back to the size she'd been when I'd met her too rapidly for belief, and kept shrinking. She became wrinkled and haggard, and her voice a rasping echo of what it had been. The binoculars hardly helped now, and from a distance she could detect only movement. Close up, she still had some recognition of colour and shape and faces. Tillmann would now spend hours on the bed, right up against his mother's face, so that she could see even just a glimmer of her precious beloved boy who loved her more than she could believe.

As the end of the summer drew closer, her bedroom turned into a hospital room. It was crammed with all kinds of machinery intended to ease her dying. Intravenous drips, oxygen masks, bed pans, you name it. We'd even managed to find space in there for a bed for the nurse.

Kate stopped refusing the painkillers. She now had a morphine drip to keep the pain at bay as much as she could. I thought she wouldn't last until school started again. Maybe some part of me was hoping that she would die with some dignity left. But she didn't.

*

I'm crying. I can feel the tears running down my face and there's nothing I can do to stop them. I pull into the next service station and just sit in the car, my head pushing hard against the headrest. Tillmann says nothing. I close my eyes.

I sit like that for about fifteen minutes, until the tears stop. I'm not physically tired. I'm weary, tired inside my head. Tired of all those memories running around in front of my eyes, in my brain. Tired of the mistakes, the guilt, the loss, the dreadful ever-lasting loss that I carry around with me wherever I go, wherever I am. Tired of not being able to escape myself. Tired of the hold she still has over me. Tired. Tired. Tired.

'We've got a long way to go, Dad,' Tillmann says.

'I know, mate, I know,' I say. 'Just let me have a smoke and I'll be fine.' It's started raining.

'I'm sorry,' he says when I get back in the car.

'For what?'

'For this. My fault. Dragging you all this way.'

'Don't be stupid. We'd have ended up driving to Mum's anyway, because they called us. And then I'd have insisted on driving up to Scotland, as well, to find out where those books came from. And maybe this'll stop me feeling sorry for myself every single moment of every single day.'

'I don't think you feel sorry for yourself. I think you blame yourself too much for what's happened. Despite your mistakes.'

'D'you remember any of what you and Kate spoke about when you used to sit with her on her bed for hours on end?'

'Not really. To be honest, I don't think we talked about anything. I don't think we spoke about things we'd done together before she got ill. It was just a sort of silent conversation, if that doesn't sound stupid.'

'Doesn't sound stupid at all.'

'All I remember is that I thought she was beautiful, although I knew she was very ill. There was a kind of light in her eyes when she opened them. And to the little four-year-old I was, that light seemed to be full of hope and warmth and understanding. And determination. And sometimes it felt like she was trying to pass all that on to me. Trying to implant that will into me, pass it on to me, before she had to die. I've never been able to put it into proper words before.'

He draws a deep breath.

'Although right at the end she did scare me. … I wish I could drive.'

'It's no bother, son. It's not as if we're rushing, is it?'

'I guess not, Dad. Let's get going again before the weather gets any worse.'

'Let's do that. And you can read some more. We need to get through these journals before we get up there.'

I nod northwards and start the car again.

*

1985

After such a long break (again), I don't know where to start.

Caitlin found herself a job in one of the college libraries. It meant we were able to find ourselves a two-bedroom flat to rent. I don't think we'll ever buy somewhere. It suits us to be able to move at short notice if we need to.

Maybe this New Year will bring us better things. We're clinging to each other at the minute, afraid of the past, and afraid of the future. I think we both sense it has to get better. We're just grateful that we found each other before we lost each other. Before our parents' hatred took final root in us.

I'm still happy at the bookshop, and Bill seems happy for me to be working there. He's asked Caitlin and me to his house a couple of times, but I don't feel ready for that sort of social interaction. I don't want any more questions about Tillmann, and no questions about my future. Or questions about what's even further past. Like Father and Mother.

I think it would break our hearts if they ever found out where we were. Tillmann's parents, whom I sometimes call, understand this. They're thinking of moving away from our old home town, but it all seems a bit up in the air. I wonder if they're reluctant to leave the house where Tillmann grew up. Even though they've got other children. It must be awful as a parent, for one of your children to die before you.

All I think about is Tillmann. I sometimes dream of what happened, and in my dream I reach him before he stops moving and manage to save him. Or sometimes I fly across that hockey field and manage to catch the ball just before it reaches his face, just before it smashes his skull into his brain, just before it kills him. Then I wake up and feel guilty that I'm still alive and he's not.

Caitlin says she misses Tom, her Scottish friend. I asked her if she's in love with him, and she told me she doesn't know what love is. But that, now, away from him, she realises he is the one she'd like to lose her real virginity to. I can't contemplate her going away again, not so soon after we've found each other, but she needs to be happy. She's thinking about it.

It's near the end of January. Caitlin has decided she should go up to Nairn to see Tom and to talk to him, to see if there is a future for them. She's not sure. It's sad. At least I've known love. She's asked me to go with her, so we've booked two weeks holiday. And we've found a cheap B&B we can stay in. Caitlin doesn't want to stay at Tom's, at least not until she's sure about what she feels for him.

The B&B place is wonderful. It's only a hundred metres from the shoreline. An old Victorian mansion house. With chickens and other farm animals in the garden. And bee hives. Peaceful. I can sit in the room Caitlin and I are sharing and look out at the sea rolling gently in from somewhere far away. It's cold outside, but the sun is shining.

Caitlin and Tom are spending a lot of time together, although she comes back here in the evenings. I don't mind. How could I? She's my older sister, and I want her to be happy. I spend most of my time walking along the sandy beach wrapped in a big black coat.

I met Tom today for the first time. He's a tall, strong man with a head full of unruly black hair. And he's what I suppose you'd call an odd-job man. He seems gentle and kind. If I were Caitlin, I'd decide that I was in love with him and stay here, although I think he's about ten years older than her. He hasn't got a brother, worse luck.

The air here's so fresh. There's none of that decay around that I've always felt in the southern towns that I've lived in. And the people seem friendly. I guess it's just not the most exciting place in the world. But what's so exciting about the real world, anyway? It's got nothing to offer but pain.

It's the last day of our holiday. Caitlin is coming back with me. She and Tom have decided they do love each other, but they want to be apart for at least a month before making any final decisions. Although they did make one decision while I was here. That's why I've been sleeping alone in this room for the past week. I'm happy for her. She looks really joyful for the first time that I can remember.

We've been back here in Cambridge for two weeks now. Caitlin says she can't move back up to Nairn, because she'd be leaving me with the bills for this bigger flat that we're sharing. I told her not to be silly; I can always get a lodger. She can't put her happiness to one side just because of money, or just because of me. She phones Tom every day. And he writes to her every day.

Tillmann's fading in my memory. I can't remember the sound of his voice anymore. It's been a gradual loss, I suppose. What do you do when people die? How do people who've been married for decades cope when their loved one dies? I don't know. At least they might have less time to forget before they, too, are taken from the world.

I dreamt of Tillmann last night, but he was silent. I dreamt we'd had a child, and that I'd decided to call him Tillmann, too. If I ever have any children, I think that is *what I'll do. But I don't think I will ever have children. I don't think I can.*

Caitlin left today. She's going to live with Tom in the rambling old cottage he inherited from his parents. I'm going to miss her, but I know that I'll be able to go up there whenever I want. And I will, whenever I can. At least I have a sister again, now, and there are invisible bonds that will always bind us.

Caitlin's been gone for five months now. I've been back to Nairn once. Caitlin and I send each other letters every week. The letters don't say much, actually, other than the retelling of humdrum everyday life. But that's enough. I think we've both had enough of extraordinary things happening to us, bad things.

In her last letter Caitlin told me she's going to marry Tom on my birthday. That's in a month. I'll be going up there, and I'll be one of the witnesses, along with Tom's best friend. I'm looking forward to it.

Caitlin says she's happier than she's ever been. The wedding was bigger than I expected. Tom's very popular in Nairn. She's chosen well. And she looked great in her cream pencil skirt and top. I guess that's one thing we're different in, our taste in clothes. I only like black, so black is all I wear. Maybe that's why I've been so unhappy. But I won't change that. I think the colour suits me, and I look less fat in it. Or at least I think I do. Weighing eight stone isn't too bad, is it?

It's coming up to Christmas. I've found a lodger. I actually chose a man. His name's Richard, and he's from the North. He's a student here. He's only eighteen, but he seems nice enough. And I don't feel threatened. He plays hockey, too. Maybe that's why I chose him. He's very homesick at the moment. I think he's got a girlfriend at home. We don't really talk that much.

1986

Richard came back from his Christmas holiday yesterday. His so-called girlfriend finished with him. Said he was too conventional. So now he's had his ears pierced. I don't think it'll make much difference, though, actually. Because he's a nice boy, not a rebel. I hope he gets himself a girlfriend down here. He deserves it.

I think Richard has found a girlfriend. He's only here some nights. I daren't ask him, because I don't want him to think I'm prying. Hey, I must be getting old. I feel like his mother.

It's over two years since Tillmann died. I have been asked out lots by students coming into the shop, but I've always said no. To be honest, I wouldn't even know where to start. The thought of dating someone again scares me. I don't think I'd be nice enough to anyone. I'd probably frighten them off with the stories of my life.

Maybe I shouldn't ever tell anyone about my past. That's probably best. I'll just make something up.

Making things up doesn't help much. I finally decided to say yes to someone who asked me out, and I ended up in some dreadful pub. He got very drunk. The things I made up about my past obviously weren't exciting enough for him because he ended up going on a pub crawl with some friends of his who came into the pub an hour after we'd got there. One more try?

This date was more promising, because I didn't have to make anything up. The guy – he's called Andy - was only interested in what plans I've got, not what plans and dreams I'd had. He's got a cute smile and smells nice. And he took me to a restaurant. Which was better than a pub. And he didn't mind when I insisted on paying my half of the bill. We're going out again in a week.

Caitlin's last letter was a bit alarming. Tom and she had decided to try for a baby from the day they married. But nothing's happened. She's never been on the pill, so she's starting to think there's something wrong with her or Tom. They're going to go to a specialist. I hope they don't get bad news. She's very down about it all. Wish there was something I could do.

Andy and I go out for dinner once a week now. This has been going on for about two months now. The last time he walked me home, I asked him in (Richard's hardly here anymore, but carries on paying his rent). We sat listening to music and drinking coffee. He asked me if would mind him kissing me. I didn't mind. It was good to kiss someone again. And to have a cuddle. That's all we did. I think he might start asking me about my past if I carry on acting like a wounded animal desperate for help when I get some affection from someone else. Because I actually cried when we cuddled, because it's been so long since I've been close to a man, to a man who cares. Maybe I should finish it.

Andy won't take no for an answer. I don't know if this is a good thing, or not. He's asked me why I cried the first time he held me, and I said it was because I'd not felt so close to someone for a long time. I think he might have taken this the wrong way and assumes that I'm in love with him. Which I'm not, actually. Not yet, anyway. I just like him very much. He's asking me out nearly every day now, and I keep saying no. Maybe he'll get pissed off about the way I'm acting soon, and then I won't have to make a decision about us. I'm such a coward.

Caitlin says that it's her fault she can't have children. There's nothing wrong with Tom, apparently. And they can't afford IVF. And I can't afford to help them. It's so unfair. Maybe there's a way out.

Are all men bad? All except Tillmann and Tom? Andy really wouldn't take no for an answer. Yesterday, we went out as usual and had a nice evening. I asked him back up for a coffee and a kiss and a cuddle. He tried to touch me, tried to force himself on me. I kicked him, stabbed him with a fork that was lying around. I probably didn't injure him much, but I did hurt him enough for him to stop. I think that's over now, then. I don't think I can ever go through with something like this again. He called me horrid names and threatened me. I don't feel safe now.

Caitlin says that even if they could afford IVF it wouldn't help. There's something wrong with her insides. Tom understands. He says they should try to adopt. She says she'll think about it. She's very disappointed.

I heard from Bill that Andy had been suspended from university. Apparently he'd tried it on with some student girl who'd actually reported him to the authorities. How can I have been so wrong about him? It makes me think I might've been wrong about Tillmann. NO. No way was I wrong about him. We were going to get married.

Caitlin has written to tell me that she and Tom are going to be foster parents to start with. She feels that if she can help children who've been deserted by their parents to make better lives for themselves, then that's almost as good as being a mother herself. I wish her luck.

Just got back from Nairn. Caitlin and Tom have got their first foster child. They're very happy, although it's very challenging for them. I wonder how things will turn out. But despite their happiness, I thought I saw the small fog of despair in her eyes.

I'm nearly twenty-one. Life has passed me by forever, I think. I'm not going to go out with anyone anymore. I feel flattered that I keep being asked, but I can't face another disaster like with Andy. Hell, I'll grow into an old spinster and like it! Decision made.

Richard has split up with his girl. He's not very lucky in that department, I don't think, although this one has lasted almost a year. I'm sorry for him, because he does try so very hard. He's actually a very nice boy. Or should I say – a very nice man?

Caitlin and Tom now have three foster children. The cottage is big enough, and the allowances they get mean they can afford to have that many children at once. Caitlin says she's really tired all the time, but that it's satisfying to do something that might stop children being abused like she was.

Christmas is closer. It doesn't actually mean anything, though, does it?

Richard is staying in Cambridge for the holiday this year. He says he can't be bothered to go home. He says he doesn't feel like bumping into his old girlfriend back home and being made a fool of. We'll have Christmas dinner together. It's nice to have a friend. What with Caitlin so far away.

Richard and I did have Christmas dinner with each other, although it didn't actually quite go as planned. We got a bit drunk, started talking about our disappointments without mentioning them by name. And we kept eating and drinking and talking until Christmas Day came. When we gave each other our presents just after midnight, we touched by accident. We sat there for a second, afraid.

Then we lay down on the floor and started to kiss. We both moved towards each other at the same time. He held me tight, and I held him, too. He cried. I cried. Over all our pasts, over all our mistakes and heartaches. And then, just as the bells started ringing at the end of Midnight Mass, we asked each other to his bed, because I couldn't ask him to the one I slept in with Tillmann.

So now I have a lover – again. What am I going to do?

*

'Wow!' Tillmann says. 'That's a lot of past to be getting on with.'

'Mmm,' I say, preoccupied with what I've just heard. It's seven o'clock, and we've been driving for Heaven knows how long. It's been dark for an hour, and I hate driving in the dark. The countryside has grown sparse around us.

'Time to find somewhere to stay,' I mumble.

Half an hour later we pull off the road into the car park of yet another roadside motel. We'll still have five hours driving to do in the morning, I reckon. So many roads leading into nowhere. I wonder what'll happen tomorrow.

Tillmann looks back through the journals while we eat. He's given up scribbling into his notebook for the time being. Not that I'd have noticed if he had been scribbling while we were driving.

'Didn't Mum ever mention that your name was almost identical to a place in Scotland she knew?' he says.

'Nope,' I say and take another swig of my lager. 'Like I said, she never said anything about the past.'

'Still seems weird that she'd not even mention that, though. It's not as if she'd be telling you anything she'd told herself not to tell you. She could just've asked you if you knew there was this place in Scotland. No need even for her to have mentioned that she'd been there.'

'But the journals tell us now that she wasn't just that secretive about the past with me, but with everyone. Not that that's surprising in itself.'

'People have been through worse,' he says without emotion. He surprises me.

'I didn't think I'd hear you say that about your mother.'

'Put it this way. I know now she'd been through a lot, but her sister got an even rougher deal. Just imagine being abused by your father. It's gross.'

'Worse than gross, mate. But I get what you mean. I was just surprised you said what you did.'

He shrugs.

'The way she writes is quite interesting,' I go on. 'It's not overly emotional. They're not really the journals of a young girl, Dear Diary stuff and so on.'

'I reckon she just wanted to write down the important things in her life, keep a record of them, rather than using her diary as a friend she'd tell anything to.'

'How did those journals get back up to Nairn, though?' I say. 'Did she send them up there when we got married or before, or just before she died, or what?'

'We'll have to read them all to work it out. I don't think there's any point just leafing through the rest of 'em to see if we find something interesting, because then we'll lose the thread. And I'm sure it's the thread that's important. This passing from one age to the next. That's where her secret is.'

'Do you really think she's still alive?'

'Yes, I do. Although I know that I'm probably setting myself up for a big fall. But you yourself have said that there's no such thing as coincidence, so all this happening now has got to be for a reason.'

'Maybe Caitlin just thought it was about time we learned about Kate's past, that you're old enough now to understand.'

'If she knows how old I am.'

'I can't imagine that Kate wouldn't have told her older sister about you – if they were still in touch.'

'Even if they were still in touch, Mum might not have wanted to hurt Caitlin's feelings. Imagine how that would feel, to be barren and then be told by your sister that she's pregnant. … And the abortion. How d'you tell your sister who can't have kids that you've just got rid of one? No, I can't believe she'd have told Caitlin about any of those things.'

'What if she didn't have an abortion?' I say without understanding where the question has come from.

'That's impossible,' he says, sitting up straight.

'Why?'

'You told me she'd said she was ten weeks pregnant when she met you, that she'd had the abortion a few days after you'd met.'

'What if she made it up? You've read it yourself. At one point she decided she'd have to make up the past so that she wouldn't have to share her real past with anyone.'

'Then why not make up something totally off the wall, something that wouldn't make you jealous, that was totally ridiculous and meaningless?'

'She didn't know I'd be jealous when she told me, did she? She didn't really know what kind of bloke she'd married. Just like I didn't know, don't know, what kind of woman I married. I don't even know who I married, to be honest.'

'What d'you mean? I don't think she lived in a totally imagined world. I think when she met you she really and honestly fell in love with you. But that she didn't want to burden you with what she'd been through when she was younger, didn't want you to feel you had to be with her because you pitied her.'

'How could a woman that beautiful ever think someone would fall in love with her and stay with her out of pity?'

'Why do any of us feel we're not good enough for someone else?'

'Like you and the girl at school?'

'Maybe. … But I don't think your theory about the non-abortion works. She'd have had to have had the baby before you met her. A long time before you met her. Because, even though she was so thin, she'd have had to lose weight afterwards. How long did it take her to get back to normal after she had me?'

'Six months or so,' I say.

'See, it doesn't fit. I'm sure she'd have chosen something less controversial than an abortion to make up when you asked her to tell you the saddest she'd ever been. I can't imagine anything sadder. And she was worried she couldn't have babies. If she'd already had one, that doesn't make sense either, because she'd have known she could have kids. This is just confusing the issue.' He shakes his head.

'I guess you're right.' I finally concede. 'Ok. So she did have an abortion. But that one truth still doesn't explain how close the link to Caitlin was after she'd met me.'

'No, it doesn't. But that'll be in what we've got left to read.'

'Tomorrow.'

'Tonight, please. We've got to cover at least a couple more years before we sleep. There's still four years to go before she meets you. And I want to find out if that Richard bloke is the bloke who told her to get rid of the baby.'

'Not sure I want to,' I grunt.

'Come on, Dad; it's done and dusted. It's just ancient history now. But it's important for our peace of mind.'

'Ok. As long as I can have some wine and smoke out of the window.'

'You would anyway,' he says. 'I know you better than you think.'

Chapter 9

1987

I woke up this morning, turned over and looked at Richard lying next to me. He's really quite beautiful when he's asleep. And I mean beautiful, not handsome. His face relaxes and his skin grows smooth, and the wrinkles disappear from his face. When he's awake he looks quite ordinary. Why he has wrinkles when he's younger than me, I can only guess. Maybe it's something to do with all those lost girlfriends. Silly boy. Kind boy.

The post office was crowded with homesick students back from spending the Christmas break with their families. I had to wait for ages to get a stamp. I sent a letter to Caitlin telling her about Richard. I'm sure she'll be happy for me. Not that this feels like it's the big love of my life, because none now will ever be, not after Tillmann. But it's a gentle companionship along with some nice loving. I suppose I'm lucky.

Why am I so happy just working in the bookshop? Richard asked me the other day. I get to meet people. I like Bill. I love books. And to be surrounded by books all the time is just the best thing that could've happened to me. It's all I need. Richard got a bit concerned when I said that. He asked me if I didn't need him. I told him to stop being so silly; that what we had was something totally different. I'm not surprised he's got so many wrinkles if he keeps analysing every single word someone says. I'm sure I'll manage to change him.

Yesterday we moved Richard's bed (well, it was Caitlin's when she was still here) into my bedroom, which is the bigger of the two. And moved my bed into Richard's room. We're going to get a lodger now that we're together. That'll help with the bills. It's sad, actually, that the bed I lost my virginity in with Tillmann will be slept on by others now, but I really couldn't face using it with another man.

Maybe I'm strange. Richard, of course, doesn't know the exact details of why we're moving the beds, but I don't want to tell him. I know just how he'd react. I've just told him Caitlin's old bed is more comfy, but that I want us to be in the big room.

Our new lodger – I suppose it's really my *new lodger, seeing as Richard will still be paying rent – moved in today. She's called Louise, she's nearly six foot tall, and she's a swimmer. I chose her because she intimidates Richard. Her family's quite rich, and I think this is just the first step to them buying a house in Cambridge for her. She's only eighteen and a first-year student. Quite odd that her parents have let her live in digs rather than in university accommodation. I've a feeling she hasn't been easy to get on with.*

Louise is settling in. Spring's coming. Richard is going through his annual soul-searching about leaving university because it bores him, but he'll stay. He's clever enough to stay on here as a lecturer. That's what makes him a bit snobby sometimes. He keeps asking when I'll leave the shop. I don't think I will.

Spent Easter with Caitlin and Tom. They've decided to try to stop fostering by the end of the year. Caitlin says it hurts too much to take in these children without knowing for how long, caring for them, loving them back to almost normal, and then having to give them away to their adoptive parents. So they're going to try to get their own adopted children by the beginning of next year. They're quite hopeful. Having fostered should give them an advantage over others wanting to adopt.

I've mentioned Caitlin to Richard. He doesn't know she's my sister. I've told him she's just a friend from way back when. And that's it. He wasn't overly happy when I said I'd be spending two weeks away from him, but if he wants our relationship to be long-term, he's going to have to get used to it. I told him I've got my friends, just like he has his. How many pasts will I have to invent? No more, I hope. But I expect I'll have to.

The cricket season's started. I don't mind cricket, although it's just as dangerous as hockey. It's not the game itself, though; it's the season it's played in. I can just sit in the sun, read a book and look interested in what they're doing. Tillmann's accident has put me off all team sports played in the darker time of the year.

The dreams about Tillmann are rare now. And they're not about saving him anymore. They're not about having children with him anymore. They're just about meeting him somewhere, not in Heaven, but out in some street, and embracing like old friends. Old friends with a slightly melancholy look. Old friends who know that they had a chance to be lovers forever, but somehow missed it. And after we've found out that we're both doing ok, we walk away from each other. Without looking back. I do still miss him, but I won't share his memory with anyone. It's too precious for that.

Good news from Caitlin. They've been accepted as adoptive parents. It helps that Tom's business (not that he'd ever call it a business) is going from good to better, because more folk are letting holiday cottages which need maintaining. Caitlin said that if they manage to save enough money, they might think of buying one, too. Knowing her, they will, and they'll manage to make some money on it, too. Good for them. It looks like they've got life sorted out.

Richard and I are going to go abroad for my birthday. Only a cheap package holiday to Dubrovnik, but it's better than nothing. I'm quite looking forward to it.

Louise has asked if her boyfriend can stay at the flat while we're away. It'll only be for the two weeks, she said. It's fine by me. I've told her that me locking my bedroom door for two weeks isn't a sign of mistrust. It's just a habit, and a way of keeping temptation out of people's way. I must admit that I now keep lots of really precious letters and memories in a safety deposit box at the bank. Because I want to keep them secret and safe. Like Tillmann's letters. Like most of Caitlin's letters, and certainly pictures of Caitlin and me together. Although I love my sister deeply now, I don't want anyone to know I've got a sister. I just want to be me. Like I've come from nowhere. Just like I'll disappear into nowhere when my time comes.

The holiday with Richard was great. The hotel we stayed in was a half hour boat trip from Dubrovnik. It had its own private beach. Richard lay on the beach all day, while I sat in the shade of the trees and read lots of books. The food was exotic and good. I even taught myself a few words of Serbo-Croat so that I could at least be polite to the locals. And the cigarettes were unbelievably cheap.

Dubrovnik is a wonderful city. It's got walls going all the way round it. And those walls border the sea on two sides of the city. The other two sides border steep hills. In fact, part of the town rises up into the hills. I loved those steep streets when we walked them, because they felt safe and secret, especially at night. I know that doesn't totally make sense, but I know what I mean. I'd like to go back there some day.

Louise has given notice. Her parents have bought her a house overlooking Parker's Piece. They must be very rich. She says she feels bad, but I tell her she shouldn't. I know she doesn't, anyway. Her parents live some way away, so I think the boyfriend's going to become a fixture in that house. I'm not sure I'll bother with a new lodger. Richard pays his half of the rent, and that's good enough, really. I could use that second bedroom for books. Or just for being alone in.

Autumn term has started. In some ways, it's my favourite time of year. We get lots of new faces in the shop. Hopeful faces, sad faces, faces that are young and full of striving. Tearful faces full of homesickness. I try sometimes to cheer those up a little. It doesn't always work, but I feel I have to try. The world's been good to me, after all. Cambridge has been good to me. Thanks to Tillmann. Without him I'd never have got here. He gave me courage and encouraged me. What was I then? Just a runaway with a couple of school exams under my belt. And now I'm running the History

Department in a big bookshop. I've got an awful lot to be grateful for. And I'm still only twenty-two.

One other thing I love about autumn is the smell of the burning leaves. All the gardeners and groundsmen at the colleges collect the falling leaves and burn them on their many bonfires. How many bonfires there must be each autumn here. I love to wander around the colleges and the parks in the afternoon sunlight, just wallowing in the scent of the Cambridge autumn. Richard thinks I'm being sentimental. I just think that I know what I like.

My best Christmas present was from Bill who asked me if I'd like to become the deputy manager of the shop from January on. The old deputy manager is moving to one of the shops in Oxford. I like Elizabeth. She'll do well. I told Bill that I'd do it as long as I could keep History as my speciality. His eyes twinkled when he told me that's what the plan was, anyway. Maybe one day I will go to his house and see what he's like with his wife. I imagine they love each other dearly. And that he'd do anything for her.

It's Boxing Day morning. Very early morning. Richard's asleep in our room. I'm sitting here in front of the desk I bought for the spare room. I couldn't sleep. I'm wondering what to do about Richard. You see, I've grown very fond of him. And I've decided that I want children at some point, even if that decision sometimes seems like betraying Tillmann. But I don't think my life will be complete without my own children. And I need to find out if I've got the same problem as Caitlin. What if I have? I don't think I could adopt.

I have spoken to Caitlin about some of this. I've been worrying that she'll hate me again if I do ever have children of my own, because she couldn't. She told me not to be so stupid. She's got the man of her dreams, she said, so if I manage to have children, we'll be even. I must go to see her again soon. I will.

I'm not going to say anything to Richard about children yet. I'm still young enough to be able to wait a year or two, so there's no point scaring the poor boy. I wonder what he thinks, though. I suppose we'll cross that bridge when we come to it.

1988

Caitlin says their twins (TWINS!) arrive at the beginning of February. I've asked her how she'll cope. She says they just will. The cottage is big enough. Tom's earning enough. The twins will be six months old when they become Caitlin's and Tom's children. I've already decided to go up there in March.

Bill's had a second safe installed at work. He says every deputy manager should have one. He's a sweet man. He's also promised that he'll keep the safe there, no matter what, at least until he retires. I think he paid for it himself. He's also promised to tell no-one of the things he knows about me. I think he treats me like his daughter. Because he's never had one. Just sons. Three of them.

Surprises never come in ones. Richard took me to a restaurant last night. His parents were there. I was a bit shocked, to be honest. Does this mean he's getting more serious about us? Difficult to tell. His parents, or Eric and Janet as they want me to call them, seem quite nice. Mind you, I can understand now why Richard is as he is. They are quite old, really. It was a nice evening.

Caitlin and Tom have finally got their twins (I still can't believe it – TWINS!). They've called the boy Alfie after Tom's grandfather, and they've called the girl Kathleen after Caitlin and me. I'm really moved by that. Apparently they've both got lots of black hair and scream a lot – just like Caitlin and me. I don't envy those two their task with those little ones. I can't wait to see them in March. Caitlin and Tom have asked me to become the twins' godmother and guardian. I hope it never comes to the guardianship. Dreadful, having to look ahead to your own death – I nearly said looking forward.

The twins are lovely. Spending two weeks up there – Richard complained again, idiot – was such a revelation. I was able to hold them, help feed them. The thing that got me most is the way these infants look at you when you hold their bottle for them. And their warmth against my belly was so comforting. They look tiny when Tom holds them in his big hands. Caitlin looks happier than ever, thinner than ever.

The christening was fun, too. Lots of Caitlin's and Tom's friends turned out. The godfathers were two of Tom's drinking mates. Good men, both of them. Built as solidly as the new father. And we celebrated the new arrivals with some Laphroaig whisky. A dancing singing christening. I've never felt such joy.

Back to reality. My reality. It was good to see Richard again. But I hate the way he always wants to know each and every thing that I've done while I'm away. I want my own life, too. The only problem is that I have to make up more and more past, create more and more stories that people have to believe. Because I won't share everything that I've got, anything that I've had, with anybody.

*

Tillmann interrupts his reading. 'I suppose she never told you about that safe, then?' he says. 'Maybe we should go there on the way back and ask Bill if we can have a look in it.'

'I don't think he'd let us. Anyway, we don't know if it's still there.'

'It's gotta be. Surely.'

'If it is, I'm sure she'd have sent him instructions on what to do with what was in there. When she found out she was dying.'

'What, telling him to send out these journals to Nairn in time for them to be sent to Gran eight years after Mum's so-called death? I don't think so.'

'Look, mate, I don't think she's alive. The journals got to us somehow, but I don't understand for what reason.

I think the whys and wherefores need to wait till tomorrow. What gets me more and more is that she consciously decided to hide her life not just from me, but from everyone she ever met. Except maybe your namesake and her sister.'

It's getting late. I'm tired. I wish we could leave reading more of the journals till tomorrow. But we can't, because we need to have been through them all by the time we get to Nairn tomorrow afternoon. That means we won't get much sleep tonight. But maybe it'll be worth it. Maybe, by this time tomorrow, I'll finally know who my wife really was.

*

Tillmann's parents sent me a letter letting me know that they'd moved now, after all. His mother says it was a huge wrench, but that they'd decided they had to make a break from the past. Even if it's just to stop their grief affecting their other children. I can understand that. Although she's given me their new address, it might be a good idea not to be in touch with them again. To let them really start anew again. Sad. But life goes on.

It's May again already. All the students are getting ready for their exams, including Richard. He's getting more nervous every day. It irritates me, although I know I was like that when I did my school exams. The thing is, though, that I didn't know whether I was clever or not. He actually knows he's clever. What he's not so sure about is if he's attractive to women. And that's stupid. I mean, we've been together for a year and a half now. But that's what makes him so insecure, this constant worrying about if he's good enough for me. That's why he's so possessive.

I sometimes have the feeling that he follows me, that he watches me through the shop window, that he tracks my every step. It's not a nice feeling. It's horrible, actually. Maybe I should do something about it.

I think Bill's a mind reader. Today he asked me if I was growing tired of Cambridge. I said not really. Just… Just that boyfriend of yours, he said. Bit of a clinger, isn't he? All I could do was nod. I am fond of Richard, but… But a bit of distance would help. Anyway, Bill said that he'd hate to lose me, but that he was aware of a vacancy coming up at one of the shops in London. Charing Cross Road, to be precise. That it wouldn't be a deputy manager's post, but that I'd still be able to specialise in History if I chose to go up there. I didn't even think about it. I just said yes straightaway. Bill said he'd sort it out – on one condition; that I'd finally accept the invitation to have dinner at his house with him and his wife. I went to London the next day and was offered the job at the interview – starting date to be arranged.

Bill's wife is not what I expected. I was expecting someone shorter than Bill, some cuddly old lady who kept house. But she's not like that at all. She's called Kari, she's Norwegian, and she's taller than him. Although she's been in England since she was fifteen, she still has a slight Norwegian accent. She actually lectures in Norwegian and in Norwegian history, which I know hardly anything about. She's got very long brown hair, and is as thin as I am. I hope I'm in such good shape when I'm her age.

Anyway, she and Bill were together in the kitchen when I arrived – all the boys have left home, so they're on their own in a big brick house outside town. They were laughing and giggling like teenagers. I was a bit early, so I got to watch them making food together. Which was sort of cool, actually, really, because they were like I'd have liked Tillmann and I to be. And then the three of us went for a walk round their garden. They didn't ask any BIG questions, which was a relief.

After we'd eaten, they asked me if I'd like to stay there the night, so that we could have a few drinks and not have to watch the clock. I phoned Richard and told him, and he got quite cross. I told him not to be so stupid, and put the phone down.

We sat outside in the warm evening dark and talked about the future. And the immediate past. Kari knew everything about me that Bill did, and it didn't worry me in the slightest. But only because I understood there and then that these were two people who were so close to each other that anything they said to each other was just for themselves, not for anyone else. And because, like I trusted Bill from the first time I met him, I trusted Kari. It's as simple as that.

The house is so big that I got a choice of bedrooms. Before I went to bed – it was almost light – Bill and Kari told me that one of their sons had found a small flat in North London which he was leaving at the beginning of the summer. The landlord was quite happy to let the place to me. And the best thing is that I'll be able to keep the flat in Cambridge, although it'll mean taking in a lodger again. I'm sure Richard can cope with that. As a last surprise, Bill told me that I start in six weeks time, at the beginning of July. I was so thankful to them both that I cried a little. But I didn't mind. If there's anyone in the world besides Caitlin who are allowed to see me cry, it's those two people who've been so kind to me.

I told Richard about the new job as soon as I got home. He was very surprised, but I guess I *would've been if someone had told me they were moving to London after eighteen months of living with me. He'll be fine. I told him I'd come back weekends when I wasn't working. And that he could come up to see me, too. That I wasn't finishing with him, but that I needed to take advantage of such a good offer. When he'd finished sulking, he apologised. We'll be fine.*

Because I'm keeping the flat in Cambridge for Richard and a lodger, Bill and Kari have offered me one of the bedrooms in their house to store all my books and papers in. Just until I know whether or not I'm going to settle in London. I don't want to take all my stuff with me – not yet. They even said I can lock the door to the bedroom and take the key with me. It's very kind of them. I don't quite understand why they're being so kind.

Knowing me, I'm sure I'll build up a big collection of books for this new place quite quickly, anyway. The bed's comfy enough. There's a football ground a couple of streets away, but that doesn't worry me too much. Not that I'll ever go to a game. Not that I'll ever be here on Saturdays.

I sat by the window overlooking the long street in the evening sun, smoking. Had a glass of wine. Being all by myself again was actually better than I'd expected. I think I'll like it here.

My first day at work was cool. Being just a few doors down from 84 Charing Cross Road is quite something, although there's no bookshop there anymore. I've read the Helene Hanff book about 84 Charing Cross Road so many times. It's every bookseller's dream to source books for someone thousands of miles away.

The people in the shop are nice, and we go to the pub every Friday evening after closing. It makes for a better team spirit, John, the manager says. And we do all get on well with each other.

It's my twenty-third birthday tomorrow. It'll be the first time Richard has come to see me in London.

Oooo, he can be SOOOOO *nice!*

Since I moved to London, Richard's got a lot less clingy. We can go for weeks without seeing each other, although we do call each other twice a week.

Being in London is great. There's so much happening that I don't get time to write it down. I even went to the ballet for the first time last week.

I've never been in London at Christmas time. They have special supervisors at pedestrian crossings telling people when to cross and when not to cross. I've never seen so many people!

I spent the Christmas holidays in Cambridge. I wanted to. I had one lovely evening with Kari and Bill. And an even nicer evening with Richard on Christmas Eve. He bought me silk underwear. I gave him T. S. Eliot's Collected Works. Signed. Richard's a lecturer in English at the university now. I told him that I knew he'd make it.

It's New Year's Eve morning. One of those nights I can't sleep again. I'm here in London, looking out over the deserted streets waiting to party tonight. I'm thinking of Tillmann. I still miss him, but it's only a gentle pain.

I'm thinking of Caitlin, too. I talk with her every week, but I've had so much going on that I've not been up there since the twins' christening. I've promised to go in February. Caitlin says not to worry so much. She can feel me inside her like I'm a part of her. I feel the same about her, to be honest.

What would I do now if I didn't have Caitlin? I think I'd die.

*

'Right,' says Tillmann. 'One more year and she meets you.'

'And has the abortion,' I say. 'That'll be interesting - not.'

'Dad, don't go off on one. This is all good therapy for both of us!' He laughs.

'I suppose you're right.'

'Y'know, I feel I know much more than most kids my age. Why's that?'

'You've been through a lot. You do a lot of reading – like Kate did. You're a pain in the arse, but you're a clever pain in the arse. That's why. Any more questions?'

'Is Richard the father of the abortion?'

'Odds on, I reckon,' I say, feeling that familiar knot of anger in the pit of my stomach.

'I want to know how this ends.'

'I don't think we've got to the end of it by a long way. I don't think we'll get to the end of it until we've got home.'

'I'm not sure I know where home is anymore,' he says and opens the next book.

Chapter 10

1989

Will this year be any different to the others? I doubt it. I believe we're all fated to plod our weary ways through one similar day to the next until the light goes out and tomorrow doesn't arrive. I try to believe in a heaven, in a next life after this one, but it's difficult. And it often seems just like an excuse not to be afraid of death when it does come. But we will be afraid. We'll be so frightened that we'll not be able to draw breath, that we'll shrink and shrivel under the weight of it. And be gone.

Did Tillmann ever see that ball? Did he have time to think anything just before it hit him? And in that long time it took him to die, did he register anything from this side or the other? I can't tell, because he didn't speak. And then again, those occasional dreams about him make me think that maybe he is alive somewhere in some other dimension. As a ghost? As a real person? I can't answer those questions. I'd like to be a pale ghost haunting someone's house. A ghost to fall in love with. Maybe then, finally, I'd not be afraid of the past or the future anymore. Maybe then I'd feel complete.

Richard says it's weird teaching kids only four years younger than him, but I know he's revelling in it. Especially the attention he gets from the girls. He likes to be flattered. He likes the obvious signs of attraction, because he can't read the more subtle signs. Our relationship is much easier now, because he's grown used to not having me around. Maybe he's grown up.

I've just spent two weeks in Nairn with Caitlin, Tom, Alfie and Kathleen. We celebrated the first anniversary of the twins arriving. They're crawling now, and Caitlin says they should be walking soon. We went for long walks on the paths along the beach, Caitlin and I pushing prams, Tom in between the two of us. He said he felt like he had a harem and laughed a bellowing laugh out into the ocean. I can see why Caitlin feels safe with him. He's a big gentle man who loves being alive. Caitlin deserves to be happy. Why can't I find someone like Tom whom I could tell everything to?

Maybe it's because Caitlin escaped from Father by accident. She'd never planned it, so she lived her life much more raucously than I did. To forget about what was going on in that dark house of ours. Maybe it's because she's actually the abused one who needs to share what she's been through so that she can come to terms with it. Whereas I'm just the nearly-abused one who just wants to leave it all behind.

Maybe it's because I'm the widow, and to love someone enough to tell them about all of me would be a betrayal of what Tillmann and I did have for such a very brief moment. Maybe I should become a nun. But that wouldn't work. I enjoy the present too much. That's what it is, when I think about it. I discard the past both because I hate it and because I don't want to betray it. And I can't see a future yet. I just want to live in the now without a thought for anything else. Surprising really that I've not led a more destructive promiscuous life if that's really what I'm like.

We're all contradictions. We're all neither one thing nor the other. We're just reeds blowing in the wind, swaying in the direction that's the easiest. However much we believe we're different or strong or unconventional or extraordinary, we're not. None of us have the strength to push against the wind.

We're just mortal lumps of flesh and bone with no visible purpose other than procreation. Maybe that is our only happiness. I don't know if I'll ever find out. And yet something inside me tells me that I want to try, that I want to be a mother. Some time. Before I'm thirty.

Will Richard and I ever become a proper couple? I don't know. I'd like to, but his anger worries me. How can I marry someone who isn't secure in his knowledge of himself, who transfers his insecurity onto others? But then he hasn't been like that since we started living apart. Complicated. All too complicated.

I didn't want to leave Caitlin and her family. They're my family. That's what I just realised. They are *my family. I've got no-one else. But I haven't got the courage to just leave everything down South behind and live up there in almost the middle of nowhere. And I don't want to lose the chance of having my own family, one without roots in the past. A whole new family that's just mine, that I can watch grow, unencumbered by the shadows and the cold.*

Richard was happy to see me in Cambridge last weekend. He didn't ask any questions, didn't make any accusations, just took me in his arms and loved me. He's growing more confident, and he's lost that puppy-fat look about him. I think I'm falling properly in love with him. How do you tell?

Caitlin says they've bought a holiday cottage in Nethy Bridge, twenty-five miles south of Nairn. Tom's doing it up. It had got a bit run down. It should be ready by the summer. They're planning on letting it out all year round. It means spending a bit more money on fixing it up so it stays warm in the winter, but there's a better chance of making more money from it this way, too. I'm glad they've managed it.

I don't think I could ever buy my own house. It seems too permanent somehow. I always need the chance to escape, the chance to move on, even if I don't use it. Maybe I'll change my mind when I have children, maybe I won't. Maybe I won't have children. Life is a fleeting glimpse.

There seems to be less and less to write about. Maybe it's because I'm actually living. Not thinking.

Autumn again. The parks here in London don't have that Cambridge burning scent about them. That's why I've been spending all my free weekends in Cambridge. In Richard's new house. I've given up the flat, and now everything that was in it has gone to Bill's and Kari's. Not that there was much left there, anyway. Richard decided he wanted to have a more permanent place. Maybe he's thinking of asking me to marry him. I doubt it.

He seems happy the way things are. Bill and Kari think it's odd that I still see him. I tell them he's changed. I hate trying to explain things. That's why I make them up.

*

'Nothing more for that year?' I say.

'Nope. Looks like she's at the stage where she's not sure she wants to carry on writing things down. It feels like she's not sure that she's made the right choices. Especially when it comes to hiding her past.'

'I think she's decided more than ever to hide it. Like she's sick and tired of having to talk about the real world. Like she wishes she could just make everything up. Live in her own little bubble. Like she doesn't want to be real.'

It's nearly midnight. I've not been in touch with the real world for the last few days. Some might say never. I don't pay any attention to politics. I don't listen to serious radio stations, just music stations. I read, but to escape. I worry about war, but I never think I can do anything about it. I'm non-committal about everything.

And it's worse than ever at the minute because I've finally got my head into Tillmann's quest, because I'm hoping to find some sort of answer at the end of it. Probably not the same answer as him, but freedom. Freedom from the pain of grief. Freedom from the world that looks at me in my flat and asks me why I haven't remarried yet. Maybe I want to be just like Kate comes across in those journals. Someone who doesn't want to be anyone, but someone who longs for something meaningful. But was our marriage ever meaningful? I'm starting to think it wasn't.

'I'm not sure she ever pretended with you, Dad,' Tillmann says, hearing the despondency in my voice. 'She had your child, and she loved you. I know that.' He quickly turns back a few pages in the journal we've been reading. He points at the page. 'I knew that rang a bell. Nethy Bridge. Maybe she took you up there that time because she wanted to start telling you about Caitlin, about her past.'

'There's a lot of holiday cottages up there. And if she did want to start telling me about those things, why didn't she?'

'Something may have happened to change her mind. Maybe she didn't have the courage. Maybe she bottled out of it at the last minute.'

'You could be right. But I always saw her as the most courageous person I'd met. She had so much energy, so much drive. That's the puzzle, though, isn't it? Who was Kate really?'

We both say nothing for a while. We're both tired, in our heads and in our bones.

'Now, are we going to carry on or call it a night?' I say. 'We do need to leave by about eight in the morning if we're gonna have a chance of doing anything when we get up there.'

'We've got so far,' Tillmann says, 'that we can't really leave the year she meets you till tomorrow. Let's just do that and then turn in. And I'm sure it won't make much difference if we don't leave till ten.'

'Ok,' I say, close the window and lie down on the bed next to him again.

*

1990

I feel a deep sense of unease. I don't know what it is. I've tried to work it out. I've talked to Caitlin about it. But nothing. Which is why I'm writing again now. I'd just about decided to stop when I last wrote because everything in my head was getting too complicated, because my life was turning into one huge pretence.

Maybe that's where the uneasy feeling comes from. I just can't put my finger on it. On the surface everything seems fine.

Just back from my annual February pilgrimage to Nairn. The second anniversary of the twins' adoption. More whisky. And snow. Maybe I should *move up there. The holiday cottage has been occupied every single week since Tom finished fixing it up. They're thinking of buying another one in the same place. I'm envious, but not in a horrible way. More pleased than envious, really.*

I asked Caitlin how she manages to be so happy. She told me she thought it was because, after the way Father and Mother had treated her, she wasn't expecting anything good from life. When she'd ended up in Nairn by coincidence and met Tom, she'd been so low that she couldn't have got any lower. But she'd met someone who lifted her up. Yet, to this day, she says, she doesn't expect anything. She's glad she wakes up every morning alive.

Caitlin's hair and mine is the same length now, halfway down our backs. Tom's joined in and grown a pony-tail. The twins run around everywhere and cause chaos. This time we could walk along the sand on the beach, not the path, because we didn't need the prams. Still made me feel broody. I'm getting old. I'll be twenty-five this year. And Caitlin will always be my big sister.

Perhaps I should try to be more like her. Not expect anything after I'd had my life all mapped out for myself. Only to be disappointed by real life. Because real life was nothing like the plans I'd made.

Twenty-five today. I dreamt of Tillmann last night. It was the usual kind of dream. We met in a street in some place that I don't know, and he asked me how I was. When I said I didn't know, he told me that he was sure that whatever troubles I had would soon be over. But he also said that things always got worse before they got better. What does that mean?

I asked him how he was, and he said that he was fine, just fine. That he missed being able to touch things. That he missed feeling my warmth in his arms. And he told me he thought it was time for him to move on, time for me to remember him but not see him. And time for me, he said, to move on, to do what I wanted, what I needed. For Kate's children, he said. He disappeared as I was looking into his eyes. I was crying when I woke up.

I've been very stupid. Richard came up to London for my birthday yesterday and took me out. We got back here after a lovely evening. I felt so close to him, closer than I ever have before. And then it happened. We got carried away. I didn't ask him to put on a condom, because I was desperate to feel him as part of me. And he was desperate to love me. It was one of the most gentle and *passionate hours of my life, perhaps* the *most gentle. We fell asleep joined together. And now I'm worrying.*

That was three weeks ago, and I missed my period last week. Stupid. STUPID. I'm such a fool. I haven't told Richard.

Six weeks. Just missed another period. Perhaps it was meant to be. I've got three of those pregnancy tests, and I'm just writing to calm myself down before I do one of them.

I've done all three. And they all came out positive. I need to think. I've not told anyone this. I'll call Caitlin.

Caitlin says to tell Richard when I next see him. I don't know if I dare. But if it was meant to be, then he'll ask me to marry him. If it wasn't to be, then I'll have to decide what to do. I think I'd have to have an abortion.

No, no. That's not the way it'll work. Richard will marry me, or be with me. He's been so much gentler of late. And his jealousy's gone.

Richard and I have been invited to a party in Newbury in a couple of weeks. I think I'll tell him there. I keep thinking I should tell him before I go to the party, but maybe it'll be better coming from me when we're in a happy mood, not in an everyday mood.

The party's tonight. I'm just packing my bag, and then I'll set off. I'm more nervous than I've ever been in my life. Breathe, I keep telling myself, breathe deeply. That'll stop my heart from thumping up into my head.

*

There's a paper napkin glued into the next page of the journal. A cheap white one, with ink leakage through the back of it.

'Unfold it then,' I say to Tillmann, impatient and afraid.

He unfolds it very gently and slowly. I think we're at the point of no return.

*

It's the morning after the party. What a disaster. What a bloody disaster. There, I've said it. I just can't go on. Just can't. It's all over. Everything.

Where should I start? I thought it was all going to be ok.

I got there early, like I always do, because I hate being late. I walked up the drive, trying to calm myself down before my big moment with Richard. My breathing was nice and slow by the time I got nearer the house. That house with big high windows, so I could look into it quite easily, especially as all the lights inside were on. Maybe things would have been different if I hadn't walked so slowly.

Richard was already there. I could see him talking animatedly to someone I couldn't quite see. I should have gone inside then, not waited around outside to find out who he was talking to. If I'd gone in and made a noise going in, I might have avoided what I saw next.

I saw him reaching out, a big smile on his face, eyes wide open. I saw some thin tanned fingers grabbing hold of his, watched as he pulled the hand, the arm, the body towards him, almost in slow motion. And I saw him wrap his arms around a thin tall woman all dressed in clinging red silk. Then I saw him kiss Louise. And I mean kiss. I shook my head. I must be imagining things, I thought.

My heart was racing again. I started walking away. NO, I said to myself, don't walk away. There must be some mistake. But when I turned back to the window, they were still kissing, and her hands were cupping his face.

That was when I decided that I'd have to talk to him anyway, even though I'd already understood that I'd been lied to, made a fool of. But I was already past caring.

I clattered in through the door, shouted a loud hello, walked into the room where he'd been with Louise – she'd disappeared by now, of course. And there I told Richard that I was about ten weeks pregnant with his child.

'Get rid of the effing thing,' he hissed at me. 'You stupid, stupid woman. Do you really think you could get your claws into me by getting pregnant? You're such a cold, calculating bitch. Trying to turn me into an old man before my time. Just piss off, will you?'

I wouldn't give in. 'Why's Louise here?' I said. 'We were invited, not she.'

'Because it's her friend who invited us, stupid,' he said. 'And I'd thought that maybe I could have both of you in one night.' His grin was ugly, his face a grimace. I didn't know him. 'Because I've done it on successive nights before, just without either of you knowing.' He wasn't even drunk, just horrible. Like Father. Just like Father.

All I did was spit in his face before I turned away from him. I guess I'm a single woman again. And pregnant. And there's no way I can have a baby that's his.

Time to go. There's a train to London in half an hour.

*

Tillmann and I say nothing for a couple of minutes after

he's folded up the paper napkin again. I'm shaking. He tries to put his skinny arms round me but doesn't quite succeed.

'That was worse than she told me it was,' I finally say.

'Bugger.' He pauses, ruffles my hair – my kid son ruffling *my* hair! - breathes deeply again. 'More?' he says, doubtfully.

'After that, yes,' I say, trying to be positive. 'After that I need to know what she was thinking when she met me.'

He turns the page, pats it gently down on top of the napkin, and we start reading again.

*

Is it possible to hold light and dark at the same moment? Is it possible to feel joy and despair in one breath? I didn't think it was. Despair has always been there, and there's never been any relief. But I believe it now, because it's happened to me. Is there such a thing as redemption?

After I left the B&B, I walked down to the station. I must have dawdled on the way, because I heard my train pulling into the station when I was still a minute's walk away. I ran up to the narrow station entrance and almost crashed into a man who was also rushing for the train. We both exploded onto the platform just as the train was pulling out. He swore at the same time as I did. As loudly as I did. I actually felt like crying. I stamped my feet.

We got talking, and he said some strange things. Like he was always missing trains, like he was jinxed, like he was shy. I don't think he was joking. I bummed my first cigarette in three weeks from him. And my second. And more. We shared a compartment up to London. He's a bleached blond, I think. And he's no taller than I am. When he told me his name I nearly fell off my seat. I don't think he noticed, though.

And why did I nearly fall off my seat? Because he's called Nairne, that's why. NAIRNE. And he's got these hurt-looking blue eyes that go right through you if you look at him for long enough.

In the end we had lunch together. And dinner. And, fool that I am, I asked him to stay the night with me. Which he did. But he only kissed me and held my hand. And then he slept on the sofa. I was so glad he was with me. And so glad he seemed to understand that the last thing I wanted was sex.

It's like my fate has been decided now. Like everything that's ever been doesn't exist any more. Because I love this stranger. Love? How can I tell? There's no rational explanation. Love at first sight never existed for me. Even Tillmann was just a gradual recognition of something great and pure and gentle. But when I looked into Nairne's eyes, when I touched his hands, it was as if all the energy and passion of the world was flooding into me. I can't explain it.

But how can I, with another man's seed germinating inside me, love someone as strongly as this? Is it right? And is it right to terminate that life growing inside me to eradicate all that's left of the past that I no longer need? I don't feel I have a choice. I can't tell Nairne. That would risk killing everything I think he feels for me.

The less said and thought about my brief visit to the clinic, the better, but it's over. I'm no longer pregnant. It's a sad relief. So much hope. So much tragedy. Such a waste. And what if I can never have children again? What if this was my only chance? I can't believe it can have been.

But I'm free of burden now. I'm free for Nairne. I've decided to start taking the pill, even though I don't think we're even at the stage of needing it yet. This love's such a gentle thing, but not fragile. Such a caring thing, but not afraid. I think about him all the time. I distract myself from boring hours by day-dreaming of him and the touch of his hand around mine. It's electric.

There can't be any such thing as coincidence. These things don't just happen. These moments are shaped by the movement of ancient stars and earths. And the moment I looked into his eyes will stay with me for all my time.

Caitlin says I've done the right thing. She was livid when I told her about Richard, excited when I told her about Nairne. And just as convinced as I am that it must have been meant to be. From Nairn to Nairne. She sounded happy for me.

Nairne comes up here every weekend now, just about. He must be spending a fortune. He says he'd be coming up to London, anyway, to hang around in record shops. He says my sofa's so comfortable that I may never be able to tempt him into my bed. He's a funny smiling man. He brings me flowers and food and wine and laughter. Maybe I've finally grown up, to be loving a man who's five years older than I am. I can't help smiling, sitting here writing, thinking about him.

We've decided not to spend Christmas with each other. A sort of test, I suppose. It was his idea, and I agreed with him. I've been invited to spend the Christmas week with Bill and Kari, and I think I will. It'll be good to see them again, to talk with them. Because they won't ask any awkward questions, because they'll understand.

The week in Cambridge was restful. It felt strange to be sleeping amidst all my belongings in a house that I don't actually live in. Bill and Kari said everything that I've now accumulated in 'my' bedroom can stay there as long I want it to. Bill's even had my safe moved from his shop into my room.

I gave them each a plain silver ring for Christmas. Friendship rings, I called them. Surrogate parentship rings, they called them. They gave me a key to the house as a present. Why couldn't they have been my real parents?

The year is coming to a close. I feel happier than ever, more optimistic. At last I feel I have a future again. I thank Tillmann for promising me this in my last dream about him before he went away. I only dream of Nairne now, and of things that haven't happened yet. Before I met him I dreamed of the past and all its evil and all its guilt over and over again. Not any more.

*

We're up reasonably early. We get away by nine. Just like the day before, the days before, I don't pay much attention to what passes by us outside the car windows. I'm too wrapped up in my thoughts. Too wrapped up in wanting to get to the end of this long long drive. Tillmann sticks in some weird music that he likes. The Postal Service the band is called, and he says it's good driving music. Lots of electronic sounds, some soft voices, and a steady beat to match the white lines that disappear under our tires. We leave the middle of the north of England behind, start climbing up the slopes towards the border.

It's not raining anymore. We're steadily accumulating miles and time and distance. We don't say anything for almost an hour. Tillmann puts the same CD on again. How much further? Only at least another four hours.

'Should I start reading again now, Dad?' he says when he thinks I'm wider awake. 'Or d'you want to talk about the last thing we looked at?'

'No need for that, I don't think. It's pretty obvious from what she wrote that she felt the same way as I did when we first met. I was a very lucky man.'

I just don't understand how we could have messed it up so badly. How I could have messed it up so badly. Is love fated from the beginning to become a shadow of itself? Or does love always remain fresh and exciting, and it's we lovers who grow old and fearful and empty?

'You still are lucky,' Tillmann says and starts rummaging in his bag.

Chapter 11

1991

I've been wondering if I should find myself a job where Nairne lives. There are bound to be some bookshops there. I'll keep a watch on the papers. I want to live with Nairne. Forever.

But however much I love him, I really don't think I'll be able to ever tell him about Father or Mother or Caitlin. Or Tillmann. Or anything that happened before I met him. I just feel that it could destroy everything. But won't I risk the same by not telling him? I don't know. I know nothing, really. That's the really frightening thing, that none of us ever know anything with any certainty.

One minute I was without fear, and the next I'm petrified.

I've applied for a part-time job in a bookshop in Newbury. I've got enough money to survive on that job for a little while.

Last weekend was wonderful. I drove to Newbury on Friday afternoon, had an interview at the shop, and then went on to Nairne's flat afterwards. I've been there before, of course, but he'd made an even bigger effort than ever. Not that any tidying up's needed, because there's hardly anything in there.

I think it's touching that he lets me sleep in his bed while he sleeps on the sofa in the living-room. Because we're still not ready, not mentally. Despite our bodies' hunger.

Saturday was cold and sunny, so we drove up onto the Downs and went for a long walk. He lent me a big baggy jumper of his to put on under my coat. There's always a wind blowing up there. He said I looked even more beautiful with my hair whirling around my face and shoulders. We stood on a high rock arm in arm and looked down into the clear morning. We could see for miles and miles in all directions. It took my breath away.

It's only been a week since I had the interview, but I've already heard that I've got the job. At the interview I said I'd like to start at the beginning of March, which was fine by them. It gives me time to go up to Nairn in February, and then back down South to tell my Nairne that I'm moving in with him. There's not much to take from London anyway, so that bit won't take long. I can drive it all down there in the car.

Caitlin and Tom have had the twins for three years now. My visit this year was different, because I think we all knew that I felt like I'd left something behind. I spent hours on end talking to Caitlin abut Nairne, asking Tom what he thought, unrolling my whole feelings for them to see. They said they understood, that they were pleased that I was at last properly happy, at last.

They're such lovely loving people. Maybe I will tell Nairne about them, get him to meet them. Maybe – one day. I'm scared of what he might ask.

Tomorrow I'm going to tell Nairne about the new job. I'm quite nervous about it, actually. What if he's changed his mind? What if I'm wrong about him, like I was about Richard? But I don't think I am. It'll be fine, I know it will. I can feel a bond between us that I've never felt before, not even with Tillmann. But Tillmann and I were children. I'm a big girl now. A woman.

Who am *I writing this for? For me? I'm not so sure. I don't like my past, don't like what's been and gone. Sometimes it feels like I'm already preparing for my death, writing down my justification for the way I've been, for the way I am. So that those who will follow me can understand. Just making notes of the stepping stones, the crossroads, the decisions in my life. I don't think there will be any more after this.*

Maybe it's for Caitlin, because I'm sure she'll live longer than me. Or maybe it's been for Nairne, all this time, because it really feels like I was waiting for him. And he for me.

Whatever the reason, I can't destroy these books, even though I often feel threatened by them. What exactly is it about my past that makes me not want people to know about it? It could be that I'm ashamed of having been mentally abused, that I feel guilty that my older sister sacrificed a part of herself to physical abuse in order to protect me. Was I so weak? How could I be so weak? But I didn't know.

Caitlin often says I take this secrecy to extremes; that it's not normal, not natural, to be the way that I am. That it's dangerous, because all this badness I feel inside will eat itself into me like a cancer. When I was up there, she said that I should have therapy or just talk with Nairne about it. I wish I could, but with each passing day the secrets get stronger, and it gets more difficult to let go of them. Maybe I'll be brave enough to tell Nairne when we live together. When we're married? When we have children? When we're dying? When, then?

Poor old Nairne. He thought I was going to break up with him when I told him I'd got a new job out West. When I'd calmed him down, he said he'd thought I was moving out to America. His problem is that he stops listening when he's convinced he knows what's coming.

But he said YES. He said he wanted us to live together, to be together always, just the two of us. He was as excited as I've ever seen him. He may even have cried a little. He said I was all his dreams come true. His own mystery woman.

And then we kissed. And then we touched like never before. And dragged each other to my bed. And hardly slept. He said it was like the first time for him, because he'd never felt such pure love for anyone before. I told him I'd never felt before. And then I *cried until he held me even closer. He kissed my forehead and told me he loved me. That made me cry even more.*

I've decided to surprise Nairne and move in before he expects me to. I can't bear just to sit here waiting until the date we'd agreed. The timing was all because of work anyway, so I persuaded my boss to let me finish sooner than we'd actually arranged. She could tell my mind's not on the job anymore anyway.

The car's all packed. The flat's bare. All I need to do now is walk out the door, pull it shut and push the key back in through the letter box. When I hear it hit the floor, I'll know I've started my new life.

Nairne's asked me to marry him. I thought he was going to take me on holiday when he asked me for my passport. I got home from work in the afternoon, and there he was, holding a thick envelope that he asked me to take into the bedroom and read on my own. I opened the envelope and found a written marriage proposal, a marriage licence, and an appointment card. It's in three weeks. And I can't wait. Because I said yes.

It's the first week of June. We're just back from our honeymoon in Venice. It's one of the most beautiful places I've been to. We stayed in a little family-run hotel near the Fenice theatre. And walked round the back streets where no tourists get to. Hot chocolate for breakfast every day. And a thunder storm the night before we flew back here. We're wife and husband now, and I've *stopped taking the pill.*

July. I'm still not pregnant. I'm starting to worry that something's wrong with me. That the scrape damaged my insides. That I'm being punished for having the abortion. That I'm the victim of a god who can't forgive me my past. I'm frightened that there might be such a vengeful god.

We went to Cambridge last weekend. I wanted Nairne to meet Bill and Kari. We went out for lunch, the four of us. They liked each other. That's good. I think Nairne was quite surprised that I allowed him to see into my past. That I lifted some of the mystery. But he doesn't know how deep the mystery really is. Maybe he never will.

*

We're a couple of hours into our drive. I pull over. I've had an idea. I thought of it last night, but it was too late to do anything about it. It's not too late now. Bill should be in the shop by now. I feel guilty for not having been in touch with him since Kate died. I felt guilty when I heard his voice again on Saturday, when I remembered what a kind man he is, when I saw him treat my son gently and thoughtfully.

I text directory enquiries to get the bookshop's number. Then I call and ask for Bill. I tell him where we are, and about the journals. He didn't know about their existence, but he doesn't sound surprised.

'Kate was always full of secrets,' he says. 'Even we don't know anything about her, really. Only what happened in Cambridge. But that's what made her so interesting.'

'We've just read about that room in your house that she used,' I say straight out. There's no point in holding back now. 'Is it still there?'

'Oh, the room's still there, Nairne, but it's empty. Kate came up about nine months before she died and had it all shipped off somewhere. Didn't tell me where.' He hears me sigh. 'Sorry.'

'It's ok,' I say. 'It was just a thought.'

'Nairne,' he says, and he sounds as if he's standing next to me. 'Kate was like a daughter to us, and that makes you part of our family. Promise me you and Tillmann will come and see us on your way back.'

'I promise,' I say. And I mean it.

Tillmann's looking at me strangely.

'What?' I ask.

'I thought you and Mum waited until that autumn to decide that you'd have a baby.'

'We did,' I laugh. 'She'd obviously decided before then.'

*

August. I'm still not pregnant. I cry a lot. Nairne's confused and tries to console me, but he can't, because I can't tell him the real reasons I'm crying. He doesn't know yet that we're trying for a baby. Am I really twenty-six already? I'm feeling old, and I still don't have a child.

September. Still nothing. It's frustrating. Should I start praying?

October. A blank. I talked to Nairne about having children. He said he thought we'd decided to wait a while before we had one (ONE?) so that we could spend some time together, just us, alone. I told him I was desperate for a child, that I wanted a part of him growing inside me. Isn't it the greatest proof of love to carry your man's child for him? I asked him. That's when he agreed.

November. Nothing. Now that Nairne knows we're trying for a baby, our lovemaking is even sweeter than it was before. Am I a witch for keeping so much of myself to myself? Will he hate me if he ever finds out? About any of this?

Bill's forwarded a letter to me at work. I think he's quite amused by my little subterfuges. The letter's from Tillmann's mother. She'd sent it to the shop in Cambridge because she couldn't think of any other way of getting in touch with me.

Father and Mother are dead. They had an accident in their car. Wrapped it around a tree in France. It happened at the end of September. Tillmann's mother heard from a friend who still lives where our old house is. Our old home? It was never a home. There's a number for a solicitor in the letter, too. Tillmann's mother ends the letter by saying she hopes Caitlin and I are fine. She doesn't mention Tillmann. Maybe she's forgotten him.

I've called Caitlin. Good riddance is all she said. I can't disagree with her.

I've been to see the solicitor. It meant telling him where Caitlin lives, but she's safe now, isn't she? We both are. The solicitor said that because Father and Mother died without making a will, there might be a large tax bill to pay. I can't imagine that they've left much money. I told him that he should sell their house and work out everything. Caitlin and I will just take what's left.

December. No sign. Just blood. As always. Does Nairne really want a baby? He doesn't seem too worried about me not being pregnant yet. Although he tries to help me by telling me lots of things about women's bodies that I already know. I do *love him. Men just don't understand women. It's as simple as that.*

Caitlin and I will get about 150,000 pounds each after taxes and bills have been paid. That's so much more than I expected. But it means that I won't have to go back to work straight after the baby's born. If I ever have a baby.

We've got the money. Caitlin and Tom used some of hers to pay off the mortgage on the cottage, and to buy another one. The rest they've put in a high-interest account. I've opened another account for mine. Correspondence address is Caitlin's place. I don't know why I've done this. It's just another secret to keep.

Nairne treated me to so much this Christmas. He made it special. Our first Christmas together. The first of a life-time of Christmases. What more could I ever want? I love him so much it hurts. I love him so much – and still I can't force myself to share my secrets with him. Maybe I never will. Maybe I'll never get pregnant because of it. But then again, maybe I'll be pregnant by the New Year.

*

We're driving again. We've left Edinburgh behind. We're getting closer. Only another couple of hours to go till we reach the north coast of Scotland and Nairn. What will it be like?

'She never told you about that money, did she, Dad?' Tillmann says. 'Not even when she was dying?'

I shake my head. I don't understand anything anymore.

'Did she really love me?' I say. 'I know she says she did, but maybe she was just kidding herself. I feel like I never knew her, not really. That I was in love with someone else.'

'Maybe you were in love with her just as she was. Maybe you loved her *because* you knew nothing of her. Because she was a mystery to you. Your very own mystery woman. And she loved you because you never asked her who she was, who she'd been. Because you loved her for who she was when she was with you.'

'Perhaps,' I say, but I can't get the feeling out of my mind that I'd watched a stranger die all those years ago. That the woman whose hand I'd held in those last few moments of her life hadn't been my Kate.

*

1992

January. I'm still bleeding. I'm losing all hope. Maybe there's something wrong with Nairne. He says that that's possible, but that we shouldn't panic. He thinks we should try for a year, and if nothing's happened by then, we'll go to the doctor.

Even Caitlin's saying that I shouldn't worry. It's not like my insides haven't ever worked. But, I almost scream at her down the phone, but maybe they got wrecked when I had the abortion. I shouldn't ever have had the abortion! I should have told Nairne about it. He'd have understood, then and there. He won't now. Not now.

I've littered my life with lies. And now I'm paying the price. And the price is too high.

Caitlin says Nairne and I should go up to Nethy Bridge in a couple of weeks, in mid-January. We don't need to go to see her and Tom and the twins, but there's always that option. She thinks that maybe a change of scenery for me might help me relax into being able to conceive.

I've told Nairne that I've booked a cottage for the two of us in Scotland, and that we're leaving in a week. He's excited about it. He's never been to Scotland before, he said. Of course I've not told him who owns the cottage.

Caitlin says she understands that I won't be able to come back up for the twins' fourth anniversary. And that she's trying to understand why I am the way that I am. But that she wishes I could just share everything with Nairne so that we could all be a big happy family. I wish I could, too.

March. I'm pregnant! I know I am. I knew I was pregnant that first morning in the cosy cottage in Nethy Bridge after Nairne and I had made love on our first evening there. We'd gone for a walk first, but I knew we couldn't wait to get to bed.

I knew I was getting pregnant when we made love. I was so ready, so desperate, so open and soft and needing. And Nairne was like an angel come out of the shadows to console me, to wipe away all the scars and bruises of my other life. An angel sent by my god to tell me he's not a vengeful god, after all. Oh God, I love him so much I would die for him.

I nearly took Nairne to see Caitlin, but I weakened at the last minute. Instead, I drove across to Culloden with him. We wandered around the old battlefield there for hours. He was fascinated by it. Said it had the feel of the ghosts of the slaughtered still wandering around. I didn't feel anything like that in the fog of that late morning. I'd told Caitlin we were going, so I knew she was following us with her eyes from somewhere. I wanted at least for her to be able to see what my husband looked like in real life.

Caitlin called me after Nairne and I had got back home. She says that Nairne looks like a fine man, that she got the feeling from the way he moved that he sees nothing of the world except for me. But she warned me that soon it would be too late to ever tell him about the past, that I was fast getting to the point of no return, That if I told him too late, he would never be able to forgive me for not telling him in the first place. I think I've already passed that point. I'm hurting her as much as I'm betraying Nairne, really, aren't I? But it's too late now, too late.

I've given up smoking, of course. We went for my scan today. I've even held off telling Caitlin until now because I don't want to take any risks at all. Nairne cried when he saw that little body wriggling across the screen. But behind his tears I also saw apprehension, a sudden recognition that we'd never be alone together again, the two of us. I think he's afraid of that. But he'll grow used to it, having to share me with his child.

I've told Caitlin. She said she knew already. Just knew. She also said she hopes to meet my child one of these days.

The funniest thing is that it's Nairne who's being sick every morning. Sick as a pig, actually. I'm feeling fine. Better than ever. And now I'm starting to grow, it's like my whole body is in bloom. I can feel a new life inside me, and it's not taking my energy away. It's not sucking my *life from me, but it's giving me more life. It's making me wide awake and more aware of the world around me.*

When we go for walks now I can smell scents that I never knew existed. I can see colours that I'd never guessed the shades of before. When I touch things, especially when I touch Nairne, I feel pulses of nature that I've never had an inkling of before. I'm filled with life. I'm full of life. I'm what I've always wanted to be – at last.

I've put on lots of weight – nearly thirty kilos. And there are still weeks to go until the baby's due. I know already that if it's a boy I'm going to call him Tillmann. I feel it's my duty. I know it will always remind me of my first Tillmann, but it will be a happy remembering. And a thanks for his last message to me in my dreams. And a farewell of sorts.

My birthday was spent wrestling with the overactive child inside my womb. It kicks and bounces and hiccoughs. It laughs and cries and snores. Nairne has taken to putting his mouth to my stomach and talking with his unborn child. 'So it gets to know me,' he says.

And he plays music to the bump all the time. 'So it's born with some taste,' he smiles. I love those moments, lying on the bed in the sun, my husband's hands on the outside of me, and my child's hands on the inside of me.

I've grown impatient of carrying this weight around with me. October's soon over, and I don't want to go into November with this. Maybe it'll be easier next time. Nairne and I have tried all the old remedies to start labour, but nothing seems to work.

We've just got back from the Downs and I can feel my womb contracting. I think it's time.

It's a boy! After leaving him nameless for two days or so, we've called him Tillmann, just like I said I would. He's the most beautiful thing in the world that I have ever ever seen. I will never let him go, and I won't ever let anyone hurt him. Do all mothers feel like this? I can't remember the pain of birth.

Nairne's father has died. He never even got to see Tillmann. Nairne is trying to be strong, but he can't. I have to look after him and the baby. It's wearing, but I'm revelling in finally having someone who relies on me. The funeral was bad, and Naomi is shattered. I don't think she'll survive for long.

Nairne is trying to focus only on me and Tillmann and his work. But he can't concentrate. Whenever he thinks of his father he cries. Hardly surprising. But it's making him irritable, too. When I say he's doing something wrong with Tillmann, he goes off in a sulk. I hope he manages to begin healing himself soon.

Tillmann looks like me. He has masses of curly black hair – as well as a bald patch on the back of his head where it rubs against his cot sheet. That'll grow back. He'll be tall, too, I'm sure of it. But his eyes are his father's, I'm sure of it, although there are three of us in this family now with blue eyes. But he has kinder eyes than

I have, just like Nairne. Mine are the cruel eyes of a watcher and taker. Of a witch. That's how I feel, anyway, when I look in the mirror.

Our first Christmas with a baby. We spent it on our own and then went to spend New Year's Eve with Naomi. Tillmann, of course, doesn't yet understand about Christmas, but Father Christmas brought him something, anyway, to add to the presents we'd got him.

I'm tired. I don't know if I can write any more now. I've not become as free as I thought I would become. The past still grabs at me and scares me.

1993

I'm broody again already. I find Tillmann easy to look after. Nairne doesn't. I think he regrets giving in to me already. I'll have to wait a long time before I start talking about having more babies. Caitlin says I shouldn't be so impatient, but I can't help it. I have a taste for it now.

Things are so busy with Tillmann that I never feel like writing anymore. My doubts about telling have almost completely disappeared, because I've decided that I'm right to do what I'm doing, to not tell.

I called Caitlin on the twins' fifth anniversary. She's worried about Tom. She says he's working too hard, still doing too much himself, although he's now got five people working for him. The second cottage is proving just as successful as the first. The best thing is that they've got people coming back year after year, but there's still a lot to be done. And there's no real living to be made just out of two holiday cottages. And, anyway, she says, Tom likes to be outdoors. I think she's trying to kid herself. He's getting old, I think, and the hard work he's had to do has started taking its toll. I hope she talks to him, and I hope he listens to her.

I miss Caitlin. I wish she could share Tillmann with me, watch him growing every single day. I'm sharing him with Nairne, of course, but I've not known Nairne all my life. And I don't think fathers really see their children at this age. They're barely aware of them. They certainly don't see them as people. They see them as babies, without any power to think or act or be a person in their own right.

But we mothers, I think we start talking with them through our skin from the moment they're born. And before. And through our eyes each time we pick them up and feed them. There's a bond here that no man could ever truly understand. Be aware of, yes. Appreciate, yes. But never ever understand. And that's why men are so jealous of their children. Because they'll never have us back as wholly and completely as before. Before we've become mothers.

To be honest, I'm surprised marriages last, because men and women are so basically different. Totally incompatible in what they want from life, in what they treasure. I guess we find freedom in different things.

I got a birthday card from Tillmann this morning. I told him how clever he was to be able to write Mum in big letters inside the card and on the envelope. Nairne laughed at that, a big loud laugh that made me believe that he has healed himself again. It's the first time he's laughed since his father died. I've been missing that carefree man I married.

He said he thinks that he's not a very good father, and that he wishes he could be, but just doesn't have it in him. I kissed him and told him that everything would be alright, that it always took time to get used to change. He looked at me and said very quietly 'But I miss you.' Although we started making love again six weeks after Tillmann was born. But I know what he means. I just don't feel exactly the same.

This has been the summer of fools. We've been so happy since my birthday that I have a feeling it can't last. That something is going to come along and spoil it. But I've been so lucky to have a son and a husband who love me to the exclusion of everything else. Because, to be honest, it's been harder than I thought. But it's been worth it. And I want to do it again. Soon. Soon.

I've got a hangover. I've not had one for a long time. Yesterday was Tillmann's first birthday. Unfortunately it wasn't all happy. The past caught up with me, because I got drunk and was feeling vulnerable and giving at the same time. Because I wanted to give something to Nairne for his patience with me and his patience with himself. And now I have a jealous husband of the kind I never wanted.

The day started off alright. The three of us went to the caff where Nairne says he consumed a massive breakfast the morning after Tillmann was born. Tillmann, of course, not knowing what was going on, just sat in his highchair and made a mess. Nairne and I stuffed our faces with whatever food we could lay our hands on. Tillmann threw chips at us and laughed. Half-sucked soggy chips.

The rest of the day we wandered around town, happily taking it in turns pushing the pram. We bumped into a few people we know, exchanged pleasantries, showed off our growing son. Whom I had baked a huge chocolate cake for.

Nairne took pictures of Tillmann with his hands deep into the cake, chocolate smeared all over his face, grinning at us with his teeth white against the brown, and his big blue eyes staring at us over his hands. I thought how sad it was that we've only got a few people to send the pictures to. And I'll be sending one to Caitlin secretly.

We bathed Tillmann together. All three of us ended up in the bath and had a water fight. It was such great fun. And Nairne put one of his feet where he shouldn't have, which actually made me want him, and made me laugh so loudly Tillmann looked at me very strangely. He went to sleep very quickly after that.

Nairne cooked me a lovely dinner. Crispy Peking Duck; the

works. He'd bought a magnum of champagne which we drank slowly, but still too quickly. We got very drunk. We made love there and then, just after midnight, on the living room floor. And then I made the mistake of asking him if he was glad that he'd married me. He looked so lovely, so vulnerable, and I felt that I had to, that I wanted to, give him something more than just my body and my soul of the now. I wanted to give him my entire life.

And before I knew it I'd told him about the day before I'd met him, about the day I'd met him, and about the abortion. I can't remember exactly what I said or how I said it, but the words were out of my mouth before I understood what I was saying. He probably thinks I didn't notice him change there and then, but I did. And when we woke up this morning I could tell that he wasn't the Nairne that I had confessed to last night. It was like he'd suddenly grown a shell, a carapace to wear over his feelings.

Nairne is so distant. We still hold hands, make love, laugh, and all those things that people do when they're in love. But he's irritable, and he's impatient, and he annoys me. I can't change the past. I wish now I'd never told him. Caitlin was right. I've passed the point of no return and now he hates me. Caitlin's always been right. Even when I thought she hated me, and I her, even then she was right, because she sees things that I can't.

I pretended to have a headache for a week. I just couldn't face dealing with Nairne in his mood. And his mood's affecting Tillmann so badly that he can't sleep at night any more. He's awake nearly all the time, screaming and throwing tantrums, and wanting more milk. A few weeks ago I just happened to suggest to Nairne that Tillmann might get less windy if he held the bottle slightly differently. He just screamed at me and walked out of the house in the middle of the night. I feel like I've had enough. So much for wanting more children. At this rate we'll not even get round to trying again.

We've been happy again for a few months now. My one-week

mother's strike seemed to have an effect, because Nairne grew gentle and kind again. And patient. Tillmann's sleeping better again. Still doesn't leave me much time to write.

There is so much going on in my life now that I'm losing track of time. Another year is coming to its close. I'm as happy as can be expected, I suppose. It's better than Father attempting to molest me, and better than grieving endlessly for Tillmann The Older, as I suppose I should call him now. I have been warned about revealing the past, because it's already started exacting a price that I'm not prepared to pay.

*

We've got probably ninety minutes of driving to do before we get to Nairn. And we've got another six years of Kate's life to go. We've made good time, though. It's only just noon. I decide to pull into a service station so I can have a smoke and we can eat something. Tillmann brings his bag with him.

'Didn't you notice sign posts for Nairn when you were up in Nethy Bridge?' he says as we walk across the car park.

'No,' I say. 'I was too wrapped up in staring at your mother, wondering how I could make her wish of having a baby come true. Asking myself if it was my fault that she wasn't getting pregnant. Wrapped up in my own little world, as usual.'

'And at Culloden?' he carries on, as we walk into the modern building, the noise of the traffic suddenly fading. 'Didn't you notice anyone following you?'

'Tillmann, there are always lots of people up there. It's a national monument. And, anyway, what she says about me that day is true. I got this overwhelming feeling of being there just after the battle. There was an immense bank of fog rolling in over the battle field. It was impossible for me not to feel that I'd gone back to the time just after the battle. So, no, I didn't notice anyone following me. And if I had the feeling of being watched, it was the feeling of being watched by ghosts.'

'D'you feel like ghosts are watching you now?'

'Definitely not.' I laugh. 'Why?'

'Because we're getting close. Because, by this evening we may have found what we're looking for. And if there's no ghosts watching you, Mum can't be dead. She'd have followed us to her sister's.'

'Hmm. I suppose I can't tell you that ghosts are a load of old bollocks after what I've just said. We'll just have to wait and see. Wait here while I pop out for a smoke.'

'D'you have to? I'll go on up to the restaurant. I can't be bothered to stand here in a draught watching you kill yourself.'

'Fine. See you in five.'

I stand outside in the wind. Even though we're far up North, we're on a main road, and it's busy. I see the tree tops bending to the wind. I see the clouds scuttling along the horizon like sheep being chased by a wolf. Inside my head, I'm empty. Drained. Hearing Kate's voice through my son has deeply moved me. Hearing her point of view after all these years has made it even more obvious to me how much I must have hurt her in the years leading up to her death. Her sad and lonely death. Even with me there holding her hand. Because by then there was nothing left.

My cigarette flies through the air into the sand-bin provided. Its small plume of smoke carries on rising. I turn and follow Tillmann up the stairs. I need to ask him some questions. I need to hear the rest of Kate's story. There's not much time.

He's sitting at one of the many tables in the restaurant. He's bought me a snack and a coffee. Apple juice and a snack for him. His bag's on the table next to our food. I sit down opposite him.

'Feeling better for that?' he says.

'Stupid question,' I mutter into my coffee. Take a big gulp of it. 'Did you notice how she said she'd pretended to have that one-week headache episode that you probably can't remember?'

'Yes. I thought that was weird. And how she called it a strike. Does that mean that all her other headaches were pretend as well?'

'Just what I was thinking. And if they were, how could they have been a symptom of her cancer?'

'Maybe they weren't.'

'Weren't what?'

'Pretend or symptoms,' he says. 'I think it's weird. I think you were both weird. I still can't understand why she didn't tell you everything or nothing at all. And I can't understand why you reacted so badly to something she said only because you asked her to.'

'Just make me feel better, why don't you? How do you think I feel now? I'm suddenly realising that I didn't know her at all, and not because of her past, as she calls it, but because it's like I never made an effort to find out what she was thinking of what was our present then. Like I just took her for granted. That once I'd got her, I just ignored her.'

'Ok. I think that answers that question.'

'And Till; you'll find out soon enough that people hardly ever talk to each other about their real feelings. I've no idea why. I never will understand. But it's something that just happens generation after generation, divorce after divorce, fight after fight.'

'Should we read on?'

I nod. If we get through the rest of the journals before we get to Nairn I'll be happy. He opens the next book and stops. Shows it to me. Shrugs. Reads.

Chapter 12

1994

The year has started. Maybe we're on the way back together.

Caitlin's had the twins for six years. They're almost seven.

Tom's still working too hard.

Tillmann's started walking. He's two in four months.

I'm twenty-nine today.

Life moves along. We're happy, I suppose.

A nothing year. Is life really like this?

*

'Is that really all?' I say, surprised.

Tillmann nods. I grab the book and turn all the pages.

'I don't think there's invisible ink there, either,' Tillmann says. 'Life got busy, didn't it? That's what you always say about that time. Years can just pass by, you said to me once, and I believe you.'

'Why did she start a new book for every year if she never filled them up?'

'I reckon she always started with good intentions, that she meant to fill up every book, but never managed it.'

'Hang on a minute. Get out all the books and put them on the table.'

He grabs them from his bag.

'Put the ones we've read into one pile,' I say.

He does. There are only two left to make up the unread

pile.

'Where's the book for the year she died?' I say, my voice rising, panicky. 'Empty your bag out.'

'Dad, there aren't any more books. Keep your voice down. People'll think I'm with a madman.'

'Sorry. Check your bag, then.'

He rummages, piles heaps of things on the table. Gets me to look into the empty bag.

'That doesn't make sense,' I whisper a shout.

'I know,' he whisper shouts back at me. Puts all his stuff and the read journals back into the bag.

I get myself another coffee, him another apple juice. Sit down next to him. 'Let's read those last two now, then,' I say. 'Maybe she never wrote one in that final year.'

'Maybe, maybe not. Maybe she just took it with her.'

*

1995

Life plods on. I've not started work again. I couldn't. Tilly's too much fun to be with. He's growing so quickly. And saying words. He's becoming a little person. He's not a baby anymore. Can I ask Nairne to help me have more children? Not yet.

Some days are wonderful, some days not. Nairne is still the best man I've ever known, despite that hard core he's made for himself. He's thoughtful. He cooks. He loves me gently. I can feel the anger simmering in him, and I know that, one day, it'll just blow, but he never stops being gentle and kind. I'd like to grow old with him. He's the only person I'd want to have near me when I die. To hold me and comfort me when my breath starts to stop. I do love him.

Nairne and I have just had the most massive row. He sounds like he hates Tillmann. Although I know he doesn't, not really. He's stormed off down to the pub. We were just sitting in the garden, enjoying the last of the sun after Tillmann had gone to bed. And then he got angry when we started talking of how much we meant to each other, how we'd changed each other's lives.

He accused me of loving Tillmann more than him. I don't. A mother's love for her child is so different from her love for her husband, her child's father. She can't choose to love one more or less. She just loves. She protects the child and caresses the father. She needs to be there for her child. Always. The father has a sense of time. He can look after himself. He can reason. Her child can't. He's unsure of everything, except of his mother's love. And he loves her back unconditionally. He doesn't count the times she's told him she loves him, he doesn't think or know about the past, he doesn't judge her. For him, she just is and always has been. Nairne can't understand that. For him, minutes I spend with Tillmann instead of with him are lost minutes. Minutes we could have spent loving, laughing, leaning against each other, listening to each other breathe.

And then he started talking about the abortion. And all his anger flooded out of him on one spiteful hissing torrent. Things he should have said then, when I told him about it, or never said at all. Things he shouldn't have kept bottled up inside him until he exploded. And yet I feel it's my fault for not having told him everything, EVERYTHING, when I first met him. My fault for making up my new life and pretending I'd never had a past. Would telling him have changed anything? Now I think it might have. Caitlin was right. I wish she was here now.

But he's never said anything about his past to me. Not after the day we first met. When he told me he was afraid of women. When he said he'd been serially monogamous for years. And afraid of being hurt. We don't know each other at all, do we?

Like all stupid arguments, this one just went round and round and round until neither of us was talking to the other. And so he left. He'll probably come back drunk after I've gone to sleep. I wish I could just walk down to the pub and get him, but I can't leave Tillmann on his own. And I should just leave Nairne to himself for now. I'll never tell him anything again, ever. I'll never invent anything again, ever.

I heard him stumble in late last night and put on his headphones and listen to Another Girl, Another Planet *while he drank more. He was playing that song when I surprised him by moving in sooner than he'd expected. It's always been our song. And I heard him crying.*

I didn't say anything this morning. Just kissed him while he was still asleep. I watched him wake up. He doesn't understand that I would love him if he couldn't walk, couldn't talk, couldn't feed himself. That I'd wipe his backside, clean up his mess, stay with him through everything. Why does he do this to himself? To me?

He bought me flowers. He brought me the receipt for a holiday in Brittany that he's decided we're going on – I'll be spending my birthday in France. But he didn't say the words I wanted to hear. He didn't say he was sorry.

When we got back from our holiday – which was lovely and happy – I decided that I had to go and see Caitlin. I told Nairne I just wanted to get away for a week. I didn't expect him to understand. Perhaps I even knew what he would think. But I have to go. Something has told me to. I don't really want to leave Tillmann, but Nairne has promised to look after him well. I leave early tomorrow morning.

It's so brilliant to see Caitlin and Tom and the twins again. They've been a family for seven years now. And Tom is finally taking it easy. Caitlin says it was his New Year's resolution, and that he's been sticking to it. They have so much more time together now. And they look good, too.

Alfie and Kathleen are a handful. They've just turned eight, and they can be real terrors. But they're fun, and it's obvious they adore their parents.

When we were having dessert after dinner this evening, Tom was talking to us about what we could do tomorrow when he suddenly stopped in mid-sentence. He tried to carry on talking, but nothing other than slurred sounds came out of his mouth. Then he slumped across the table. Caitlin called an ambulance. By the time the ambulance arrived, we'd managed to get Tom onto the floor on his side. The paramedics checked him over. They said he'd had a stroke. Caitlin has gone to the hospital with him. Thank God it's only a couple of miles away.

The twins have finally gone to sleep. I'm sitting up waiting for Caitlin to call me. But I've heard nothing.

I must have nodded off in the chair. Caitlin came back at five this morning. Tom's critical. Caitlin cried. We sat together drinking coffee until it got light. I told her she should sleep. She slept for a couple of hours.

Caitlin came back from the hospital after dinner. She said Tom had been trying to speak. And seemed better.

The phone rang half an hour ago. Caitlin's just rushed to hospital outside visiting hours. Oh God!

Tom's dead. He'd had another massive stroke. That's why they called Caitlin. He died fifteen minutes after she got there. She's totally beside herself. He was only forty-five. He looked younger. She said she should never have told him to take it easier. She said she'd killed him because she tried to change him.

How do you console your older sister? How do you console someone who has made so many sacrifices for you, and who had finally achieved happiness? Only to have it taken away from her in the most cruel way? How do you? I can't.

The twins just watched. They tried to understand but they couldn't. They still can't.

I'm back with Tillmann and Nairne now. I couldn't even stay with Caitlin to arrange the funeral. I'm going to go back up there for the funeral, though. I owe Caitlin that much. I don't know what Nairne will say. I suppose I could lie and say that Kari or Bill had died, but he'd soon find out that it's not true. I wish now, I wish so much I'd had the courage to tell Nairne everything about me on that day we met. I did think about it, but I stopped myself. I stopped myself because I didn't want to destroy what, even then, I knew would grow into something more than just a coincidental day out together.

I've let everyone down. It's all my fault. I've made this world a place of lies and deceit. It's me. It's been me all along. Caitlin would never have suffered at Father's hands if it hadn't been for me. How often must she have wished she didn't have a little sister? I'm sorry.

Nairne and Tillmann wouldn't be suffering either, if it hadn't been for me. If I'd told the truth then, Nairne might have loved me even more instead of becoming the withdrawn insular man that he is now. He's a good father, but he doesn't have that spark anymore, that spark of loving his child because of its mother.

And me? And me? Maybe I was the one who tempted Father to begin with? That must be it. That's why he said I was a slut. That's why I'm so ashamed of everything that's happened, because, deep down, I know, I understand, that it was I who started this dreadful course of events, this descent into the pretend world that I inhabit, and that I've forced everyone that I've ever loved to share with me.

Maybe I should just leave. Leave everything behind. Bring this pretence to a final end. Like I should have done when Richard rejected me. Drive to the Severn Bridge and jump. That's what I must do.

I don't have the courage to be a jumper. I need to find the courage to make it up to all those I've hurt. I've got to try and salvage something from this whole tragedy that I've caused.

Caitlin says I should stop being so stupid. How can it be my fault that Tom died? How can it be my fault that Father was a deviant? How can it be my fault that he abused my sister and not me? How can it be my fault that Nairne, despite all his kindness, is a man who won't forgive me for something that happened before he met me? She tells me to get with it, to stop feeling sorry for myself. She insists that I should tell Nairne everything, that it's the only thing to do.

I can't.

I'm travelling up to Scotland every other weekend now. I leave on the Friday and get back on the Monday. Nairne hasn't once asked where I go, but I know what he fears. I see him doing the washing, looking through every piece of my clothing for the signs that he hopes he won't discover. And he won't discover any. Because, despite everything, despite my whole mixed-up living, despite his growing remoteness, I do still love him.

Caitlin's coping. Just. She's now running the business that Tom had. The twins are almost self-sufficient. She's told me that I don't need to come up so often anymore if I can't manage it. Because she thinks that I should try to mend some fences with Nairne. Even after just having seen him once, she thinks that he must be a wonderful man. That she'd have liked to know him better. She still hopes she will. Because she has more faith in me than I have.

I'll spend Christmas at home. I've told Caitlin that I'll come up again for the twins' eighth anniversary in February next year. She says she hopes that I'll be bringing Tillmann and Nairne with me. I doubt I will, somehow.

*

'Jesus wept,' Tillmann says. 'This is a sick joke.'

He picks up the book and throws it down onto the table again. His eyes are red.

'Life *is* a sick joke, ' I say as calmly as I can. I can't believe what we've just read, what we've just experienced.

'Why didn't she come to you? Why didn't she talk to you?'

'Would you have done if you'd been her? After the way I'd behaved?'

'Probably not. Although, if she was building bridges, or mending fences, wouldn't that have been the natural thing to do?'

'You don't know me very well. I really had, by that point, retreated so far into myself that I don't think she'd have reached me. She'd have thought that to talk to me about all of her past would just have destroyed what we'd managed to build up again.'

'She could've tried. What did she have to lose?'

'You,' I say. 'Simple as that. … And her chance to have more children with the only man she thought she'd ever really loved.'

He leans against me. I put my arm round him. He is a child, after all. Still. And will be for some time yet.

'I don't think we can blame her for the way she behaved,' I say. 'I'm surprised she didn't leave me and take you with her. I think she had more belief in the power of love than I ever did. That's what made her stay. I'm sure of it.'

We both look at the last unread journal lying on the table. Tillmann reaches for it. Changes his mind.

'You open it,' he says. 'You're the one who needs to know the end of her story more than I do.'

'We both need to know it, Tillmann. Because I'm her husband and you're her only son. And because as long as you're with me, I still have some of her.'

I slowly open the book and see the shapes of her words swim in front of my eyes.

*

1996

I feel calmer. I spoke to Caitlin this morning. New Year's Day. The twins brought her breakfast in bed. She says she's got a headache. Must be all the drink, she says. Tom's friends surprised her last night and brought whisky, more whisky, and beer. And food, but obviously not enough. They held an impromptu Hogmanay ceilidh at her and Tom's house (because it is still Tom's house, after all, she said). And celebrated the past, because, like Caitlin says, the past is only the path to the future. I wish I'd believed that before.

Nairne and I had a peaceful time with Tillmann over Christmas and New Year. We're growing together again. Or is it just the calm before another storm? There's no point in thinking about that. There's no point in worrying about what might be waiting for us.

For the first time ever, Nairne and I made love crossing from one year into the next. That must be a good sign, mustn't it? He's so kind and gentle and thoughtful when he's loving me that I can't understand where all his anger comes from. At the moment it doesn't matter, because we're happy together, all three of us.

I'm leaving for Scotland tomorrow. Again, Nairne doesn't ask any questions. It's like he's deliberately fighting against his jealousy, against all those things that bring out the man in him that I don't know. He talks in his sleep, which is when I hear him calling to his demons of fear and anger, when I hear him battling against them physically. I hear his frightened voice begging them to leave him alone. And then I hear another voice of his, a strong and clear and powerful voice forcing them to give way, forcing them to bow before his love. But I don't know if he ever remembers those dreams the next morning.

The cottage is empty without Tom. Caitlin's thinner than ever. But she seems cheerful. She's so much stronger than I am. I sometimes wonder how two sisters so similar can have such a differing degree of wisdom in their bones. But she doesn't look well. She keeps having headaches, she says. And she feels tired all the time.

When I asked her if there was anything I could do, all she said was that I should forgive myself. And that she wanted Nairne and Tillmann to be with us. She said she was sure that she'd have been very fond of Nairne. And of Tillmann. I've brought as many photos as possible of the three of us with me for her to see. She looked at one of Nairne on his own for a long time. And looked at me. It was meant to be, she said. It was meant to be. She looked very very sad and old. She frightened me.

We're in the middle of what feels like a long hot summer. Tillmann starts school when this summer is over, and I'm already afraid for him. He's only a small boy. He might get lost in the playground. He might get picked on by the older children. He might hurt himself. And I won't be there for him. It's a blessing that the school is just across the road. I suppose I'm being foolish. I suppose every mother feels like this when her first child goes to school for the first time. Even when it's only nursery school. I think Nairne worries, too, but he doesn't show it.

Today's been my birthday. Everyone's asleep now, and I'm sitting alone, with just the desk light on. Nairne had arranged a surprise party for me that I really knew nothing about. Didn't have an inkling of it. I am thirty, after all. He'd asked Bill and Kari to come down from Cambridge. It was a lovely surprise to see them. We've only been up to Cambridge a few times to see them since Tillmann's first birthday. I hadn't been expecting Nairne to do anything special at all. I was quite taken aback. Tillmann played with Bill and Kari in the garden, while I just sat in the sun and watched, a glass of white wine in my hand. And while Nairne was in the kitchen. That man can cook.

I feel old. That's what's kept me awake. I need to have more children. I feel incomplete. And the thought of not having any children in the house during the day time while Tillmann's at school scares me. I think it'll soon be time to talk to Nairne about it again. That scares me, too.

Yesterday was Tillmann's first day at school. He cried when I left him there. And he looked all alone and small and lost in that tall white hall that's his classroom. Nairne tried to seduce me when I got back across the road, but I pushed him away. And then I cried and I cried and I cried. And Nairne held me close to him and told me to let it all come out, to cry my troubles into his broad shoulders. Like he always does when I cry. So why can't I cry my broken past into him, why can't I destroy all the pretend things and let him pick me up and take me away from the pieces? Because I have no belief in myself, I guess. I know.

The crying has gone on for weeks now. Tillmann's and mine. Nairne seems to think I'm being weak. He said that it's important for Tillmann to learn to be independent. For him to start learning things for himself. But he's not a grown-up, I screamed. He can't figure things out yet. He's still a baby, really.

It's getting easier. Tillmann's beginning to enjoy himself over there. And I'm calmer. Nairne and I make more use of our mornings alone. We go for long walks round town like we used to do before Tillmann was born. Only then it used to be in the dark so that we could look in through other people's windows if they hadn't drawn the curtains. And we'd make fun of those people's taste in furniture and television programs. And get back to a flat made cosy by the fire we had lit before we started out on our walk.

The daylight doesn't let us look into other people's homes quite so readily. So we enjoy the wind, the flowers, other people's faces as we pass them in the street. So we walk out of town into the fields beyond, and try to guess what this place looked like before the town came. And we're happy, just the two of us, knowing, at last, that our son has become old enough to be himself without us.

Sleeplessness is becoming a habit. Nairne and I made love in the middle of the day. In our bed, with the sunlight coming in through the windows. It was wonderful. And when we were lying there, afterwards, I realised that this was the moment to talk about having another child. I looked at Nairne, and he looked all befuddled and sweet and vulnerable. And we talked about it sensibly and lovingly. And he said that I'd already made my mind up, obviously. And there and then I saw the thought cross his face that he could live with another child, that his heart wanted another child, that, deep down, he was feeling as incomplete as I am.

His blue eyes came alive in a new way, and I expected him to say that we would, that we really finally would try for another child. And I saw the thought linger in his mind and behind his eyes as he bent down to me and kissed me with a smile on his lips. But he never turned that thought into words, never uttered what I wanted to hear. Didn't even acknowledge what his heart was saying to him. And after we'd held each other, after we'd slept for a while, after we'd picked Tillmann up from school, after all that, he drove off and came back with more condoms.

And here I sit now, restless with sleeplessness, asking myself if I really did marry the right man, asking myself if the man I live with now is the same man I married. And wonder if he really does believe that more children would destroy him even more than he feels he has been destroyed already.

I'm so tired from my lack of sleep – which neither Tillmann nor Nairne seem to notice – that I feel less and less like making love, feel less and less like doing anything, actually. We've stopped going for walks as often. We've stopped running around the garden or the flat like idiots. It feels like we've become numb. Like I've become numb. Some nights I have allowed him to make love to me, but I don't feel anything.

And now, when I look at Nairne when he undresses at night, I ask myself if I still find him attractive, if I still really fancy him. Because there was something about his body that I could always admire, that I would always want while I thought there was a hope for another child. Because I saw him as giving me life when he gave his body to me. Do I still love him?

Caitlin says her headaches are getting worse. I think she's not coping very well with her grief. I've not bothered her with my problems, but I think she can sense them. I've told her to have counselling and go to the doctor. She's probably thinking I should do the same. But my headaches are excuses, and my problems of my own making.

My hands are shaking as I write this. Nairne and I have just had a massive row. Started by the innocent Tillmann of all people, because he asked if he was getting a baby sister for Christmas. Later on, I thought I'd try one last time with Nairne, to seduce him, to talk him into having a baby. Maybe I thought I'd be able to get him so passionate that he'd forget about the condoms. Instead, he spat such a venomous tirade of hate and abuse into my face that I told him I never wanted him to share a bed with me again. He thought I'd put Tillmann up to asking for a sister, accused me of having numerous lovers, told me to get a baby from one of them if I was so desperate for one.

He's sleeping in the living room on the sofa now. I don't want him in here. I don't want him anywhere near me. I'm not even sure I want to be in the same house as him. I've got to leave him. And I've got to leave Tillmann. Because Tillmann reminds me of Nairne. And I love them both. But I can't, I just can't be with them any longer. My past and my present are killing me, and I don't want to die.

*

I close the book. Gently. Because I know now that I drove her away. I know now for sure that I killed her. She'd never have got ill if I'd given in to her, if I'd given her what she wanted. If I'd just made an effort to understand who she was. But I didn't. I just took it for granted that my mystery woman, my magical coincidence woman, my beautiful Kate, would be with me for all time. And now she's gone.

Tillmann doesn't say anything. He just packs everything into his bag, almost mechanically, and gets up. He's waiting to leave. I get up, too, and follow him back out to the car park. We get into the car. He gets the atlas, shows me where to drive and sticks one of his endless CDs in the player.

We're on the last stretch of our odyssey now. Getting closer to Nairn all the time. It's like I know where to go. I don't see the traffic. I don't notice the cars overtaking us. All I see is Kate. Like she was the day I met her. Like she was the day she died.

I can't wait to get this over and done with.

Chapter 13

The last few weeks of Kate's life were a torture for all of us, but most of all for her. Because everything changed. One moment she'd be lucid, the next not. She started talking about things that I knew nothing about, muttered half words about things she'd done that were strange to me.

I made a last effort to get her doctor's notes, but I was told that she'd signed a privacy form which listed the people her doctor was allowed to discuss her condition with. There were no names on that form. She'd made sure she dealt with this on her own. There was nothing I could do, the doctor said, except go to court. And at this late stage – he could tell me that because it was obvious – it was hardly seemly or worthwhile to contest my wife's right to privacy in court.

By now her body looked hollow. It wasn't Kate in that bed. It was a monster made only of skin and bone. Even at night, with the door closed, I could hear her breathing scratching through the whole house, as she fought to drag air into her failing body. And sometimes I would be woken in the middle of the night by a scream that was somehow louder than it should have been from a body that shrivelled and faded. But I couldn't go in to her in the dark. Couldn't comfort a stranger. I think the nurse tried to.

We both insisted that Tillmann start back to school as normal. I, because I didn't want Tillmann to have to go through the pain of seeing his mother decay in front of his eyes. Kate, because she, in one of her more lucid moments, had said that he needed to learn to be without either of us. Tillmann, already rebellious, had said that he didn't care what either of us thought. That he'd go back to school because he wanted to, and because he wanted to tell his friends about how ill Kate was.

One day I remember in particular. Tillmann had just come back from school. He ran into the house as soon as I unlocked the front door, threw his bag onto the floor in his bedroom, and tiptoed into Kate's room. I sat down in the living-room to read something or other while the nurse went out for the hour or two she'd get to herself at this time of day. After about half an hour I wondered why everything was so quiet.

I crept to Kate's door. Tillmann was lying on the bed with her, had somehow managed to squeeze himself between all the wires and tubes, just to get as close to her face as he could. He was lying there, on his stomach, his eyes an inch away from her eyes. And he was stroking her wrinkled blotchy head as gently as he could. He just kept stroking her, as if she was some fragile tiny animal that he'd found and was looking after. Running the palm of his hand across the tufts of hair that had started growing again. And just humming that gentle *shhshh* song we all learn when we have babies to put to bed or to console. And he drew his child's love all around her disfigured face with those little smooth hands of his – over and over and over again.

He moved even closer to her, rocking, as gently as he could, his small body into the curve of her almost corpse, as if he wanted to give her all his warmth, as if he was desperately trying to make her better. And as if he was longing to be a part of her body again. Trying to heal her with his little boy's love, with his undying unconditional unquestioning and unfathomable love. And all the while her lips were moving. And all the while her grimace of pain had softened into the semblance of a smile.

I stood there and watched the two of them in their gentle embrace for two hours or more. I know it was two hours, because I occasionally glanced at my watch. What I saw moved and appalled me. Why couldn't I have loved her so unconditionally? Why couldn't I have loved them both this unconditionally? Why had this abyss opened between us two lovers, we two who had always, from the first, believed that we had been meant for each other? Seeing Tillmann and Kate saying goodbye to each other the way only those who love without limit can, broke me.

How do we make our choices? Are we really meant to love others? Or do we merely decide, at some point in our lives, that we don't want to be alone, that we don't want to grow old alone, that we don't want to die on our own? I have tried, ever since Kate died, to make sense of what we chose to do. Because, to be honest, I think I let her die on her own, without any comfort, without any feeling of love or need or want. Because she knew as well as anyone that I'd left her the moment I began to doubt her, the minute I'd stopped listening to her, the day that I hadn't listened to my heart when my heart told me I actually did want more children. I walked away from her at the very time when I should have realised that my love for her knew no bounds. But I refused to release my love from the cage I kept it in, and released my demons of jealousy and selfishness instead. Failed to become one of those lucky few who love without limit. And now it's too late.

Tillmann has always said that he remembers those few hours he was there with her, near the end. That he stroked and caressed her, although by this stage she revolted and scared him, because he felt he needed to. Because he felt that *she* needed him to. I find that incredible, but I believe him.

A couple of nights later, at the beginning of October, the nurse woke me at about two o'clock in the morning. She told me she thought the time had come. Kate had grown restless, her breathing irregular, even stopping for a few seconds. Tillmann was already with Kate. He'd not been able to sleep. All the lights in the room were ablaze, and the nurse had lit a couple of candles.

I didn't really know what to do, so I sat down on the edge of Kate's bed. She opened her eyes and looked at me. Her skin was dark, and the blue of her irises seemed sharper than ever, staring at me from the yellow of her eyes that had been white. Other than her eyes she looked like an old woman. Suddenly her breathing grew rapid, and her hand, which I was holding, grew almost too hot to hold.

'Why are you leaving me?' she sighed as life started to desert her, as she grew too weak to hold on to her self any longer. It was the last thing she said. Her breath rattled through her teeth. I remember worrying what this would do to Tillmann, but he seemed totally untroubled by what was happening. He just carried on stroking her face and talking quietly to her. And then she stopped breathing. Just like that. And then she was gone.

We left her lying in her bed until the next day, when the undertakers came to take her away. Tillmann didn't cry. I did. The nurse did. But not Tillmann. He kept saying we'd see her again soon. Kept telling me not to be sad because we'd all meet again, somewhere, some time. That night his dreams began.

In the ten days up to the funeral Tillmann kept telling me that he'd been speaking with Mummy in his dreams, and that she was fine. He still didn't cry. It was only after we'd been through the service and the cremation that he started crying, and only after some more dreams. The dreams of her going away. The dreams of her telling him she wouldn't be back. Eight years of dreams and tears and loss and grief. Until he told me that he didn't believe she was dead. Until now.

*

We're nearly in Nairn. We've listened to Tillmann's endless CDs crammed with old and new tunes. We've driven up a slope without seeing anything, and now we're at the top of the slope looking down at the sea, looking down at this small town that I hope will be the final stop in this journey. And the sun reflects red from the sea up onto the road we're driving down. A long road with lazy bends that gently wind their way down towards the houses and the piers beyond, and the dunes beyond that.

I open my window although it's cold outside. I feel the salt breeze drifting in from the open ocean, scent the freedom that Kate must have felt whenever she came up here. And I wonder why she didn't come up here, why she didn't decide to live with that part of her past that meant the most to her. Why she didn't lay her weary mind to rest up here, where the endless sea beckons, where she could have started her life afresh, and kept alive the past that she wanted.

The sun makes me squint as we make our slow way down the road into the town. We follow the signs for the city centre, looking out for those blue parking signs. We hope we can find somewhere close to the post office. It's about three in the afternoon, and there are still a few hours of daylight left for us.

As we're coasting down the hill, I notice the hospital on the left. That must be where Tom died. And shortly afterwards we cross the railway line and come to a junction where Tillmann spots a sign to the right for the cemetery. We both wonder if that's where Tom's buried.

'Maybe we should bring Mum's ashes up here to be reburied,' Tillmann says at the same time as I'm thinking that very thought. 'Or scatter them into the sea from those dunes.'

'I think that's a good idea. There's a feeling about this place.'

'Oh aye,' he mocks me with a fake Scottish accent. Coughs. 'I actually mean it,' he says, seriously.

'So do I. So do I.'

After driving aimlessly round the town centre for a few minutes, we decide we'll use the car park nearest the sea. That way we can work our way back up the hill if we need to, and know we've got a downhill return journey to the car. We've become lazy. But not just that. We both want to take a few minutes out from this quest, just to go and stand on the shore and feel the wind of the wild in our hair, to let nature take some part of us, to feel at rest for a few precious heartbeats.

We park. I throw some money into the machine. We do allow ourselves a few minutes by the sea, to catch breath, to pretend we're just on holiday, to rest. Tillmann finally turns to me.

'That guest house Mum and Caitlin came to,' he says. 'That must be around here somewhere.'

'It's a long sea front. Could be anywhere along here. It stretches for miles.'

'But I can't think they'd 've been far from the centre. And remember, she said that the hospital was only a couple of miles from Caitlin's and Tom's house.'

'We'll see, won't we? Let's find this post office first.'

He's already got his bag over his shoulder, has got his picture of Kate ready in his hands.

'Why've you got that out?' I say. 'I thought we'd just ask the post office if they remember someone sending a package to Yorkshire a few weeks ago.'

'Dad, I know this place is small, but not that small. D'you really think the people at the post office have time to look at every address on every small package they send?' He looks at me and shakes his head. 'Besides, there might be a family resemblance. We know there is, hair and all that. So Caitlin must look a bit like Mum.'

'That picture's over thirteen years old,' I say.

'I've got others, more recent.'

'But they're all at least eight and a half years old. And we don't know how much older than Kate her sister is.'

'That's true. But it's worth a try.'

We start walking up the gentle hill, back to where the town seemed busier. We get to the roundabout where the main road we came in on takes a right-angled turn to the right – where we turned left to find the sea. The High Street must be along here somewhere. We find it after some false starts.

We start trying to spot locals. We approach one of them, an elderly lady, and ask where the post office is. She tells us it's a couple of streets away, on the junction of the High Street and Cawdor Street, just a bit more up the hill. It's nearly four o'clock. I'm worried the place might close before we get there. Now it's Tillmann who tries to calm me down.

'Dad, we've got plenty of time. It'll only take us a couple more minutes to get up there.'

We find the place. Tillmann was right, of course. It doesn't close until half past five. It's not a huge place, but, nevertheless, there are three or four open counters. I hesitate. Tillmann's braver than me. Because the place is almost empty, he just goes up to one cashier, with me trailing behind him.

'Do you know someone who looks a bit like this?' he says, sliding Kate's wedding picture under the thick glass, not expecting a positive answer.

'Och aye,' the man behind the pane says. 'That'll be Caitlin Drummond. She lives out at Balnaspirach off the Balblair road. D'ye know her?'

'I think she might be my aunt,' Tillmann says. 'Although I've never met her.'

'Well, don't you worry,' the man says. 'She's a fine woman. Loves kids.'

'Can you tell us how we can find her place?' I say. 'We've never been here before.'

'Ach, I guessed that,' he smiles. 'You parked down on the sea-front?'

I nod.

'All you need to do is take the main road back out of town, take a right just before the hospital, and you'll be on the Balblair road. Then it's a couple o' miles along there, through Balblair, and you'll see a little sign-post pointin' to the right. Turn off there and Balnaspirach's at the end of the track.'

'Thank you very much,' Tillmann and I both say.

'Nae bother,' he smiles at us again. 'Glad to be of help.'

We leave the post office. I'm covered in sweat. Tillmann looks as untroubled as ever. I'm glad of the cool fresh air. We head back down the hill again.

'I'll give you directions,' Tillmann says. 'I think I managed to write it all down ok. Nice old bloke.'

'Very friendly. But then the further north you get on this island, the friendlier people seem to get.'

We walk towards the sea. The sun's weaker now, and the blue sky promises a frost. And night-time. What will we find at Caitlin's cottage?

Dusk has fallen pretty rapidly by now, creeping unnoticed up onto land from the sea. By the time I get the car out of the car park it's pretty murky. I miss the turning the first time, and have to negotiate my way round a warren of side streets before we make it onto the Balblair road. The traffic's picked up by now, too, so that I feel pressured into driving too quickly when I should be going slowly.

I miss the turn to the cottage as well. Tillmann shouts at me to go more slowly, but I'm getting myself into a real state by now. We end up in a place called Easter Lochend, where I have to turn again. We're now looking for a turn on our left. At last there's nothing behind me and I can drive as slowly as I please.

'There it is,' shouts Tillmann. 'Here. Turn left.'

I slam the brakes on although I'm going slowly, and the car hops off the tarmac onto a pot-holed dirt track. I slow down even more, but it's still a very uncomfortable ride. I wonder if the car will ever be the same again after this.

What seems like an age has passed. It's even murkier outside. We finally get to the end of the track which opens out onto a wide gravel drive in front of an L-shaped stone-built cottage.

'This must be it,' Tillmann says. 'This must be it.'

I drive as close to the front door as I dare. There's a clapped-out Land Rover parked there. I shut off the engine and the headlights. Now that we're here, I don't know what to do. There's a few lights on in the cottage but no-one seems to have reacted to the sound of our car pulling up. I get out and tiptoe across the gravel. I don't know why, I just do.

The cottage looks like it has a few rooms on the first floor, gabled windows peering down at us. But most of the house seems to be on the ground floor.

'Go on,' Tillmann whispers. 'What're you waiting for?'

He's got his bag draped across his stomach like a leather shield.

We move gingerly across to the front door. I knock. Once. No response. I wait. Still nothing. I knock harder.

'Come in,' an accentless female voice calls. 'The door's open.'

I push the door handle down and push open the door. The hall's bright with lights.

'In here,' the voice calls, off to the left. We follow it.

The ceiling's quite low. This is someone's real home. Not like our modern converted flat where nothing ever feels quite right. This place has been someone's home for centuries. And still is.

We walk towards the warm yellow light and the scent of something cooking. My feet sound loud on the quarry tiles as we walk across the threshold into the kitchen. Across from me, the other side of a huge wooden table, a tall woman bends over a range cooker, tastes something out of a spoon. She turns round very slowly, painfully slowly, and walks into a pool of light by the table.

Oh God! She looks exactly like Kate. I grab hold of one of the chairs my side of the table. I'm shaking. Try to control it. Tillmann says nothing. He's rooted to the spot. The woman smiles at me. Smiles at Tillmann. She has huge blue eyes set in a thin pale face. Waves of long black hair tumble down her back and down the sides of her face.

'You must be Nairne,' she says softly. 'Welcome to Balnaspirach.' She chuckles. 'No, I could never pronounce it properly either.'

She turns to Tillmann. 'And you must be Tillmann.'

I think I see her tremble slightly, but maybe it's just a trick of the light.

'Sit down,' she says. 'You can have dinner with us.'

'But,' I try to say more. Nothing comes out.

'We were twin sisters,' she says. 'I'm older by half an hour. I think she always reckoned I felt superior because of that. But I didn't.'

'Take your coats off.' She smiles. 'Just chuck 'em on some other chairs.'

We do as we're told. She beckons us to sit down with a hand I think I see shaking, and sits down herself. There's a bottle of red wine open on the table. She raises a questioning eyebrow at me.

'Why not?' I say, my voice suddenly grown hoarse. I sit down, heavily and without elegance.

'There's soft drinks in the fridge,' she says to Tillmann. 'Or water in the tap. And glasses in the cupboard to the right.'

The absence of any more words is awkward. Just feet and chairs scraping across the floor. I really can't speak. I feel like leaving.

'I was wondering when you'd come,' she says after we've got comfortable. 'I didn't really know what to do with Kate's journals, but when I realised Tillmann was coming up to being a teenager, I thought it was best to send them. To try to make up for lost time.'

'So why not send them straight to us?' I say, starting to feel a little angry.

'I'm sorry, but I thought a little bit of a mystery might be useful,' she says, not reacting to the tone of my voice. 'And I wanted to give you time to consider what you might do. Rather than sending a letter with them that told you to come up here so I could finish Kate's story for you.'

'And what is Kate's story?' Tillmann says before I can say it. 'Because *I* think she's still alive.'

Chapter 14

There's an awkward silence after what Tillmann's said. I don't think Caitlin was expecting him to say anything like that. She picks up her glass with her long pale fingers. She's wearing a plain gold band on her ring finger. Kate and I had plain gold bands, too, but we burned hers with her. I still wear mine. The silence is heavy.

Before any of the three of us can say anything, there's a loud clattering outside in the hall, and six children come rushing into the kitchen. Caitlin stands up as these kids stare at us as if we're from Mars.

'Don't stare, kids,' she says. 'This is Nairne, your uncle, and this is Tillmann, your cousin. Kate's husband and son, basically.' She gesticulates vaguely in our direction. 'And these,' she says to us, gesticulating vaguely again, 'are my children.'

I'm looking at three sets of twins.

'These two are Alfie and Kathleen. They're seventeen now.' She turns to the second pair. 'And these two are Thomas and Jacob. They're eight.' The smallest pair are hiding behind their bigger siblings. Caitlin gets them to come to the front of the silent gaggle. 'And these two sweeties are Imogen and Jennifer. They're six. And Jennifer hates being called Jenny.'

'Hi, gang,' Tillmann says, instantly at his ease.

The gang smile at him, gather round their mother. I'm lost for words. So I just smile, sort of. Caitlin takes control.

'Right, food's ready. Kathleen and Alfie – plates. Jacob, Thomas – glasses. Jennifer and Imogen – forks. I'll get the water.'

The kitchen is a sudden explosion of activity. Tillmann and I don't really know where to put ourselves. Caitlin plonks three cork mats along the centre of the table. And three jugs full of water next to them.

'Nairne can sit in the middle on this side,' she says. 'And Tillmann can sit opposite him. The rest of you just sit where you can.'

I end up sitting between Thomas and Alfie. Tillmann's between Kathleen and Jacob. The two youngest sit themselves at the end of the table to my left. Caitlin dollops huge ladles of something into three big bowls, which she then puts on the mats on the table.

'Fried rice and bacon. A staple in this house. Easy to cook, easy to eat, easy to heat up the next day.' She sits down at the end of the table to my right. 'Go on,' she says. 'Help yourselves.'

When all our plates are full, a hush falls over the kitchen. I'm starving. Tillmann's eating like he's never seen food before, and Caitlin's family seem to be used to eating without talking or even breathing between mouthfuls.

I watch Caitlin eat. I watch her move. It's a weird thing to see someone so familiar and yet so strange so close to me. She could be Kate, albeit a countrified Kate. And yet she is foreign to me. I get this ridiculous idea that if I'd met Caitlin before Kate I might just as easily have fallen in love with her. They have the same kind of mellow still voice, they both move slowly, they're both beautiful. Or should I say were. Because the one I love is dead. And I'm having dinner with her twin sister. An older version of Kate.

I finish my plateful, take a sip of warm red wine. I take a look round the table. I never thought it could be like this, like almost fun, to be surrounded by seven children. I shake my head and smile to myself. At least I thought I was smiling to myself. I hear Caitlin chuckle. So I look at her. She looks back and doesn't look away.

'It's not this peaceful all the time, you know,' she says. 'But it can be fun most of the time. I just had to keep adopting. It was the only thing to do, because it was the right thing to do.'

'Kate would've loved this,' I say. 'All these children around. If she were still alive.'

'Yes, she would.'

Tillmann smiles at me from across the table.

'I take it you never remarried then, Caitlin?'

She's not shocked by the direct question. 'I've only ever loved one man. Just because he's not here with me, it doesn't mean that I don't carry him around with me. There's no-one else to love.'

'I feel the same,' I say, feeling slightly hypocritical.

Caitlin just smiles. 'I'm sure you do. I'm sure you do.' She helps herself to more wine and a bit more food.

'So, tell me, how d'you manage with six kids?' I say. Like I've said before, I'm not very good with small-talk.

'We do ok, don't we kids?'

They all nod. Tillmann seems amused by this large family huddled around the table, this unknown feeling of collective responsibility. We've become too much like cynical hermits, Tillmann and I.

'I've got three cottages now,' Caitlin goes on, like she's trying to avoid the silence. 'And they're all paying for themselves. I've still got the business that Tom used to run. And that's not going too badly, either. And we manage to watch the pennies by not being too extravagant with our wishes, desires, and purchases, don't we, Alfie and Kath?'

The two oldest ones dutifully nod and blush, as if there's some unspoken family joke being told here.

'Right, folks. Nairne and I are going to step outside for a smoke while you clear the table and sort out the washing-up.' She gets up, pats the table with both her hands. 'Let's go, kids! And then I'll show Nairne where he and Tillmann can sleep.'

I follow her back out through the hall to the front door and out of the house. She closes the door. We're alone for the first time since I arrived.

'You sure we're not imposing?' I say.

'Why should you be imposing? It's because of me that you're up here in the first place.'

'Well, Tillmann and you.' I tell her the story of the whole odyssey from when Tillmann woke up last Saturday morning and told me we had to go and find Kate. I've started to tremble again.

'And he's been having these dreams ever since?' She shivers. It's getting colder.

Some crazed part of me wants to reach out to her. And stops.

'Just about, and most nights. Every night.'

'Didn't you think to take him to a child psychiatrist?'

'Not really. Why? I don't think they've harmed him. I don't think they will harm him. He seems like a healthy, well-adjusted, standardly rebellious twelve-year-old to me.'

'You know him better than I do.'

'He knows me better than I know him. Seriously.'

'I believe you. I really do.'

'Why wouldn't you?'

She looks at me as if she is going to say something. Changes her mind. Looks at the ground. Draws the final draught of smoke deep into herself. I can't break this silence. I don't want to. Talking to her feels like blasphemy. Her boot grinding the sparks into the ground scatters the quiet. She turns to go back into the house. Then stops so suddenly I nearly walk into her. 'I think you're a good father.'

I'm so close to her I can feel the warmth of her skin. I take a step back. She laughs.

'Sorry. I'm always accused of invading other people's private space.'

'Don't worry. It's fine. Thanks.'

Back in the warm house, she shows me where the

living-room is, says she'll be back in a minute. Then quickly checks on the kids in the kitchen.

It's more a library than a living-room, really. Bookshelves up to the ceiling, round every wall. No television. A long leather couch. Wooden floor. A solitary photograph over the open fireplace. Of Kate and Caitlin. You can't tell them apart. They look the same in every way. I wander round the low-slung room. Pull books out from the shelves. Some of them have Kate's name in them. Some Caitlin's. Some Tom's. I push the books carefully back into their place when I've looked at them. My eyes keep turning back to the photo. I stand in front of the fire, warm myself on its flames and on the smiles of the two women in the photograph. It's quiet.

I don't hear her come back into the room. She's suddenly next to me. I can almost hear the electricity crackling when she puts her hand on my shoulder.

'This is where Kate's stuff from Cambridge came, then?' I say. I don't turn to look at her, because I want her hand to stay on my shoulder.

'This is where she sent it, yes. Everything she had, everything she was so afraid of sharing with you, came up here.'

This time I do turn, and she takes her hand away. 'Why was she so afraid of telling me about you, about the past, about all this? And I don't mean after I'd made my mistakes, but I mean right at the start, right there and then in London that first day?'

'I don't know. She loved you so much. And I kept trying to persuade her to tell you. I've been trying to solve the mystery, and I think she was on her way to solving it when she died.' She sits down on the couch. Her breath is hard and fast, a succession of painful sighs. She closes her eyes. Covers them with her hands.

'And?' I say, sitting down at the opposite end of the couch.

She opens her eyes again. They shine, but they don't look at me. 'Just stop thinking about yourself now. Just stop. They weren't just your mistakes.'

'What?'

'I don't think what happened means anything anymore. Stop blaming yourself. There's no-one to blame. Think of the good things. Think of what you were both like when you first met. How much you felt, what you felt. That's all that's important. That passion. … Because that's all that ever counted, all that should have mattered. … And her past was so painful, so … desperate, that she should have told you about it straightaway … You saved her from it, you could have redeemed her, taken all that guilt from her shoulders, all those burdens … because I couldn't, I never could … never.'

'But you ... your dad…'

'She blamed herself for that as well, you know she did. Such a waste of energy and emotion. There was nothing she could have done about it. It could have been either of us he picked on. He was a sicko, and Mother too weak. She should have told you about what went on in that lovely family ours. She should have told everyone she knew. That way she'd have got rid of it. She would have stopped carrying it around with her, eating away at her. Damn it!'

She's angry. Red in the face. Animated. Like she's been wound up and won't stop till she's exhausted herself. I want to calm her, but I can't interrupt.

'It's what Father said about being a slut that stuck the most, you know. Although she wasn't, although she never could have been, she went through her whole life feeling like one, feeling that she wasn't good enough for anyone. That everyone and anyone who found out about her past would automatically recognise her as the slut Father said she was.'

'That's ridiculous.'

'But it's true. That's the way it was always going to be.'

'It wouldn't have been if she'd told me.'

'She did tell you, in the end.'

'I …'

'You reacted the way she assumed everyone would react.'

'She shouldn't have lied to me.'

'She didn't lie to you. She just left things unsaid. Would you have reacted any differently if she had told you everything the first time you met?"

'I don't know.'

'Exactly. And she couldn't know how you would react; wouldn't risk breaking this new love she had found. Happiness was what she wanted more than anything else.'

'We were happy – for a while.'

'You're both to blame for that. You didn't even listen when she said that you were her light in the darkness. In the end, you just heard her story about the darkness and decided that she'd betrayed you before she even knew about you. You couldn't accept that you were her light. You were as insecure as she was. You still are. You dress up the past in jokes and empty words. You both never loved yourselves.'

I just grunt.

'It's something you have to deal with, Nairne. Otherwise Tillmann will turn out just like you. He won't be able to have any meaningful relationships, won't be able to love.'

'But I'm teaching him not to be like me.'

'That's not the point. He needs to have it spelled out to him, not the not being like you, but the being loved, being cared for, being secure.'

'I've told him this trip. He knows I love him.'

'Good.'

'I go through every day knowing that I killed Kate with

the way I was. I understand why I didn't follow through that urge to have more children. I didn't want to become even more emotionally vulnerable than I was. I didn't want to give my entire being to anyone else. Because that's what having children means – you have to give yourself entirely up to them. You have to become unselfish, uncomplaining, don't you? You have to forget your self. And I couldn't face that. The fear was there every day – what if he doesn't come home? What if he stops breathing in the night? All those what ifs. Always. For the rest of your life.'

'Why didn't you ever tell her that?' she says, looking at me, straight at me.

'Because she'd have thought I was betraying her? Because she'd have thought I was weak for not choosing the difficult path? I don't know. Why is it that we find it so difficult to show our feelings to those we love, but manage to show them so easily to those we hate?'

'It's much more difficult to love someone than to hate them, that's why.' She stops talking abruptly and slaps her hands onto the couch. She gets up. Conversation over. Just like that. She doesn't seem angry anymore. 'Come on, let's go see what those kids of ours are up to now.'

I follow her out of the room. The kitchen's empty and tidy.

'You've got 'em well-trained,' I say.

'I wish.' She shrugs. There's music and shouting coming from upstairs. 'Ah,' she says. 'That's where they've got to.'

We climb up a narrow staircase, up into a corridor with several doors along it, opposite a row of windows.

'Shhhh,' she whispers, and smiles.

We creep up to the door from which the music's coming. It's open a little way. We peek in. The two youngest are dancing crazy dances around the floor, while the five older ones are sitting on the two beds in the room. As we pull away, our hands accidentally touch. It's like an electric shock. We both start and pull back.

'Let's leave them to it for an hour. I've put Tillmann in with Alfie, along there.' She points, ignoring our touch. 'And you're in the spare bedroom downstairs next to the living-room. I sorted it out before.'

'Thanks.' I ignore that electric shock, too. It's too crazy to be real. After she's shown me the room, I go out to my car to get our bags in. I leave Tillmann's at the foot of the stairs. I'll take it up later.

Caitlin's sitting in the kitchen, nursing another glass of wine. She pours me another one, too.

'I was wondering what you were like, when we were reading Kate's journals on the way,' I say. I sit down at the table opposite her. It's peaceful down here.

'Well, you know now.' There's a tremble in her smile. She seems suddenly afraid. Probably all that talk about the past. 'How long will you stay?'

'How long do you want us to stay?'

'Stay as long as you like.'

'I've still got to persuade Tillmann that Kate really is dead. That's the only reason I agreed to his mad idea of driving round to look for her.'

'I don't know how you can convince him.'

'It's something he's just going to have to accept.'

'Have you accepted it?'

'I know she's dead.'

'What I mean is, have you accepted that she's gone? Or do you think about her every day, try to recall her touches, try to think of the good times you had with each other, the small words you gave each other when you were happy? That's what I mean.'

'Just because I do all those things doesn't mean I don't accept she's gone. I still have our wedding picture by our bed. I try to hear her voice, try to feel her hands stroking my back when I'm going to sleep at night.'

'And can you sleep?'

'Most of the time, no.'

'Maybe you will tonight.'

I look at her. She's not promising me anything. She's just saying what she feels. Could she feel her sister's pain when she died? How did she find out about her death? Those secretive phone calls with the door closed? Or did she just know? I haven't the energy to ask her. I'm tired. I wish I had someone. I wish I had Kate. I wish I hadn't messed up. But it's too late now, always will be.

'Are you strong enough to tell me about her dying?' she says.

'Are you sure you really want to hear it?'

'I wish I'd been there. But she forbade me to come. Wanted to keep her big secret right to the end. I couldn't contradict her. I loved her, you see.'

So I tell her about Kate's last few days, about her last moments. About her and Tillmann on the bed. About Tillmann's superhuman efforts at loving her until she'd gone. When I look at Caitlin, she's crying. She wipes her face with her sleeve.

'Thank you,' is all she says. Takes a few deep breaths.

'Do you think you've changed since then?' she says. 'Do you think you'll make the same mistakes again?'

'I don't think there'll be an again. And you?'

Her face is paler than ever. 'I probably feel the same as you,' she says.

'If I could just have one more moment with Kate, I'd ask her to forgive me for being such a fool. For not thinking about who she really was. For taking her for granted.'

'I think she'd forgive you. I'm sure she would.'

'I've nothing to forgive.'

'You can't be sure of that.' Caitlin shrugs and leans back in her chair. She looks exhausted, all of a sudden.

The air crackles again. Time to change the subject. Time to move on.

Later, after arguing with the children about bed-time, I finally get to have my last cigarette of the day, on my own. The sky is clear, and, without street lights to pollute my view, I can see millions of stars up there. One of them is Kate. And soon one of them will be me. I hope.

When I get to my room and turn the light on, I see a notebook on my bed. I pick it up. It's just like all the others. On the front, *Kate's Journals – 1997.*

Chapter 15

1997

I thought I had it all sorted out. In my head. What I was going to do. I'm on my way up to Scotland now, and I'm not sure I want to be. I'm not sure I can go through with what I'm planning. Not sure I can do what Caitlin wants me to do. Even though it's probably for the best. And I can always change my mind, can't I? Even after the fact. Anyway, it's the now that matters.

Caitlin looks dreadful. She's wearing a wig because she's already cut off all her beautiful hair. To prepare herself. When she told me a few weeks ago that she was ill with a cancer they couldn't cure, I cried. She'll start having treatment, but she's not sure for how long. What she suggested then seemed monstrous, but I should have seen it coming. The twins don't seem to have noticed the difference in her.

Caitlin and I sat down last night after I'd arrived. Talked about what we should do. Whether we could do it. We are women, after all, and leaving our children isn't something we do lightly. Won't they notice?

Caitlin says that she doesn't want the twins to have to be looked after by strangers after she's dead. She wants me to look after them. And if I won't reveal the past to Nairne, that means staying here. Things have gone too far with Nairne. He would never understand now. And he would never accept more children, even if they were adopted.

How can I leave Tillmann? He's the only thing that's left to me of the life I dreamed about. Caitlin says that I'll be able to find my way back to him in good time. How can we be so cruel? I feel like we're two witches casting spells on those we should love. Instead of which we're betraying them in the worst possible way. Won't all our children come to hate us? And won't we hate ourselves?

But then I look at Caitlin's pain and her fear. She's the one who's going to die, not me. Shouldn't I repay her sacrifice? She's the one who stopped me being raped by Father. She's the one who was raped instead. She's the one who sacrificed herself for me. I have to repay that debt, no matter how much it might cost me. There is nothing left for me down there, with Nairne and Tillmann.

Caitlin says that Nairne will be a good father to Tillmann. That I shouldn't worry. And, she says, it's a chance for me to make a new life. With nothing to regret or repent. She was always wiser than me.

When I left Nairne, I held Tillmann so close. That I should never again be able to do so is unbearable. He's my flesh and blood. He grew inside my body. And now I've left him. Will he ever forgive me? Will he ever know?

Caitlin and I sat with each other all day yesterday and told each other our entire life histories. She told me of all the things she's ever done with the twins. She'd even prepared notes, crib sheets full of memories and hints. She'd written down everything that would allow me to lead her life for her. Because I don't have a life anymore, I've not written anything down. She's read my journals up till now, and that's all she needs. Because she isn't going to lead my life for me. She's going to die for me, so that I can disappear. Isn't this the biggest lie?

Caitlin leaves tomorrow morning. Will either of us be able to cope? I've given her everything of mine. My passport, my driving licence, all my credit cards, everything. And she's given me all her things. We've swapped clothes. I've told her where everything is in the flat. I know where everything is here. We've told each other how our respective washing machines work. We laughed when we did that. That there should be such triviality in our plan.

We've set our alarms for very early. I've said bye to the twins.

We're standing in Caitlin's bedroom. We're still in our nightshirts. Caitlin's clothes are laid out on her bed for me. Mine are next to hers. We're naked now. Identical, even naked, except that Caitlin's body is beginning to show signs of her illness. We'd always been amused that we're so absolutely identical. Even our sweat smells the same. If we'd have had a happier life, we could have had a lot of fun fooling with lovers and enemies. But there'll be no lovers for us now, not ever again. And our worst enemies are dead.

We put on our clothes and stand in front of the wardrobe mirror. I'm Caitlin now, and Caitlin is Kate. The time has come.

We changed our plan at the last moment. Caitlin said she couldn't go without saying good-bye to the twins. She took off her wig. We sat downstairs and she trimmed a bit of my hair off and put it in the bin. We heard movement upstairs. And then turned on our laughter. When the twins came downstairs we told them that Kate had decided to get her hair cut, and that Caitlin had decided to trim hers a little. My suitcase was sitting on the floor next to the table. The four of us had breakfast together. Except that the twins were calling me Mum and Caitlin Kate.

Caitlin tried not to cry when she left. She'd already put my suitcase into my car. She put on my coat. 'Time to leave,' she said. She hugged me and almost crushed the breath from me. Then she knelt down in front of her twins. 'Look after your mum for me,' she said, and took them both in her arms. 'I may not be back for a long time.' And then she walked out of the front door. The three of us stood there and smiled and waved as the car crunched its way down the gravel drive. I'll never see her alive again.

I can't sleep. The house seems empty without Caitlin. I have two children now. They're asleep in their rooms. There is so much to do, so much to get used to. And yet my new life seems painful. And as much of a lie as my old one.

Before Caitlin left, we agreed that I would call her once a week. I called her yesterday, a week after she'd left. She told me she'd told Nairne about the cancer. That she'd been to the hospital and had herself diagnosed again. That she'd signed the privacy form and put no-one's name on it. She told me she'd kissed Nairne on the cheek and held him tight. She said that it was weird being so close to her sister's husband. Especially after having been without a man for so long.

I'm getting used to my life as a mother of twins. I miss Tillmann every day. I miss Nairne, too. But it's easy to be angry with him every time I make myself remember our last big row. Yet I can't forget our love, and I never will. Because I do still love him. I just think, now, that we're better off without each other, that our lives will go their own separate ways. All I'm doing now is waiting for Caitlin to die, and for Nairne to have to live on his own with our child.

Caitlin says she can feel herself growing weaker. She's starting to be afraid. The cancer is starting to bite into her. She says the pain is worse than anything she expected. She says this will be her last spring. She's given up the treatment. Six months to Tillmann's fifth birthday. She's transferred the last of my inheritance money from my secret account into her account in Scotland. I don't feel richer.

There's a nurse looking after Caitlin now. I can hardly hear Caitlin's voice when we speak on the phone now. I ask her if Nairne's getting suspicious about the phone calls. She says she doesn't think so. She says there's very little left.

Caitlin says she's fallen in love with Tillmann. That he's a wonderful and sweet boy. That he loves me more than anything else. I cried and cried and cried after she'd told me. I want him back, but I know I can't.

The nurse is moving into the flat tomorrow. Caitlin's just called and said that there's no real point in me phoning her any more, because we won't be able to keep the secret in front of the nurse. And she soon won't be strong enough to hold the phone. That she'll be on a morphine drip soon.

It's only the twins who are keeping me from going mad now. Because they still need so much love and affection. I really do feel like their mother now. I've applied to adopt some more children. They say I have a good chance, although I'm a single mother, because Alfie and Kathleen have become such good children. A credit to me, they say. A credit to Caitlin Drummond.

My first summer near the sea has been wonderful. Some of it, anyway. When I'm not thinking about Caitlin or Tillmann or Nairne. The fresh breeze has stopped us from overheating in the warmest months for years.

What am I waiting for? It's weird not speaking to Caitlin anymore. It's difficult not knowing if she's still alive or not. How could we have done this? Is it too late now to tell Nairne of this evil thing we've done, Caitlin and I? But it's not so evil, after all, is it? None of us could cope with our lives. And now we've changed them forever. It's five weeks to Tillmann's birthday.

I'm sitting in the kitchen alone. The twins are at school. The phone is on the table in front of me. I've stopped myself from calling so often. I don't think I'll be able to stop myself now. It's Tillmann's birthday.

I disguised my voice and asked to speak with Kate Watt. Nairne answered the phone. I pretended to be a telephone sales person. He told me his wife died four weeks ago. I apologised and put the phone down. I'm all alone now.

No more writing.

2005

It's Tillmann's thirteenth birthday soon. I have six children now, but I'm still childless.

I've sent all my journals except for this one to Nairne's mother. I know she's still alive, because I've called her at the home once a year. I'm sure she forgets she's spoken to me as soon as she puts the phone down. And if she has ever mentioned it to Nairne, I'm sure that he'll just have put it down to her senility. Will she tell Nairne about the journals? I don't know, and I don't know if I want her to.

But I miss them so much, all of them. Caitlin, Tillmann, Nairne. And I don't want this life to go on without Nairne and Tillmann knowing the truth. Maybe they'll find me. And maybe they'll hate me for what I've done. But I just wanted to protect them against me, against what Father told me I was. But now I know that's not what I am. I am Kate Watt, and I'm still alive. And while I'm still alive, I want my family to know the truth about me. All of it.

*

It's four o'clock in the morning. I need another cigarette. I don't know if I should be angry or sad. I don't understand anything about Kate, about what she's done. What will those seven children say when they find out the truth? Is that what she wants?

I let myself out of my room quietly. There's a light on in the room at the end of the corridor. I ignore it. The front door isn't locked. I walk out into the cold air. There's a frost on the ground. The first frost of the autumn. Tillmann will be thirteen in just over a week. He has a right to know the truth. He's known it all along, really. It's up to him to decide what he wants to do with that knowledge. I think he's old enough.

And me, what will I do? I can't hate Kate, but I'm not sure I can accept what she's done. But it's not mine to forgive, not mine to judge.

I face south. The sea's behind me, somewhere, a few

miles away. I can hear it, even here. I can feel the timeless wind drifting in from that endless ocean that embraces all our world's islands. It's a long way to drive home now. An even longer way to walk.

I turn back to the house. Kate's standing in the doorway, framed by light. We say nothing as we close the door behind us.

THE END

Printed in Great Britain
by Amazon

67185224R00139